TOIL AND TROUBLE

Also by Wendy Corsi Staub

The Lily Dale Mysteries

NINE LIVES
SOMETHING BURIED, SOMETHING BLUE
DEAD OF WINTER
PROSE AND CONS *
THE STRANGER VANISHES *
DOG DAYS *

Standalone novels

THE OTHER FAMILY
WINDFALL
THE FOURTH GIRL

The Foundlings Trilogy

LITTLE GIRL LOST
DEAD SILENCE
THE BUTCHER'S DAUGHTER

The Mundy's Landing Mystery Novels

BLOOD RED
BLUE MOON
BONE WHITE

The Nightwatcher Series

NIGHTWATCHER
SLEEPWALKER
SHADOWKILLER

The Social Media Series

THE GOOD SISTER
THE PERFECT STRANGER
THE BLACK WIDOW

* available from Severn House

TOIL AND TROUBLE

Wendy Corsi Staub

SEVERN
HOUSE

First world edition published in Great Britain and the USA in 2025
by Severn House, an imprint of Canongate Books Ltd,
14 High Street, Edinburgh EH1 1TE.

severnhouse.com

Copyright © Wendy Corsi Staub, 2025

Cover and jacket design by Nick May at bluegecko22.com

All rights reserved including the right
of reproduction in whole or in part in any form.
The right of Wendy Corsi Staub to be identified
as the author of this work has been asserted
in accordance with the Copyright,
Designs & Patents Act 1988.

British Library Cataloguing-in-Publication Data
A CIP catalogue record for this title is available from the British Library.

ISBN-13: 978-1-4483-1246-7 (cased)
ISBN-13: 978-1-4483-1247-4 (e-book)

This is a work of fiction. Names, characters, places and incidents are either the product of the author's imagination or are used fictitiously. Except where actual historical events and characters are being described for the storyline of this novel, all situations in this publication are fictitious and any resemblance to actual persons, living or dead, business establishments, events or locales is purely coincidental.

No part of this book may be used or reproduced in any manner for the purpose of training artificial intelligence technologies or systems. This work is reserved from text and data mining (Article 4(3) Directive (EU) 2019/790).

All Severn House titles are printed on acid-free paper.

Typeset by Palimpsest Book Production Ltd.,
Falkirk, Stirlingshire, Scotland.
Printed and bound in Great Britain by
TJ Books, Padstow, Cornwall.

The manufacturer's authorised representative in the EU for product safety is Authorised Rep Compliance Ltd, 71 Lower Baggot Street, Dublin D02 P593 Ireland (arccompliance.com)

Praise for Wendy Corsi Staub

"[A] lovingly described, quirky, small-town setting . . . Sympathetic, well-delineated characters"
Booklist on *Dog Days*

"Cozy fans will enjoy the company of Bella and crew"
Publishers Weekly on *Prose and Cons*

"This warm, small-town series will appeal to fans of the Hallmark Channel's *The Good Witch*"
Booklist on *Dead of Winter*

"A touch of the paranormal, a hint of romance, and a sweet and sympathetic protagonist will lure readers to enchanting Lily Dale again and again"
Publishers Weekly on *Something Buried, Something Blue*

"Charming . . . Anyone who enjoys Nancy Atherton's 'Aunt Dimity' mysteries will be drawn to this cozy"
Library Journal on *Something Buried, Something Blue*

About the author

New York Times and *USA Today* bestseller **Wendy Corsi Staub** is the award-winning author of more than one hundred novels, including young adult fiction, psychological suspense and traditional mysteries. She lives in the New York City suburbs with her husband, their sons, and a trio (give or take) of rescue kitties.

www.wendycorsistaub.com

For my guys, Mark, Morgan, and Brody.
For my beautiful niece, Hannah Rae Koellner, and her husband-to-be, Dylan Roche, with loving wishes for a lifetime of joyful blessings.
And especially for Scooter. You've got this, and we've got you.

Screw your courage to the sticking-place,
And we'll not fail.
>					William Shakespeare, *Macbeth*, Act 1, Scene 7

PROLOGUE

September
31,000 Feet Over Mid-America

Being sandwiched in the middle seat of the last row of an hours-delayed and completely full cross-country airline flight is bad enough.

Far worse: being sandwiched between a pair of high school girls traveling together yet unwilling to trade seats with you. One wants to keep the aisle, the other wants to keep the window, and both want to keep up a running conversation that was underway long before takeoff.

At cruising altitude, a reprieve seems inevitable when each girl pulls out her iPad and earbuds and connects to the onboard WiFi. But no, neither one is going to sink into a nice long movie or binge a television series. They're both watching influencer video snippets, laughing out loud and telling each other about them.

Your own headphones are useless when the plane lacks entertainment screens and your phone was in the carry-on bag they made you check at the gate because there was no room in the overhead compartment. The flight attendant, in response to your pointed question, said earplugs aren't available on domestic flights. And the incessant chatter makes it impossible to get lost in a book or magazine.

What's a middle-seater to do but sit here, jaw clenched, trying to ignore the girls?

'Oh, look, this is the one I was telling you about with the cat . . .'

'Wait, wait, back it up – I want to see that part again!'

'Hey, Kyleigh Chronicles just posted another dance video!'

'Yay! Is it another one about her messy roommate?'

'No, it's about some lady who bakes blueberry scones. Check this out! It's amazing!'

What's amazing is that any of this nonsense passes for entertainment.

But no, there it is – a pretty young woman wearing a blue bikini and a chef's hat, dancing alone in between clips of an equally pretty, not quite as young woman in an old-fashioned kitchen.

There are captions.

This is Bella.
Bella was blue.
What's a gal to do?

There's a shot of mixing bowls, baking ingredients, and baskets of fresh berries.

An enormous hashtag flashes onscreen: *#Bake #BlueberryScones #YumTum*

The dancing woman dances. Close up of her pretty face.

The baking woman bakes. Close up of *her* pretty face.

A memory stirs.

Those deep blue eyes aren't just strikingly beautiful . . .

They're familiar.

She's familiar.

She's . . .

Bella.

Yes. That's her. She's the one.

She's the reason everything went so very wrong. She made a mess of everything – and got away with it.

But I see you, Bella. And I'm going to make you pay for what you did.

ONE

November
Lily Dale, New York

'Isabella? Helloo? Isabella?' a familiar voice calls, punctuated by a barking dog.

Bella Jordan, wrestling with a fitted sheet in a third-floor guest room, pauses and murmurs, 'What in the world . . .?'

Her ears must be playing tricks on her.

Or maybe Nadine is.

According to the Lily Dale locals, Nadine is a mischievous spirit who's resided here at Valley View Manor for over a century.

As a relative newcomer to both the guesthouse and Lily Dale, a rural upstate New York lakeside village populated by spiritualists, Bella tends toward skepticism where Nadine is concerned. Really, where most paranormal things are concerned. She often finds a scientific explanation for the 'inexplicable' goings-on about the Dale.

But the grieving widow in her, longing for a connection to her late husband, has had a few experiences that are rather . . . baffling, to say the least.

Unlike most residents, an unwitting Bella hadn't intentionally settled down in this town that talks to dead people. Eighteen months ago, on the heels of losing her husband, her suburban New York City home, and her job teaching middle school physics, she and her son Max were driving to Chicago for a fresh start when a pregnant cat popped up in their path.

Max was certain it was the same stray they'd left on their doorstep four hundred miles and seven hours ago.

Of course that was impossible.

But their efforts to rescue the cat had led them to veterinarian Drew Bailey, who quickly became a friend – and slowly, so much more. Drew was able to identify the cat's owner, Leona Gatto, Valley View's manager.

When they arrived, they discovered that Leona had 'crossed over,' as they say here, in an accident that had turned out not to be an accident. After solving her murder, Bella accepted a temporary stint running the guesthouse. It had turned out not to be temporary.

Essentially, Chance – on the verge of giving birth to eight kittens – had led Bella and Max home, at a time when she'd believed she'd never find home again. The mediums have since assured her that felines are mystical creatures that have a way of turning up when and where you need them to be.

Now Chance and her litter's runt, Spidey, reside at Valley View with Bella and Max and their recently acquired rescue pup, Hero – who happened to have been in the right place at the right time to save Bella's life back in August.

Anywhere else, she'd consider what had happened with Chance and Hero mere coincidences. However, one of the Dale's catchphrases is There Are No Coincidences.

Now, the barking continues downstairs, and the voice persists, 'Isabella! Where are you? I'm home!'

With a sigh, Bella guesses that it belongs not to a ghostly visitor, but to Pandora Feeney.

That can't be, because today is only . . . what is today?

November 8th.

Pandora is away until December, at least.

'If we're having too splendid a time, Isabella, we may extend my sojourn through the first of the year,' she'd warned, when Bella dropped her off at the airport last week with a mountain of luggage and her Scottish Fold, Lady Pippa.

'That's a great idea, Pandora. You should extend your sojourn even longer. You know January and February can be pretty bleak around here, and I'm happy to keep an eye on your place while you're away.'

'Perhaps I shall, love. How very kind of you.'

OK, so Bella's sole motive hadn't been to spare her friend western New York's notorious blizzard season.

A recent windfall had allowed Pandora to buy Valley View. Initially, Bella viewed that as her own salvation, because the previous owner intended to sell it, leaving her jobless and homeless all over again.

Fast forward a few months. While she's still grateful to Pandora for allowing her and Max to stay on – and for making the roof replacement a home-improvement priority this fall – things haven't exactly turned out as expected.

'Just think of me as your silent partner, Isabella,' Pandora had said when the real estate transaction went through, assuring Bella that Valley View would continue to operate as a guesthouse, and that she had no intention of moving in.

Somehow, Bella had believed her, despite Pandora's proprietary attitude toward Valley View. She'd owned it once before, as a private residence where she'd lived with her ex-husband Orville, a.k.a. 'the wanker.'

Bella should have known she wouldn't be content with silent partnership. There's nothing silent about Pandora Feeney.

Or, in this moment, about Hero, hardly the most astute watchdog in the world. He's not the type of dog to bark at people he knows, or even at strangers. Guesthouse visitors have been known to step over the snoozing hound upon arrival.

'Hush, now, Hero!' Pandora scolds. 'Isabella! Where in the world are you?'

'Be right there, Pandora!'

Leaving the unmade bed, she exits the third-floor guest room and descends two flights of stairs. The first is narrow and enclosed; the second is a grand staircase at the far end of the wide second-floor hall lined with closed doors.

Most are guest accommodations, each with its own theme and décor to match. She'd recently added painted placards to the doors: the Teacup Room, the Orchard Room, the Doll Room . . .

Two are marked *Private*. Max occupies what had formerly been the Train Room, Bella the spacious Rose Room at the head of the stairs.

Heading down the carved mahogany staircase, she pauses on the landing to turn on the wall sconce beside the jewel-toned stained-glass window. It's not yet three thirty, but the day is overcast and dusk falls early at this time of year.

Below, someone has already lit the sconces, *and* the bronze Victorian chandelier suspended from a scrolled plaster medallion.

Someone?

'My goodness, Isabella, the place was dim as a cave! It's a wonder I didn't trip over all that clutter and break a leg!'

The voice is Pandora Feeney's, but it appears to have come from Little Red Riding Hood.

Bella stops short on the bottom step, eying the figure clad in a red tartan cloak, the barking dog, and then the 'clutter.' It consists of her newly acquired prescription glasses, a folded paper program from the high school play she'd seen last night, the umbrella she'd propped on the mat alongside her rain boots, a large box of breakfast pastries she'd bought this afternoon at the Sacred Grounds café, and Pandora's enormous suitcase, bulging satchel, cat carrier . . .

And a motionless, medium-sized rodent.

No wonder Hero is all worked up.

'Uh-oh, *again*?' Bella hurries to open the door to let out the possum.

Hero bounds past her onto the porch, but the bundle of fur on the mat doesn't budge. Bella grabs an umbrella and gives it a cautious poke.

'Isabella, what on earth are you doing? That's a valuable antique!'

'Antique?'

'It's a rare nineteenth century muff, hand-knit of fine Scottish yarn.' Pandora grabs it and holds it out of Bella's reach.

'Sorry, Pandora, I thought it was another possum.' She returns the umbrella to the mat and points to her glasses. 'I went to the eye doctor the other day, and it turns out I'm a little nearsighted, so—'

'You have *possums* in the house?'

'Just the one. It got in through a hole in the siding, and I meant to have it repaired, but haven't gotten around to it yet.' She returns her attention to the dog. 'Hero! Come on back in, boy! It's chilly out there!'

He ignores her, tail wagging, perched on the porch next to a pot of purple mums and a flaccid jack-o'-lantern.

'You appear to have been quite overwhelmed here in my absence, Isabella, but now that I'm home, I intend to pitch in and do my fair share.'

Afraid to speculate about what Pandora considers her fair share where Valley View is concerned, Bella says, 'Speaking of being home, Pandora . . . how did you get here?'

'I flew, of course. London to New York, New York to Buffalo.'

'But I was supposed to pick you up at the airport. Next *month*.'

'I had a change of plans, and I know you're overwhelmed here, so I arranged a car-hire.'

'How thoughtful.'

'I did try to ring you, but you weren't answering.'

Bella pats the back pockets of her jeans. No cell phone.

'Misplaced your mobile again, have you?'

'It's around here someplace.' Shivering in the brisk breeze blowing through the door, she calls, 'Hero! Come on in, boy!'

He remains rooted to the porch, and she decides to let him stay. He won't wander, and he often goes out at this time of day. Part bloodhound, he seems to catch Max's scent long before he's made his way up from the bus stop.

Closing the door, she returns her attention to Pandora, who's unfastening the gold buttons on her red cloak. She drapes it over Bella's puffer jacket on the coat tree beside the door.

Ordinarily pale, starchy, and drab, she's wearing bright yellow Wellingtons and a denim shirt dress with a red paper poppy flower pinned to the lapel. Her cheeks are rosy, and windswept strands escape the silvery braid hanging down her back.

'You look great, Pandora,' Bella says.

'Thank you, love. And you look . . . a bit disheveled, quite overwhelmed, and thoroughly knackered,' she returns, peering at Bella.

Bella sneaks a peek at her own reflection in the large wall mirror. Fair enough. She's wearing a bleach-stained sweatshirt and tattered jeans, hasn't brushed her long brown hair since this morning, and she does have circles under her eyes. Going to bed after midnight and getting up at four will do that.

What she wouldn't give for just one day of peace and quiet, rest and relaxation.

'The roofers didn't finish until Saturday, and I've had workmen here all week wrapping up the interior repairs on the third floor, so I've had a million last-minute things to do to get those rooms ready for guests,' she tells Pandora. '*And* we were up late for Roxy's opening night.'

'Ah, yes, you went to the production with your lover, did you?'

Bella cringes. 'How many times do I have to tell you that Drew isn't my *lover*?'

'Right. He's your main squeeze, as you Americans say.'

'We don't say that. At least, *I* don't say that. And yes, I went with Drew, and Max, too.'

'How did young Max enjoy his introduction to the Bard?'

'He enjoyed seeing his favorite babysitter playing the lead as Lady Macbeth, but he wasn't so thrilled with the play – or the witches.'

When Max wasn't dozing, he was shrinking down in his seat whenever the wicked trio took the stage.

'They are a bit frightening,' Pandora agrees. 'But the Bard is a sheer delight.'

'Let me guess – Shakespeare's spirit visits you?'

'No, no, Willie and I knew each other in my past life as an Elizabethan shepherdess in Stratford.'

'That's nice,' Bella says, her usual response to such tidbits from Pandora. 'So you bought a . . . muff?'

'Yes, I went up to Edinburgh to introduce Lady Pippa to her ancestral land.' She gestures at the cat carrier, which contains her coddled, cuddly Scottish Fold. 'I came across the muff and cloak in a lovely vintage shop on the Grassmarket. I purchased a smashing cloak for you as well, Isabella. We'll be twins! Well, nearly. Yours is midnight blue with silver buttons.'

'Oh, that's so . . . uh, thank you, Pandora. How kind.'

Pandora takes it from her bag and hands it to Bella. 'Go on, try it on. Let's see if it fits.'

'I'm sure it—'

Pandora envelops her in the swath of wool, steps back, and tilts her head. 'A bit snug, is it?'

'Snug!' She might as well be wrapped in a king-sized blanket.

'Oh, well. With a proper diet and exercise program, you'll be wearing it in no time.' Pandora plucks it from Bella's shoulders and drapes it over the coat tree, then digs in her bag. 'Now then, I've got a brilliant Victorian top for the lad from an emporium in Camden.'

'Isn't Camden in London?'

'Of course it is. Do keep up, Isabella.'

'I'm up, I'm up. So, you got a Victorian top for Max? Is it . . . ruffled? Or, ah, velvet?'

Neither will go over well with a boy who wants to wear the same Buffalo Bills hoodie to school every day.

'Don't be daft, Isabella. It's metal!'

'Metal? Do you mean . . . armor?' That might be better received, as he'd recently watched *The Sword in the Stone*.

Three times, in fact.

She doesn't typically like to occupy him with television, but he's had a rough time lately, missing his best friend, Jiffy Arden.

Jiffy and his mom, Misty, have been away ever since tragedy struck in mid-September. Jiffy's dad, Mike, a deployed army paratrooper, was killed in a training accident.

Bella, Max, and just about everyone in the Dale had attended the heart-wrenching funeral in Mike's Pennsylvania hometown. Afterward, Misty and Jiffy had spent several weeks there with Mike's family before heading to Arizona to settle his affairs and retrieve their belongings from the military base where they'd all lived before moving to Lily Dale.

Now, Misty, Jiffy, and their puppy, Jelly, are in a rented U-Haul, making their way back east. Sort of.

Last week, she'd texted Bella from the Dakota Badlands; the week before that, from the Texas panhandle.

As a fellow widowed mom, Bella wasn't about to question Misty's decision to pull Jiffy out of school for months on end. She'll support whatever gets them through this ordeal, and she and Max will be here for them when they return.

She did, however, ask about the meandering route.

We're doing some sight-seeing along the way, Misty replied. We're going to the car museum in Detroit, then we might take a ferry to Canada so that we can go to Niagara Falls on the way home.

Bella suggested she reach out to Odelia Lauder, the medium next door, who'd traveled that route on a romantic October getaway to Michigan's Mackinac Island with her boyfriend, Luther Ragland.

I'm pretty sure she mentioned the ferry doesn't run from November through spring, Bella had cautioned Misty.

'Ah, here it is!' Pandora holds up the souvenir she'd brought for Max. 'Brilliant, isn't it?'

'Oh! It's a *top*!' Bella smiles, seeing the old-fashioned tin toy, round with a knob for spinning.

'That's what I said, Isabella. Now that you've admitted you can't see a thing, you might want to consider hearing aids as well.'

'I said I'm a little nearsighted, and I *heard* you just fine; I just didn't understand that you meant—'

'Apologies are unnecessary. It's to be expected given your situation.'

'What's to be expected? What situation?'

'Your muddled brain, love. When one is overwhelmed—'

'I am *not* overwhelmed!' Bella bellows. 'Please stop saying that!'

Pandora winces. 'Do lower your voice, Isabella. I'm not the one who's hearing-impaired. Now, then, this top is for your young Max, and I have one for the Arden lad as well, but I see that their cottage still appears deserted. Have you had any word from Misty on when they'll return?'

'They're still on the road. And you know her; she's unpredictable. Like you, Pandora. Why are you back so soon?'

'I was quite homesick.'

'But you were homesick for *England*,' Bella reminds her. 'It was all you talked about for months. How you couldn't wait to revisit your childhood home, and see old friends, and drink proper tea and eat crumpets and spotted dick. You said you were considering dividing your time between here and there.'

'Yes, yes, I did consider it, but Charles was right. You can't go home again.'

'You mean Thomas.'

'Thomas?'

'Thomas Wolfe.'

'Never heard of him.'

'He's the great American novelist who wrote *You Can't Go Home Again*, which is—'

'Oh, Americans. I was referring to words of wisdom from our own dear Charles.'

'King Charles?'

'Charles Dickens!'

'Charles Dickens didn't write *You Can't Go Home Again*.'

'No, of course not. He said it.'

'Oh, well . . . I'm not familiar with all his quotes.'

'He said it to *me*,' Pandora clarifies.

'In a past life?'

'Yesterday, love. The dear man joined me at Marley House, my childhood home in London. He resided just a few doors down, you see. He and his wife Catherine were quite friendly with my ancestors Cornelius and Theodora Feeney.'

'Did they join you, too?'

'No, no, just Charles. He was aware that I'd been considering spending more time at Marley House now that I've inherited the property. But as he said, you can't go home again, so I called an estate agent to arrange for the sale.'

'Wait, Pandora, do you mean you're not going to keep Marley House after all?'

'I've really no use for it. I'm quite satisfied with my real estate holdings, what with Valley View Manor and Cotswold Corner.'

Cotswold Corner is her little pink cottage across the park. She's resided there ever since she lost Valley View in her contentious divorce.

Hearing a loud meow from the cat carrier, Bella chuckles. 'It sounds like Lady Pippa agrees with you.'

'Oh, that wasn't Lady Pippa.'

Well, it wasn't Chance or Spidey. Bella can see them on the window seat in the adjacent parlor, curled up together and sound asleep, as is their daily afternoon habit.

'I definitely heard a meow, Pandora, and I don't need hearing aids.'

'Ah, but it wasn't Lady Pippa.' Pandora opens the carrier. 'She's knackered from all the travel. It was Lord Clancington.'

'Lord . . .?'

'Clancington.'

A Scottish Fold kitten pokes its head out with another loud meow, and Pandora scoops him up. 'Quite a cheeky fellow.'

'Pandora, what's going on? Did you swap out Lady Pippa for a new model while you were in her ancestral land?'

'Of course not. She's been quite lonesome, you see, and I

thought it might be nice to find a companion for her. Would you like to hold him?'

'Sure.' Bella rests her cheek against the kitten's soft fur, feeling the rumble of purring. 'Hello, there, Lord Clancington. That's an awfully big name for such a tiny guy. I'm going to call you Clancy for short.'

'How very forward of you,' Pandora says, but she's smiling. 'Now, then, shall we put on the kettle? I'm chilled to the bone.'

'Oh, Pandora, I'd love to, but Max should be home from school any second now, and I've got guests arriving for the long holiday weekend, and I'm sure you're anxious to get settled back at home.'

'About that, Isabella . . .'

Bella looks up sharply.

She may not be psychic, but she knows Pandora well enough to recognize that tone.

'. . . I believe it makes more sense for us to stay here at Valley View.'

'For tea?'

'For . . . a bit longer than that.'

Bella looks her in the eye, keeping her voice even. 'I'm not sure I know what you mean?'

In truth, she's sure that she does.

But if she insists that Pandora spell it out for her, the woman might grasp that what she's proposing is preposterous and change her mind. After all, she's always going on about proper manners, and it isn't proper manners to invite oneself – and one's pets – to move into someone else's home.

Then again, Valley View isn't someone else's home.

It's Pandora's.

'Is the Gable Room still vacant?'

'Yes, but the work isn't finished yet.'

The third-floor room had suffered the worst of the leaky roof damage back in August and had to be completely gutted.

'How unfinished is it, Isabella? Are there walls? Is there a door?'

'Yes, but—'

'Splendid.'

'—it's all just primed because I haven't had time to paint, so the furniture is still covered in drop cloths—'

'Easily removed.'

'—and there are no curtains—'

'The drop cloths will do the trick.'

Racking her brain for other deterrents, Bella says, 'There are no towels in the bathroom.'

Pandora waves her hand. 'There are plenty in the hall closet, unless you've had a linen thief afoot?'

'No linen thief,' Bella admits. 'Why are you asking about the Gable Room?'

'I've done a good deal of thinking while I was abroad, you see, and I'm not sure it makes good sense for me to return to Cotswold Corner.'

'I think it makes perfect sense, since, you know . . . that's where you *live*.'

'Yes, but it's rather small for three, don't you think?'

'I don't, when two of the three can be mentioned in inches.' Bella indicates the cats.

'I shall confess that space isn't my only concern. You said yourself that you're overwhelmed trying to manage here, Isabella, and—'

'Pandora, *you* said that.'

'—I know how pig-headed you can be, and—'

'*I'm* pig-headed?'

'I'm not referring to your appearance, Isabella.'

'Well, gee, *that's* a relief.'

'It's just that you're the kind of woman who shoulders monumental tasks all on her own, stubbornly refusing to ask for – or accept – assistance even when it's clearly, sorely needed.'

Bella opens her mouth to protest and then closes it. Pandora may be right about that, but how is it a criticism?

You can do anything you set your mind to. You're the most capable woman in the world, Bella Blue.

Sam's deathbed words have echoed in her head for nearly two years now, especially in her most challenging moments. Knowing that he'd believed in her has made it easier for her to believe in herself.

Pandora is prattling on. 'Frankly, love, I've been concerned about you for quite some time, and I can no longer sit by and allow you to toil away while I—'

She breaks off, bowing her head and closing her eyes.
'Pandora?'
She holds up a palm. 'Shush.'
Bella sighs, recognizing the indication that a spirit is 'touching in' from the Other Side. With any luck, it's Charles Dickens, telling Pandora that she *can* go home again – to Cotswold Corner.

Stroking the kitten's fur, Bella notes it's the same creamy, rosy shade as Lady Pippa's. He really is an adorable little thing, with a chubby face and big round eyes. He's watching Pandora with an expectant air, as if he, too, awaits the message from the Other Side.

'Hang in there, Clancy,' Bella says softly, well-accustomed to these little interludes by now. 'This might take a while.'

Pandora is swaying as if in a trance, talking quietly to herself, or to Spirit.

There are times when Bella is amused by her friends' interactions with visitors they alone can see and hear. She rather enjoys the one-sided repartee between Pandora and her late nemesis Wallis Simpson, which isn't nearly as contentious as Pandora's ongoing rivalry with the equally feisty and very much alive Odelia Lauder.

Today, though, an uneasiness settles over Bella. The house is silent, aside from Pandora's strange murmurings and the ticking mantel clock in the parlor. Outside, ancient tree limbs creak and the wind chimes tinkle in the porch eaves.

They'd been a treasured gift from her husband Sam, cascades of blue stained-glass angels on silver chains – meaningful, because he'd often called her Bella Blue, because of her eyes, or Bella Angel, because her maiden name had been Angelo.

Now that Sam is gone, the wind chimes sometimes stir for no discernible reason, almost as if he's trying to get her attention. Trying to warn her.

That isn't the case now. It's just the wind. Beyond the window, in the park across the lane, branches are swaying, and the flag flutters atop its pole. She sees her friend Calla Delaney hurrying along carrying her laptop and a paper coffee cup, long brown hair whipping in the wind. She's an author and had been writing in a quiet corner when Bella went to Sacred Grounds earlier this afternoon to buy a big box of pastries.

'You must have one heck of a sweet tooth today,' Calla said, looking up from her screen.

'Oh, they're for the breakfast room tomorrow morning. I've got a full guesthouse this weekend.'

'You're not baking your famous scones? Your fans are going to be disappointed.'

'Good berries are impossible to find in November, and I don't have fans, Calla.'

'Are you kidding? You and your scones are viral!'

Over the summer, Bella's homemade scones had impressed a young woman who had a summer internship writing for a local newspaper. She wrote a feature: *Baker Bella's Blueberry Breakfast Creating a Buzz.*

Bella's Blue . . .

So close to *Bella Blue* that she'd read it that way at first glance. But of course the piece had nothing to do with Sam, and their old life . . . or so she thought.

It was supposed to focus on, well . . . baking.

The piece *had* featured a huge photo of her in Valley View's kitchen surrounded by far more mixing bowls than it takes to make a batch of scones, wearing an apron dusted in flour. A *lot* of flour. So much flour that it looked like she'd rolled around in it.

The finished piece contained more personal information than Bella had realized she'd shared.

'You should have said no comment when she asked you all those personal questions about your past,' Calla had scolded her. 'You really have to be careful with the press.'

'I'm not Taylor Swift. She was a college kid. I thought she was just making conversation.'

'But you agreed to be interviewed.'

'About the scones.'

In the article, the scones had become a metaphor for a widow's 'journey' as she bounced back from grief and created a new life *'from scratch. These days, the only blues in Bella's life are the berries in her scones.'* Not exactly a Pulitzer-prize-worthy conclusion, but Bella figured that would be the end of it.

Unfortunately, Kyleigh, the young woman who wrote it, is majoring in social media – who knew there even was such a thing? – and after she got back to college, she posted a series of dance videos featuring the articles she'd written over the summer.

Dance videos.

They created a stir, even the one about Bella and her scones. Not because young adults are fascinated by widows and fresh scones, but because Kyleigh is beautiful *and* hilarious, and has cultivated a massive social media following.

'It's so amazing that you *know* her, Bella!' Roxy had said not long ago. 'I cannot believe she was literally here in the Dale and you didn't introduce me! I mean . . .'

Roxy often punctuates comments with a dramatic *I mean . . .*, allowing the words to trail off as she gapes at the person she's talking to.

Pandora finds it maddening.

Not Bella. She's reminded of her own teenaged days, when she had her share of conversational idiosyncrasies.

'Later, dawg,' she once said to her best friend, Meredith, as she left Bella's apartment.

As soon as Meredith was out of earshot, her father scolded her.

'Why would you call that pretty young girl a dog? Do you know how hurtful that is?'

'Not *dog*, daddy. *Dawg*.'

'In my day, that's what we called an unattractive person.'

'Well, in *this* day, it's what we call our friends.'

Bella smiles, thinking of Meredith.

Now married with a newborn daughter, she'd recently moved back to their old New York City neighborhood, having taken over her parents' rent-controlled apartment.

Bella keeps in touch with her by text, but they're overdue for a phone chat.

In her most recent message, Meredith had said, You can call me anytime. Seriously – at any hour. I no longer sleep. Ever!

Pandora lets out a gasp. Turning, Bella sees her head jerk up and her eyes open wide.

'Something wicked this way comes,' she says as Bella hurries toward her.

'I've been called a lot of things, Pandora, but wicked isn't one of them.'

'Not you, Isabella. That's what Spirit is telling me: something wicked this way comes.'

Bella recognizes the quote. It's one of the more ominous lines from *Macbeth*, uttered by one of the witches.

'Ah, so the message is from the Bard?' At Pandora's blank look, Bella adds, 'Your old pal from Stratford? Is he—'

'The message is from my *guides*.'

'They're Shakespeare buffs?'

'Isabella, *please*!' Pandora's tone is sharp. 'You mustn't take this lightly.'

'Sorry. I'm just . . .'

Scared. You're scaring me.

Bella bites down on her lower lip to keep from admitting it.

Pandora looks past her, at the glass-paned door.

'Do you think the wicked thing might be a storm?' Bella asks, again noting the swaying branches, whipping flag, and twirling wind chimes. 'Now that we have the new roof, we don't have to worry about leaks anymore, so—'

'This isn't about the *weather*. I'm not Al Roker!'

'Then what *is* it about?'

'I'm afraid you're in grave danger, Isabella. Very grave indeed.'

TWO

Max climbs off the big yellow school bus just outside the Lily Dale gate.

There's an empty little gatehouse where Roxy works during the summer season, and there are brick pillars, and an old-fashioned scrolly iron arch, and a painted blue billboard.

He knows the arch says *LILY DALE ASSEMBLY* and the sign says *THE WORLD'S LARGEST CENTER FOR THE RELIGION OF SPIRITUALISM*. He can't read all those big words, but Jiffy can, even though he's only seven, like Max.

'That's because I have a genius IQ,' he told Max, and explained it means he's super smart compared to everyone else. 'But my mom thinks it's bad to say that.'

'Well, it's true,' Max pointed out, 'and *my* mom says it's bad to lie and she also says your mom has a lot of crazy ideas about what's good and bad to do as a mom.'

'By the way, my mom says the exact same thing about your mom.'

That was a long time ago, when Max first learned that *by the way* is Jiffy's favorite thing to say. It was *before* Jiffy got kidnapped and before their two moms became really good friends like Max and Jiffy.

He trudges up Cottage Row, trailing behind the older kids who live in the Dale. It's a gray, windy day. The streets are made of mud because it rained yesterday and all night long. He usually likes rain and wind, and mud, too, but everything makes him sad now that Jiffy's not around. He always has the best ideas for fun stuff to do.

Up ahead, the big boys are playing catch with an old tennis ball, and the girls are walking the way the girls always do, talking and giggling.

Max wonders how they can have so much to say to each other after riding the bus to school together, sharing a classroom and a lunch table, and riding the bus home together.

He and Jiffy don't always have that much to say, but they have a lot to *do*, even when they're walking.

Sometimes, they run all the way to Valley View and the last one there is a rotten egg. Sometimes, they walk very slowly and look for hidden clues about the pirate treasure Jiffy says is buried by the lake. Sometimes, they count how many trees they can hit with stones – though they're not supposed to do that ever since Jiffy missed the trees and broke Odelia's window. Sometimes on windy days, they tie their jacket sleeves around their necks so they blow behind them like superhero capes. Sometimes on rainy days, they jump into big puddles, pretending they're army paratroopers like Jiffy's dad.

Well, Max isn't sure they'll be doing that last one anymore, because of the terrible thing that happened after school started. Jiffy and his mom Misty have been away ever since, doing whatever it is that boys and ladies need to do after a dad dies.

Max isn't exactly sure what it is, because his own dad died almost two years ago, when he was just a little kid. He remembers crying a lot, and that his mom had cried a lot, too. Sometimes they cried together, and sometimes they tried to pretend they weren't crying.

Especially Mom. She's good at a lot of things, but she wasn't good at that.

You don't have to go away for two months just to cry, though, so there must be other stuff to do.

Without Jiffy, the walk home seems extra far and takes a long time. He's glad he doesn't have to do it again until Tuesday.

Just before dismissal, Mrs Powell, his second-grade teacher, had reminded everyone that there's no school on Monday and asked, 'Who knows what the holiday is?'

No one did, including Max.

If Jiffy had been there, he probably would have raised his hand because he's the smartest kid in the class. Maybe in the whole school.

Max doesn't know who the smartest kid is now that Jiffy's away, but he knows the worst kid.

Robby moved here last week, the day after Halloween.

On the day *before* Halloween, when Max found out a new kid was coming, he was disappointed it couldn't be one day sooner so that maybe they could have picked out matching costumes and carved jack-o'-lanterns and gone trick-or-treating together, the way Max and Jiffy would have done.

Now that he's met Robby, Max knows that never would have happened, and it isn't just because Robby turned out to be a girl.

Not that she's the kind of girl who wears pink dresses and ribbons and doesn't like to run around and get dirty. When Max first saw her, he even thought he might be able to be friends with her. She has glasses, like Max. Her blonde hair is always falling out of its ponytail, like Max's mom's. She likes to wear jeans with holes in them and scuffed sneakers, like Jiffy.

But Robby is nothing like Max, or his mom, or Jiffy. Max would never be friends with her in a million gazillion trillion years.

He turns his head a little bit to see if she's still walking behind him with her mother, who meets her at the bus stop every day.

Yep, still there.

The mom sees Max and waves. Robby crosses her eyes and makes a mean face at Max.

He turns around quickly, wondering how such a terrible kid can have such a friendly, smiley mom.

He wonders, too, why the big kids aren't making fun of Robby because of her mom meeting the bus. They don't seem to be paying any attention to her at all.

When Max first moved here, Jiffy warned Max that only kindergarten moms come to the bus stop. He said the big kids would tease Max if the mom of a first grader did that, and he helped Max convince his mom to stop doing it.

That wasn't easy, because Max's mom has a lot of rules and she likes to keep an eye on him, unlike Jiffy's mom, who has no rules and likes to let him do whatever he wants to do.

Robby is a second grader like Max, but Max didn't tell her about moms and bus stops and big kids and teasing. He was going to turn around and say it the first day, when Robby sat behind him on the way to school, but at first, he was too shy, and then he was too upset because Robby put something gross and slimy down the back of Max's coat.

'Snake!' she yelled, and Max screamed and jumped around until the thing fell out on the floor.

It was just a rubber snake. He recognized it right away. That was the day everyone was supposed to bring something for Show and Tell that reminded them of a fairy tale they'd read. Robby said the snake reminded her of *The Frog Prince*.

Amber Saxton raised her hand and said, 'Then you should have brought a frog, because there isn't even a snake in that book.'

'I like snakes better,' Robby told her.

Amber raised her hand again. 'Well, it isn't called *The Snake Prince*, right, Mrs Powell?'

Robby said, without raising her hand, 'Snakes are cold and slimy just like frogs. Right, Mrs Powell?'

Max doesn't know why Robby didn't put the snake down Amber's back instead of his, because she's the class tattletale. All the kids sitting in the back of the bus laughed, and the ones sitting in front of Max turned around to see what was going on. The bus driver, Mr Johansen, yelled at Max to sit down and be quiet.

Max sat and he pressed his head against the window and tried hard not to cry. He never, ever gets yelled at by Mr Johansen or by anyone, really. Not like Jiffy, who is always getting yelled at by everyone and never minds.

Now, Robby sits right behind Max every morning and afternoon. Max keeps his coat zipped and his hood up even though it's hot on the bus, and he slumps way down in the seat, so that Robby can't put a toy snake or a real snake down his back, and he misses Jiffy so much he feels like crying.

Especially when he sees the older boys drop their backpacks under a big old tree and hoist themselves up into the bare branches. Watching them climb, laughing and shouting at each other, Max thinks that if Jiffy were here, he'd be able to climb higher than anyone else. He's a great climber, except when he falls and gets hurt.

Jiffy's house is up ahead, and Max checks to see if there's stuff like scooters and wiffle bats and sometimes coats and sneakers lying around on the lawn, because that's how it looks when Jiffy is home.

There's no stuff, and it still seems deserted.

A lot of houses do at this time of year, because Lily Dale is mostly a summer place. That's called 'the season,' when people come here from all over the world. Some of them are sick and want to visit the local healers, and some are wondering about the future and want the psychics to tell them what's going to happen. But most of them just want to talk to dead people.

Almost everyone in town can do that, including Jiffy and his mom, Misty.

That's why she has a sign hanging over their front door. Jiffy told him that it says *Misty Starr, Registered Medium.*

Most of the cottages have those signs. Some people just live in them during the summer and some live in them all the time.

Max and his mom live here all the time, but their house is not a cottage. It's a big mansion at the end of the lane, and it has a big sign that says *Valley View Manor Guesthouse*. A smaller sign beneath has words on both sides. Today, the side that says *No Vacancy* is facing out. Max knows that means there are no extra rooms because a lot of people are coming to stay for the holiday weekend, which is Veteran's Day, according to Mrs Powell. She had to answer her own question because no one knew.

'Let's think of our brave Vets and their sacrifices this weekend, boys and girls.'

Max raised his hand to tell her that his mom's special friend, Dr Drew Bailey, is a brave vet.

But she was still talking. 'And let's especially think of our friend Michael Arden.'

Michael Arden is Jiffy's real name. All the kids at school know what happened to his dad except Robby, who raised her hand and asked, 'Who the heck is Michael Arden?'

'Michael is our classmate who lost his father while he was serving our country overseas.'

'Where did he lose him? Did he check under the beds and in the closet?' Robby asked with a snicker.

Mrs Powell said, 'Now, Robby, is that being kind?'

'Uh-huh. I'm just trying to help this kid find his lost dad.'

Amber Saxton's hand shot up in the air and she waved it so hard Mrs Powell called on her before Max.

'Jiffy doesn't like to be called Michael. And his dad isn't that kind of lost. He's dead, right, Mrs Powell?'

'Uh, right. Max, did you have something to share with us?'

He did, but now he wanted to share something different: that Robby never even met Jiffy, and that she's never being kind or just trying to help. And that Amber shouldn't act like she knows everything about Jiffy because she's not even his friend.

He would have said all those things if the bell hadn't rung just then.

Or maybe he wouldn't have. It's a lot easier to do brave things when your super-brave best friend is around. Jiffy isn't afraid of anything, especially speaking up in school. He speaks up way more than Amber Saxton, and he never raises his hand. He spends a lot of time in the principal's office.

Max is looking forward to three whole days of no school and no Robby.

Mom will be extra-busy because of No Vacancy, which means Max will probably watch TV a lot. That used to be a special privilege, but it doesn't feel so special now that Jiffy's gone.

This morning, he'd told Mom that if he had a Playbox video game console, it would cheer him up a lot, because he only gets to play that when he goes to Jiffy's house.

'Nice try, kiddo,' Mom said. 'But we still can't afford that. Maybe Santa will bring one for you.'

'Santa! But Christmas isn't for a long, long time, and Jiffy won't be back for a long, long time, and I really wish I could have Playbox.'

'No, I heard from Misty, and I think they'll be back soon.'

'Yes!' Max shouted. 'I knew that when I woke up this morning! I thought today is the day that he's coming home! Like, how soon do you think? In a few hours?'

'Not that soon, sweetie.'

'After school?'

'I don't know that it will be today, but—'

'A few days?'

'Soon,' was all she said.

Soon isn't soon enough for Max.

And he's not a psychic like Jiffy and Misty and his other Lily Dale friends, but he's still pretty sure today is the day. That's good, because he wants to show Jiffy the jack-o'-lantern he and Dr Drew carved for Halloween.

Well, Dr Drew did the carving, but Max made the face – first on paper, and then on the pumpkin with a Sharpie. He made mean eyebrows and a scary grin.

It's still on the front step, but it's turning black inside, and the face is kind of sunken in, and Mom keeps wanting to put it in the compost pile out back.

'One more day,' Max tells her every day, hoping Jiffy will get back in time to see it.

There's a smaller pumpkin on the step, too, and it isn't carved. Max had brought that one to school on Show and Tell day because it reminded him of Cinderella's pumpkin coach. He wishes he'd brought the black mushy one instead, because he could have put a big slimy chunk down Robby's back on the bus.

'Excuse me,' a grown-up voice calls behind him.

He turns to see Robby's mother waving again. This time, it's not a *hello* kind of wave, but more of a *come here* wave.

Max doesn't come there, but he stops walking and waits for Robby and her mother to catch up to him.

Robby looks kind of like Max's mean, scary jack-o'-lantern face, but her mom looks happy. She has jeans and sneakers and a puffer jacket and a ponytail like his own mom – like a regular mom of a regular kid, but Robby isn't that.

'I'm Mrs Burton, Roberta's mom.'

'Oh . . . uh, who's Roberta?'

'Hey! You're not supposed to call me that anymore!' Robby tells her mother.

'Right. It's Robby now. Sorry, sweetie pie.'

Max expects Robby to tell her mother not to call her sweetie pie, either, but she just looks at the sky.

'Anyway, Maxwell, is it? *Robby* tells me that you two are in the same class.'

She waits for Max to say something, so he says, 'It's not Maxwell, by the way. Just Max.'

'I'm so sorry. Max, then. Since Robby is new in town, I thought it would be nice to set up a playdate. What do you think?'

'About a playdate?'

'Would that be a good idea?'

Max shrugs. 'I guess it depends on who the other kid is and what kinds of things she likes to play with.'

She laughs and pats Max's head. 'You're absolutely adorable.

What I meant was, I'd like to invite you over to play with Robby.'

'*Me?*'

Max glances at Robby. She makes a face that's scarier and meaner than the jack-o'-lantern. She reminds Max of the witches in last night's play, except she's not mixing up a potion in a bubbling cauldron.

Robby's mom asks, 'Would you like to come over to our house, Max?'

'No, thank you,' he says, trying to sound polite. 'I have to go home. My mom is waiting for me.'

'Of course she is. I didn't mean right now. I just meant, one of these days.'

'Which day?'

'How about sometime this weekend?' Before Max can say that he's busy this weekend, she asks, 'Do you like Playbox?'

'Yep.'

'Do you have it?'

'Nope.'

'Robby does, and she has lots of games for it.'

Max hesitates. 'Does she have *Ninja Zombie Battle Armageddon*?'

'Robby?' her mom says.

'Yeah.'

'You have it?' Max asks. 'How about *Ninja Zombie Battle Reckoning*?'

'Uh-huh.' Robby's face looks like they're talking about going to the dentist or eating broccoli.

'I'll call your mom to set it up,' Mrs Burton tells Max. 'She runs Valley View, right? Her name is Bella?'

'How do you know that? Are you a psychic?'

She laughs. 'Me? No.'

'Well, a lot of the people in Lily Dale are psychics.'

'I'm aware. My friend Doris is a medium. She runs the Yin-Yang Inn here in the Dale. Robby and I are staying with her for a while.'

'Only for a while? Not forever?' he asks, hopeful about that.

'Time will tell, Max. I saw your mom's phone number on the list of class parents. Let her know that I'll give her a call later.'

'I will.'

For once, he's glad that his mom is so good at saying no, because he's going to tell her that no matter what, she has to tell Mrs Burton that Max can't have any playdates with mean, scary, terrible Robby.

THREE

Something wicked this way comes . . .

Bella looks from Pandora to the program from last night's *Macbeth* production, right there on the console table.

She clears her throat. 'Pandora, you must be jet-lagged, and I'm wondering if . . . well, maybe you're mistaken and that's not a message from your spirit guides. Do you think the line popped into your head because we were just talking about the play?'

'I'm never mistaken, Isabella.'

'Everyone makes mistakes.'

'*I* don't. Not about *Spirit*.'

'It just seems like an awfully big coincidence.'

Predictably, Pandora says, 'There are no coincidences in Lily Dale.'

'Well, if my life is in danger, I'd like a little more to go on than a quote from *Macbeth*, so—'

'If you'll allow me to meditate, I shall attempt to obtain additional information.'

Feeling as though a customer service representative has just placed her on hold, Bella paces into the parlor with Clancy still snuggled in her arms.

She looks around for her cell phone, wondering if she'd set it down in here earlier, when she was mopping the perimeter of floor not covered by the wool area rug.

This is one of her favorite rooms in the house, with brocade wallpaper, Victorian furniture, and a stately marble fireplace. On a day like this, a fire will make things even cozier for her arrivals.

Check-in begins at four. According to the mantel clock, she has half an hour to build a fire, find her phone, and finish making up the third-floor guest room. *And* get Max settled with his after-school snack.

Balancing Clancy on one arm, Bella reaches past Chance and Spidey to part the lace curtains and peek out. The scene is a little blurry without her glasses, but she spots Max down the way, chatting with the new girl and her mom.

Bella hasn't met them yet. Odelia had told her they're staying at the Yin-Yang Inn, which is unusual. It's run by Doris Henderson, a year-round medium, and it's always been closed in the off-season.

Odelia, who's chairing this month's Sadie Hawkins dance, was on a rant about Doris abruptly dropping off the committee, and could answer none of Bella's questions about the newcomers. 'I've told you everything I know. I was away the week they moved in, and Doris is pretty close-mouthed about them.'

'That's not like her.'

Really, it's not like anyone in the Dale, a quintessential small town where everyone seems to know everyone's business.

Max, too, has been uncharacteristically quiet about his new second-grade classmate. These days, without Jiffy, he's quiet about everything, really. Bella knows that he's just missing his best friend, but she worries that Jiffy's bereavement has also brought back the pain of Max's own.

Next month will mark two years since Sam's passing. Sometimes, the loss still feels so raw that Bella can't believe so much time has passed.

'Isabella?'

She drops the lace curtain and hurries back to Pandora. 'Did you get anything else?'

'I did, I did. Spirit has shown me a body of water.'

'Cassadaga Lake?'

It's a logical assumption, given that the lake is quite literally in Valley View's backyard.

But Pandora shakes her head.

'Smaller. A pond, I believe. Lily pads, and a small duck floating in the reeds.'

'Are you sure it's not the lake? There are lily pads, reeds, and ducks here.'

'It was a pond.'

'That's all you saw?'

'A pond, and a duck. Oh, yes, there was one more thing. A fruit-filled pastry.'

Bella points at the bakery box from Sacred Grounds. 'If that's your way of hinting that you'd like a turnover, Pandora, help yourself.'

Pandora peers inside. 'No, this isn't quite what Spirit showed me. It wasn't a triangular, flaky pastry. It was round and doughy, with a circle of jam, and piped white icing.'

'That's specific.'

'The vision was quite specific.'

'It sounds like you're talking about a Danish. I saw some apricot ones at the café and I'm sure they're still open, if you really want one.'

'No, no, Isabella, I don't *want* a Danish. I *saw* a Danish. It was quite menacing.' She shudders.

'The Danish was menacing? Was it . . . um, alive?'

'It was a pastry, Isabella. Pastries aren't *alive*.'

'The duck was alive, though. Was it menacing?'

'It certainly was.'

'What does it mean?'

'I'm not quite sure.' Pandora looks again at the door, as if expecting Something Wicked to barge in at any moment.

This isn't the first time she's shared a dire warning courtesy of her spirit guides. Nor, if it's true, would this be the first time Bella has faced a life-threatening situation here in the Dale.

But even if there *is* something to Pandora's psychic visions, they aren't always meant for literal interpretation. Like her spiritualist colleagues, she has a unique 'shorthand' – a way of interpreting visions and phrases presented by Spirit.

She'd once told Bella that when her guides show her a bowl of nuts, 'It symbolizes Christmas, because my dear Aunt Eudora always made an English-walnut-studded mincemeat pie for our yuletide feast.'

At that comment, Odelia shook her gingery head and said, 'Not for me. If I see a bowl of nuts, it means someone is bonkers.'

'*Who's* bonkers?' Bella had asked. 'The spirit that's coming through, or the person the message is meant for?'

'Most likely the medium *receiving* the message,' Pandora cracked.

Now, there's not a hint of humor in her expression as she turns away from the door with a shiver. She grabs her red cloak from the coat tree and pulls it on.

'Pandora—'

'I'll take the kitten, Isabella.' She holds out her arms. 'You were absolutely right.'

'About calling him Clancy for short?'

'About getting him home to Cotswold Corner. As much as I appreciate your offer, I can't stay here at Valley View.'

'My . . . *offer*?'

'I really must get home.' Pandora puts Clancy into the carrier and zips it closed, ignoring his mewed protest. She slings the strap over her shoulder and yanks open the front door.

'Wait, what about the rest of your things?'

'I'll retrieve them later.'

She vaults over Hero, now sprawled on the top step, and barrels across the lane, directly in the path of an oncoming car. Its speedometer is likely in the single digits, this being Lily Dale, *and* a rutted dirt road.

The driver skids to a stop for Pandora. She scurries on through the park without a backward glance, like Red Riding Hood with the Big Bad Wolf nipping at her heels.

Hero sits up and barks at the car.

'It's OK, boy.' Bella steps out onto the porch, gives him a reassuring pat, and looks toward Max, now alone and paused in front of the Ardens' cottage. He's gazing up at the little house as if he's willing his best friend to materialize.

Tonight should cheer him up, though. Drew is coming over with dinner.

'What should we have, Max?' he'd asked when he'd dropped them off after the play last night. 'Pizza and wings? Fried chicken and mashed potatoes? Chinese food?'

'I like all of those things! Can we have them all?'

'Choose one, Max,' Bella told him.

'And dessert,' Drew said. 'How about ice cream?'

'Yes! Which kind?'

'Any kind. You can choose two flavors. Let your mom know tomorrow.'

Max had a drowsy smile when she tucked him into bed, pondering ice cream flavors, *Macbeth*'s scary witches forgotten.

With any luck, the prospect of dinner with Drew had buoyed his spirits through the school day.

About to walk down to meet him, Bella sees that the car is now pulling into a parking spot marked *Reserved for Valley View Guests*. Ah, the weekend's first arrival. With any luck, it isn't Fritz Dunkle, who's reserved the third-floor room with the unmade bed.

Nope. A female driver emerges.

Still holding a grudge over the car's near-miss with Pandora, Hero barks again as the woman pops the trunk and goes around to open it.

'It's OK, Hero, she's a guest,' Bella says. 'And it isn't *her* fault Pandora ran out in front of her. Come on, let's go inside.'

The dog dutifully follows her to the tall antique registration desk. She quickly lights a pumpkin-scented jar candle and sets it beside the old-fashioned silver service bell and the guestbook that lies open with a pen in the crease. Beside it, there's a glass bowl of M&Ms and two covered jars, one filled with dog biscuits, the other with cat treats.

The moment she hands Hero a biscuit, Chance and Spidey miraculously stir from their deep sleep, materializing at her feet with expectant gazes.

'You two don't miss a trick, do you?' Bella chuckles and gives them treats, then turns to the shelf behind the desk, where a computer is open to her current reservations list.

There were no guests from mid-September through last week, while the roof work was being done. Most everyone she's expecting this weekend is a summer regular paying an off-season visit, but there are a few newcomers.

Scanning the names, she finds only one solo female traveler, a woman named Jane Anderson. She's reserved the Vineyard Room on the second floor, so named for the purple color scheme and grape-patterned wallpaper.

The front door opens and the woman steps over the threshold, pulling a rolling suitcase.

She's very pretty, with long brown hair and blue eyes. She appears to be in her early to mid-thirties, which is unusual around here.

Valley View has plenty of female guests during the season, but the solo travelers tend to be middle-aged or elderly. They're ill and seeking healing, or they're widows hoping for contact with a late husband. A few are traveling lecturers here to make presentations, or aspiring mediums attending workshops and seminars.

Spotting Bella, the woman says, 'Hi, I'm—'

She stops short, seeing the dog and cats.

'Don't worry, they're friendly,' Bella says.

Hero barks, as if to prove Bella's point . . . or perhaps to disprove it, because she notes a wariness in his gaze as he eyes the newcomer. He'd grown accustomed to strangers coming and going when the season was in full swing, but it's been a while.

'It's OK, I love animals. You have quite the menagerie. I hope your vet gives a volume discount.'

Bella smiles, thinking of Drew, who refuses to charge her for anything.

'What are their names?'

'The kitties are Chance and Spidey, and the dog is Hero.'

'Well, hello, everyone.'

After giving her a cursory glance, the cats go back to their treats. Hero does not.

'Aw, you're a good boy, aren't you?' She leans in to pet him.

He barks again and bounds past her, out the open door and down the steps.

She looks at Bella. 'Uh-oh. Did I scare him away?'

'No, my son is coming up the street on his way home from school. Hero probably sniffed him out.'

'And you just let him wander around on his own?'

Bella isn't sure whether she's talking about Hero or Max – not that it matters.

'I don't let him *wander*. He'll be right back. And the cats are indoor only. But overall, the Dale is safe,' she says, trying not to think about Pandora's warning. 'Everyone here keeps an eye on things.'

The woman takes a last look before closing the door. 'Really? It seems pretty deserted out there.'

'This is the off-season, but there are plenty of year-rounders, so . . .' She shrugs, telling herself the woman is just making conversation, not commenting on Bella's parenting or pet ownership skills.

Born and raised in New York City, Bella had taken quite some time to grow accustomed to the Dale's old-fashioned small-town vibe. Yes, she's had a few brushes with unsavory characters around here, but not because this is a crime-ridden, unsafe area. It really is the kind of place where nobody locks their doors.

The woman returns to the desk. She seems vaguely familiar. A repeat visitor?

Having hosted hundreds of people since she started running Valley View, Bella's gotten to know all the regulars, but she doesn't recall every repeat visitor nearly as well as they do her, so she's learned to introduce herself to everyone.

If they've already met, they're usually quick to remind her. She's grown adept at feigning instant recognition, saying things like, 'Oh, of course, Mrs Wellington! How is it that you haven't changed a bit since last year?' or 'Mr Busby, you must be aging backward! I didn't think that could possibly be you!'

Corny, but in this business, a little flattery goes a long way.

'I'm Bella Jordan,' she says now. 'I'm the manager here.'

'Jane Anderson.' Reaching across the desk, Jane takes Bella's hand in both of hers and squeezes it as though they're long-lost friends. 'It's *so* nice to meet you.'

Ah, a first-timer – at least, on Bella's watch.

'What brings you to Lily Dale?'

'I've just heard so much about it. I mean, hasn't everyone?'

'Everyone but me, until last year,' Bella says with a laugh, opening a file drawer filled with alphabetically arranged folders, each bearing the name of a guest room. 'I found my way here by accident.'

'How so?'

'Long story.'

'I'd love to hear it.' Jane gazes around the stately front hall, with its warm woodwork and amber brocade wallpaper bathed in golden light. 'This place is awesome.'

Her pronunciation strikes a familiar chord with Bella.

Awesome . . .

Oh-ah-some.

It's not polite to comment about someone's accent, so she doesn't ask if Jane, too, is from New York.

'How lucky are *you* to accidentally find yourself living in a place like this?'

'Pretty lucky,' Bella admits with a smile. Then, catching the wistfulness in Jane's blue eyes, she adds, 'Although nothing's perfect, right?'

'Seems pretty perfect to me. A beautiful mansion in a storybook village . . . it's like something out of a fairy tale.'

'Oh, well . . . old houses and small towns have their share of problems.'

'Yeah, well, I'd take *those* problems any day.'

Unsure how to respond to that, Bella reaches into the last folder, pulling out the welcome packet for the Vineyard Room.

It contains the code for the keypad locks on the room door and the main entrance, along with information about breakfast hours, the local area, and house rules, of which there are few. During the summer season, she includes the Dale's daily calendar, which offers a full range of activities from dawn until well after dark.

In November, there's little on the schedule except a Veteran's Day ceremony this Monday, and next week's annual Sadie Hawkins dance.

Bella slides the packet across the desk and turns back to the computer. 'Did you want to charge the room to the credit card you used to confirm the reservation?'

'No, I'll pay cash.'

'By check, app, or debit?'

'By *cash*. You do take cash?'

'We do.' Bella unlocks a desk drawer and opens the lid to a metal box.

'Here you go.' Jane counts out a stack of bills and a couple of coins. 'That's the exact amount, with sales tax, right?'

Bella nods. 'It is, and wow, thanks for being so efficient. During the summer season, I'm always equipped to make change, but at this time of year—'

She pauses as the front door opens.

Max bursts into the house. 'Hey, Mom—'

'Sweetie, wait, please wipe your feet. I just washed the floors.'

He backs up and wipes his feet on the mat. 'Mom, someone is going to—' He stops short, seeing Jane. 'Oh. Sorry.'

She smiles. 'That's all right. You must be Bella's son. You look just like her.'

'No, I don't. I look like my dad. Right, Mom?'

'You do,' Bella agrees.

Max resembles Sam more every day – same intense brown eyes, same spiky brown hair, right down to the cowlick above the bridge of his glasses.

'Well, I guess I can't be a good judge of that until I meet your dad,' Jane tells him.

'He's dead, so you can't meet him.'

'Oh . . . I'm . . . uh, I'm sorry to hear that.'

'Thanks. There's a lot of dead dads around here,' he adds in his matter-of-fact way, bending to pet Chance and Spidey as they rub against his legs. 'My friend Jiffy's dad is dead now, too.'

'That's . . . I'm sorry,' Jane murmurs again, and turns back to Bella, repeating, 'I'm sorry.'

Bella never knows what to say in response to sympathy from strangers. Not, *that's OK*, because it isn't. Not, *I'm sorry, too*, because it comes across as unappreciative. Yet *thank you* doesn't quite seem to fit, either.

She settles on a polite nod and change of subject to avoid questions she doesn't want to answer. 'Max, why don't you go into the kitchen and get your snack while I show our guest upstairs?'

'OK, but this lady—'

'I think there are still some brownies left. And please feed Hero, Chance, and Spidey.'

'It's not their suppertime yet.'

'I know, but they're going to expect treats every time a guest checks in.'

'OK, but this lady—'

'I'll be right there, Max,' Bella says quickly, because you never know what's going to come out of a seven-year-old's mouth. 'By the way, *this lady* is Ms Anderson. Ms Anderson, this is Max.'

'Nice to meet you,' he says glumly, holding out his hand to shake hers, the way Bella taught him. He turns back to Bella. 'You shouldn't say *by the way*, Mom, because it makes me feel sad about Jiffy because I really thought he was going to be here in time to play with me after school.'

'I'm sorry, sweetie. I'm sure a brownie will make you feel better.'

Max shuffles into the kitchen, trailed by the dog and cats.

Bella turns back to Jane. 'Jiffy is his best friend.'

'The one who lost his father?'

'Yes. He and his mom have been away ever since, and Max misses him. You know how it is with friends at that age. At any age, really.'

Jane nods. 'I do. Our friends are supposed to be the people we can count on, aren't they? The only people we can trust in this world. And when they turn their backs on us, disappear from our lives . . . well, it's devastating.'

'Jiffy didn't turn his back on Max, and he hasn't disappeared,' Bella points out. 'Not forever, anyway.'

'Mmm.'

Noting the strange, faraway look in her eye, Bella isn't sure she even heard.

'I'll show you to your room,' she says, picking up Jane's bag and turning toward the stairs. 'You must be exhausted from your trip.'

'Not really.'

Well, Bella is definitely exhausted, and perhaps, as Pandora kept reminding her, just a bit overwhelmed. The sleepless night and flurry of activity are catching up with her.

Outside, the wind kicks up, rattling the panes.

Bella casts an uneasy glance over her shoulder at the door.

Something wicked . . .

Darn Pandora and her warnings.

FOUR

For Bella, the last two hours have been a flurry of guest check-ins.

During the season, the new arrivals would be hurrying right up to their rooms to unpack before an early dinner and the evening program. But there are no programs at this time of year, and the regulars haven't seen Bella or each other in nearly three months. Everyone had plenty of time to linger at the registration desk, and plenty of catching up to do.

It's five thirty before she finally has a moment to light the fire in the parlor and turn on the lamps in the adjacent library, in case her guests decide to do some reading or play one of the board games that fill a section of shelves.

Back in the hall, she retrieves the bakery box.

They're pastries, not Danish. Certainly not dangerous.

She crosses the formal dining room, with its mahogany furniture and vintage crystal. An antique cast-iron fleur-de-lis doorstop props open French doors to the adjacent study. It had once been used by the resident medium for spirit readings. Now it serves as Bella's office. There's a landline phone on the desk that guests are welcome to use for booking appointments with the Dale's registered mediums, whose numbers are listed on a placard.

As she passes the study, she trips over the rug. Holding the bakery box, she doesn't have a free hand to steady herself, and narrowly escapes being impaled on the pronged doorstop.

Shaken, she looks at the box, remembering Pandora's warning. It's not Danish, but perhaps it's dangerous after all.

In the breakfast room, she gladly relinquishes it to the counter, then spends a few minutes making sure everything is ready for tomorrow.

Originally a service porch, the cheerful room has whitewashed wainscoting, café tables covered in blue-and-white gingham, and three walls of windows. In the summer, they're open and the room is breezy, scented with honeysuckle and sweet peas twined up the trellis.

Now, closed off and unused for a few months, it wafts with summer-cottage mildew. The potpourri sachets she'd placed around the room seem to have helped a little, and in the morning, it will be fragrant with coffee, filled with guests and chatter.

She turns off the light and presses her forehead to the glass so that she can see out into the backyard. The wind whips the gingko tree, threatening to scatter all but the most stubborn of its remaining yellow foliage across the lawn. The clothesline looks as though it might snap any second. Beyond, the lake is choppy.

No ducks, menacing or otherwise.

For some reason, she finds that oddly reassuring, despite her resolve not to put much stock in Pandora and her visions.

Anyway, this one was about a pond, not a lake. It might not even have been about a pond, specifically, or even about a duck. The spirit guides might have been indicating a nonspecific body of water or waterfowl.

Remembering the spirit shorthand conversation about bowls of nuts, she wonders if this vision wasn't even about a waterfowl. The word is also a verb.

Duck . . . as in, keep your head down.

Bella glances up at the ceiling. Even in the dark, she can see that it isn't caving in, and there's no enormous anvil hanging by a thread.

'Now who's nuts?' she mutters.

In the back parlor, she finds Max watching Valley View's only television. Spidey is curled up on his lap, Chance dozes by his side, and Hero is sprawled at his feet, snoring.

The room is far more informal than the front parlor, with comfortable furniture. The hardcover she's reading for this month's book club is on the coffee table. The bookmark hasn't budged from Chapter One since she'd checked it out of the library on Halloween, unless you count the time Hero had knocked it off the table and lost her place.

She couldn't even figure out where she'd left off, so she had to start it all over again. It's not that she doesn't like the book; it's just that she's been too busy to sit and read.

How nice it would be to flop down on the couch beside Max and finish the first chapter at last. But she'd probably just doze off, she acknowledges, covering a deep yawn.

This isn't the time for napping *or* reading.

'Hey, Max,' she says, 'I haven't even had a chance to ask you how your day was.'

'Good.' He's transfixed on the screen.

'How was your Stone Soup?'

His second-grade class is doing a unit on fairy tales, fables, and folklore. This week's lesson had culminated in a cooking and tasting project.

'Good.'

'Was there a real stone in the soup?'

'No.'

'Did you—'

'Can you ask me that stuff after *Ninja Zombie Battle* is over, Mom?'

'Sure.'

She retreats to the kitchen, where multiple tasks await. The drying rack is full of clean dishes that need to be put away, the breakfast things are still in the sink, the coffee pot is half-full of this morning's stale brew, and . . . aha. There's her cell phone, sitting on the counter beside her purse, car keys, and three days' worth of mail she'd pulled out of the box this morning.

She sees that she's missed a number of calls: several from Pandora, one from Odelia, and one from Drew. He'd texted as well, at five o'clock, saying he was heading into surgery on an injured dog, and will check back with her after six to see what Max wants for dinner.

Touched that he hasn't forgotten it in the midst of his busy day, Bella puts a heart on the text and responds with a thumbs-up emoji.

Then she calls Odelia, who answers on the first ring. 'There you are, Bella!'

'Sorry, I just saw that you called.'

'No worries. Your guest parking spots are full, so I figured you must be busy with check-ins. I was just calling to confirm that you're coming tonight. It starts at seven.'

'What does?'

'The meeting.'

'The book club meeting?' She could have sworn it's not till after Thanksgiving.

'The Sadie Hawkins dance meeting! Remember, I talked to you about it Tuesday morning?'

'Tuesday morning . . .'

'Election day, Bella. We ran into each other at the polls. You said you'll try to make it tonight.'

'I'm so sorry, Odelia. It completely slipped my mind.'

'And it slipped *my* mind to remind you. I'd let you off the hook, but the dance is a week from tonight, and I still haven't found anyone to replace Doris on the decorations committee. I've asked everyone in town.'

'How about Pandora? She's back from England, and—' Bella breaks off as another call buzzes in. Glancing at the screen, she sees that it's from an unknown number.

That wouldn't give her pause if the call had come in on the landline. It had started ringing off the hook as soon as Kyleigh's video went viral.

Not all the calls were from potential guests. In fact, most were not. One day of kids, cranks, and weirdos was enough. Bella silenced the phone and let the calls bounce to an automated recording.

'You've reached Valley View Guesthouse. We're closed for renovations through the first week of November. If you'd like to make a reservation after that, please do so on our website.'

Problem solved.

Since no stranger who'd seen the viral video would have her personal phone number, today's unknown caller is probably just a telemarketer.

Or a collections agency.

Sam had been a wonderful husband in every way, but he'd let his life insurance policy lapse in favor of investments that were intended to build their nest egg for a home of their own. The investments had failed, as had his health. They'd spent everything they had and extended every bit of credit, for treatments that hadn't saved his life.

Grateful for the rent-free roof over her head, she's scrimping each month to make a dent in the debt, but some bills are long overdue. The interest keeps mounting, and the collectors keep calling.

'Pandora is *back*?' Odelia is asking. 'Why is she *back*? I thought she was staying at least another month.'

'She got homesick. Listen, I've got to take this other call. I'm sure Pandora will be thrilled to help with the decorations. I'll let her know about the meeting.'

'But—'

'Talk to you later! Bye!'

She disconnects with only a slight twinge of guilt. Odelia needs help, Pandora has plenty of time on her hands, and the two women have been making an effort to get along. It's a win-win situation – especially for Bella. If Pandora is tied up with the decorating committee, she'll be less inclined to show up at Valley View making dire predictions or even worse, threatening to move in.

Bella answers the unknown call with a tentative 'Hello?'

Please be a telemarketer, she thinks, mindful of the stack of mail on the counter, mostly bills.

'Bella Jordan?' a woman's voice asks.

'Yes . . .?'

Pleasepleaseplease be a telemarketer.

'Hi! This is Kay Burton.'

'Kay Burton?' Bella echoes.

She sounds so friendly she can't be a bill collector, but Bella can't place the name.

'You probably know that our kids have become friends, and I'd love to set up a playdate.'

'Oh! That's so nice. Is your son . . . he goes to school with Max, then?' she asks, running through the boys in his class, trying to place someone named Burton. He must live outside the Dale. The school district is centralized, and Jiffy is the only other second-grade boy who lives here in town.

Kay chuckles. 'It's my daughter, Roberta. She's in his class. Oops, I mean Robby. She goes by Robby now. I keep forgetting. Anyway, we're new here and she can be a little shy, but she and Max seem to be having fun together, so I thought it would be nice to have him over to play.'

'You're staying at the Yin-Yang Inn, right?'

'We are. The owner speaks very highly of you and Max. She said you're running the guesthouse on your own. She mentioned that Max's best friend has been away, and he's been lonely without him.'

Ironic. Doris Henderson refuses to share much info about her current guests with the locals, but she's apparently not opposed to sharing info about the locals with them.

'Anyway, I was thinking tomorrow morning might be a good time, if Max isn't busy?'

'Oh . . . that would be nice. I'd be happy to have Robby come here.'

'I think they've got plans that involve Playbox. I just got it for Robby to make the move a little easier on her, and Max said he doesn't have one, so . . .'

'Ah, Playbox. I'm sure Max would love that.'

'Perfect. Why don't you drop him off at ten and he can stay for lunch?'

Bella hesitates. Ordinarily, she wouldn't let Max have a playdate at a stranger's house without her. But she'll be tied up at Valley View with her guests tomorrow morning.

Anyway, it's right around the corner in the Dale, and Doris is a friend, though she's one of those people who's always trying to help you the way they think you need to be helped – whether or not you need help in the first place. Maybe that's because in addition to being a medium and a shamanic healer, she's a social worker and therapist who'd once told Bella that her mission in this earthly life is to help women overcome repression and oppression.

She means well, but Bella often has to remind her that not every woman is oppressed. She herself is just a busy single mom who's grieving the loss of her husband, trying to run a business and take care of her son . . .

Who, while he's not oppressed or repressed, has certainly been *depressed* for a while now without Jiffy.

How can she deny Max the opportunity to play with a new friend?

'That sounds great,' she says. 'Thanks so much, Kay. Max will be thrilled. See you tomorrow.'

FIVE

When Jiffy is here, he and Max always watch *Ninja Zombie Battle* to the very end of the credits, because they like to sing along with the theme song.

We're zombies . . . our hobbies . . . are dead bodies!
We're warriors . . . without barriers . . . we're scarier!

Sometimes, they act out the song, jumping around on the couch. Sometimes, Mom hears and gets mad and comes in to say someone is going to get hurt even though no one ever does.

Except once, when Jiffy dove onto a pillow and a big heavy book was there and the corner gave him a black eye.

'It's OK, Bella,' he told Mom. 'I've got a lot of other black eyes from falling off my scooter the other day, but you can't see them because they're on my arms and legs.'

'Wow, can I see them?' Max asked, and Jiffy pulled up his jeans to show him a bunch of purple bruises.

Then Max wanted to know where the eyes were, and Jiffy acted like that was a stupid question because eyes are only on faces, and Max told him he shouldn't say he has black eyes on his legs because that's lying, and they had a big argument and Jiffy went home.

But the next day, they were friends again.

Max thinks that if Jiffy ever wants to show him black eyes on his legs again and there are no eyes again, this time he won't say it's a lie, because he doesn't want to have any more fights with Jiffy.

We're zombies . . . our hobbies . . . are dead—

Max turns off the TV and tosses the remote on the table.

Mom sticks her head in from the kitchen. She's holding her phone in her hand.

'Max? Is your show over?'

'Uh-huh.'

'Drew wants to know if you've decided what you want him to bring for dinner and dessert.'

Max shrugs. 'He can choose.'

Mom frowns. 'But he wants you to choose. You were so excited about it last night. Do you want pizza, or—'

'Pizza's good.'

'Pizza,' Mom says into her phone. Then she asks Max, 'Wings, too?'

'OK.'

'Wings, too,' Mom says. 'What about the ice cream, Max?'

'Yeah, ice cream's good.'

'But what kind? You get to choose the flavors.'

'Dr Drew can choose.' Max leans back, petting Spidey, feeling his rumbly purring under his soft black fur.

'He says it's up to you,' Mom says into the phone. 'Yes. I know. No, that'll be perfect. OK. See you soon.'

She hangs up and puts her phone back into her pocket, but she stays in the doorway, watching him.

'Max?'

'Yeah?'

'Are you OK?'

He isn't, but he doesn't want to talk about it. Mom always knows when he lies, though, so he says, 'I just really miss Jiffy and this morning when I woke up, my head told me that he was going to come home today.'

'I know, sweetie. But guess what? I have some great news.'

He sits up straight so fast that Spidey gets scared and sticks a sharp claw in Max's hand.

'Ouch!'

Spidey jumps off his lap and runs across the room. Hero bolts up and gives a worried bark. Chance opens one eye to see what's going on, and then closes it again.

Mom hurries over. 'Oh, Max, did he hurt you? Let me see.'

He shows her his hand. There's a little bit of blood coming out of the soft V between his thumb and finger.

'We have to clean it right away,' Mom tells him. 'Come on. I don't want you to get an infection.'

'Do you think I'll get a bruise, though?'

'I hope not.'

Max hopes *so*, because the great news must be that Jiffy's coming home, and Max can show him a bruise and tell him about how Spidey got all fierce and Max had a battle with him, which will not even be a lie.

'Come on. The first aid kit is upstairs. Let's go.' She gets him off the couch and steers him out of the room.

'Wait, we should call Dr Drew and tell him to get extra ice cream. And he should get the chocolate kind with peanut butter swirls.'

'He said he'll get chocolate for sure,' Mom says as they head upstairs.

'With the peanut butter swirls? Because that's Jiffy's favorite. And we should make sure he gets the wings extra hot and not just medium hot, because Jiffy likes those the best.'

'Sweetie, when Jiffy comes home, we'll get the things that Jiffy likes, but tonight, let's just get what you and I and Dr Drew will eat.'

'But Jiffy's coming home tonight.'

Mom doesn't say anything about that. She just opens a door marked *Private*. This is the bathroom that's just for her and Max to use.

'Mom? Remember? You said this morning that he's coming home soon but maybe not today.'

'Right. *That's* what I said. Misty told me they'll be home soon.'

'Well, my head told me that soon is today.'

Mom turns on the water and rummages under the sink for the first aid kit. 'Start washing, Max. Lots of soap.'

He puts his hand under the water. There's only a little bit of blood. It runs into the sink and swirls away. He pumps some soap onto his palm, and it stings a little where Spidey clawed him.

'But Mom—'

'Wait a second, Max . . .' Her head is under the sink. 'I'm trying to find the – oh, here it is.'

She stands up, holding the first aid kit. 'I guess we use this a lot more when Jiffy's around, don't we? Here, let me see that hand.'

Max turns off the water and holds it out to her. She pours some liquid from a brown bottle onto a cotton square and starts patting the cut with it.

'Ow!'

'Sorry, sweetie. We need to clean it with peroxide to make sure you don't get an infection.'

He squeezes his eyes closed and turns his head until it's over.

Then she dabs some goop from a little yellow tube into the cut.

'How does that feel? OK?'

'Yeah, it doesn't hurt anymore. Can we be done?'

'As soon as I bandage it up. Let's see, we've got Batman, Spiderman, Superman . . . which superhero do you want?'

'Spiderman,' Max says. 'Because Spidey's the one who hurt my hand. He didn't mean it, though. He just got scared when I jumped up because you said you have some great news about Jiffy coming home tonight.'

'I do have great news, sweetie.' Mom peels off one side of the bandage. 'But not about that.'

'That's the only great news I want.'

'Stay still, OK?' She puts the sticky side on his hand. 'I know how lonely you've been, so I've set up a playdate for you—'

Max stops staying still, because he'd forgotten all about that until just now.

'With Robby?' he asks, just as Mom says the very same words.

'With Robby. Yes. Stay still.' Mom peels off the other side of the bandage. 'Her mother called and invited you over to their house tomorrow.'

'No! That's terrible news! It's the worst news ever!'

'Max! Stay still!'

'That's the thing I was going to tell you about when I got home, but you kept interrupting me and that's not even polite!'

Mom is finished with the bandage. She leans back and looks at him. She looks really, really tired. And really sad. He feels bad about yelling at her.

'Sorry,' he says. 'You're usually always polite.'

'Oh, Max. I'm sorry, too. I thought you'd be happy about the playdate. Robby's mom said you two are friends.'

'We're not friends! I don't even talk to her.'

'Well, her mom says she's shy.'

'She's not shy. I don't like her.'

'Why not?'

He considers telling his mom about how she put a fake snake

down his back and made everyone laugh at him and how he got yelled at because of it.

But Jiffy says you shouldn't be a tattletale.

Max shrugs. 'I just don't like her.'

'Well, it's not easy to be new in a school where everyone knows everyone else. You know that, because that's how it was for you, Max.'

'Uh-uh. I knew Jiffy.'

'You were lucky. It sounds like Robby can use a friend, too, doesn't it?'

'I guess, but it can't be me.'

'Is it because she's a girl?'

'No!'

'Good. Because a friend is a friend, no matter what they look like on the outside. It doesn't matter whether it's a boy or a girl, or what color their skin is, or how old they are, or where they came from. We can make friends with all kinds of people. The only thing that counts is what's on the inside.' Mom taps the spot over her heart.

'I *know* that. You always tell me that. But . . .' He wants to tell Mom that Robby's insides are not friendly, but that doesn't seem like the right way to say it.

'Oh, and Max, guess what? Robby's mom says she has Playbox. You were just talking about how much you miss it.'

'I only miss Jiffy's Playbox. I only miss Jiffy.'

All of a sudden, Max's scratched hand hurts very badly, and so does the rest of him. He looks down at the floor, feeling like he's going to cry.

'Oh, sweetie . . .' Mom puts her arms around him. 'I know. I'm so sorry. I—'

There's a loud bang downstairs.

For a second Mom looks so afraid that Max is afraid, too.

But then he hears the bell ding on the registration desk, and a man's voice calls, 'Hello?'

'It's a guest,' Mom says. 'Go hang out in your room until I get him checked in, and then we'll talk.'

Mom hurries downstairs.

As Max shuffles down the hall toward his room, he sees something move at the far end of the hall.

Something – someone – is there, at the foot of the stairs that go up to the third floor, and then they're gone.

Guest or ghost?

Whoever it is goes up the stairs very slowly, as if they're being sneaky and trying not to make the steps creak.

Guests don't do that. Ghosts probably don't either.

What if it's a witch?

Heart pounding, Max hurries into his room, closes the door, and locks it behind him.

SIX

Bella would have recognized the stout, gray-bearded man waiting for her by the registration desk even if she hadn't been expecting him.

Fritz Dunkle had checked into Valley View on her very memorable first day here.

A college English professor from Pennsylvania, he'd come to research a book he was planning to write about Lily Dale.

Bella had been pleased when she'd seen his name come up on this weekend's reservations list. She's often wondered about him.

'Sorry about the commotion, Bella,' he greets her, removing his black brimmed hat, revealing a head that's grown considerably balder since last year. 'There's a wicked wind out there. It grabbed the door and slammed it closed.'

Something wicked . . .

No. Pandora claimed her message had nothing to do with the weather.

'Welcome back to Valley View, Professor.'

'Thank you. I almost didn't recognize the place. It's looking considerably spruced up since my last visit.'

She smiles. 'It's a work in progress. Speaking of which . . . how is yours coming along?'

'Oh, I'm not a homeowner.'

'I meant the book. I have a writer friend who always calls hers the "work in progress," so . . . how is yours coming along?'

'My academic responsibilities were so demanding these last few semesters that I had to put the book on hold, but that was for the best. Time and distance have provided some much-needed perspective.'

'That's what my writer friend says about writing.'

'You're referring to Calla Delaney? The novelist?'

'You know her?'

'I know that she's based here – Odelia Lauder's granddaughter, correct? And she moved back to the Dale last year?'

'You know a lot.'

'All part of my research. And I read Calla Delaney's novel. It's quite good. I'd love to meet her. Do you think you can introduce me to her?'

'Oh . . . ah, sure. If she's around.'

'That would be terrific. I have a few questions I'd love to ask her. Pick her brain a little, if you don't think she'd mind.'

'I'm sure she'd be happy to chat with a fellow writer.'

'Would-be writer,' he says with a chuckle. 'But I'm taking an academic sabbatical in the spring, so I'm planning on revisiting the Lily Dale book with a whole new angle.'

'Well, you're in the Jungle Room on the third floor,' Bella says, going around the desk and opening her file drawer. 'It's nice and quiet up there, in case you want to get some writing done this weekend.'

'Excellent.' He helps himself to a handful of M&Ms. 'I was glad to find out you're still here running Valley View. I thought this was just temporary last summer and that you and Max were moving in with your mother in Chicago?'

'My mother died when I was just a baby. We were planning to move in with my mother-in-law, Millicent.'

Back then, her secret nickname for Sam's formidable mom had been Maleficent, and she was their last resort.

For years, Bella had seen Sam's mother as cold and unyielding. She's changed. Something – age? grief? – seems to have blurred those sharp edges.

Perhaps Bella, too, has changed and softened, willing to forge a relationship with the woman who shares her profound loss and her maternal concern for Max.

'That was the plan, but . . .?' Fritz prompts.

'But Lily Dale felt like home, so we stayed.'

'Interesting. It doesn't seem like the ideal place for a young widow to settle down to raise a child.'

'Well, my husband and I both grew up in cities, and they have so much to offer, but they're expensive, noisy, crowded . . .' She shrugs. 'We dreamed of raising our son in a small town.'

'There are plenty of those that aren't . . . *Lily Dale*.'

Bella stops thumbing through the folders in the drawer and looks up to see him regarding her with narrowed eyes, stroking his beard.

'Are you questioning my choice because I'm not a spiritualist, Professor?'

'I'm questioning it because you don't strike me as a reckless person.'

'What do you mean?'

'This is a dangerous place.'

'Because of what happened last summer? Leona's death?'

'Leona's *murder*.'

'Those were extraordinary circumstances.'

'My research has shown me that there have been quite a few *extraordinary circumstances* since then. Grifters, kidnappers, art thieves . . .' He ticks them off on his fingers. 'It seems to me that this town is a magnet for criminals.'

'And it seems to *me* that you're way off base.' Bella grabs the welcome packet from the Jungle Room folder and shoves the drawer shut. 'Lily Dale is a tourist town. Anyplace that draws outsiders is going to draw its share of crime.'

'Fair enough. But statistically speaking, Lily Dale draws *more* than its share.'

She decides to ignore that comment. She's running a business, and Fritz Dunkle is a guest.

'I'd like to speak to local law enforcement while I'm here. Do you remember that nice young man who investigated Leona's murder with you last summer?'

'You don't mean Lieutenant Grange?' He isn't nice, or young, and he didn't investigate anything *with* Bella. She's had many a run-in with him since last summer, and he usually behaves as if he's investigating Bella herself.

'Yes! Lieutenant Grange. Is he still around?'

'I don't think so,' she lies.

'That's a shame.'

Pasting on a smile, she nods toward the stairs. 'I'll show you up to your room.'

'After you.' Ever the gentleman, he makes a sweeping gesture.

She leads him up two flights and demonstrates how to unlock the electronic keypad.

'Oh, and the code for the front door is in the packet. You'll need it to come and go after hours.'

'Last time I was here, there were just old-fashioned iron keys,' he observes. 'It was quaint. Why the change?'

'Oh, you know . . . just sprucing up the place, like you said.'

He sets his bag on the luggage rack and looks around, taking in the green frond-patterned wallpaper, leopard- and zebra-print fabrics, paintings of animals grazing on grassland and savannah, and faux fur throw rug.

'I certainly see why you decided to call this the Jungle Room.'

'I can't take the credit – or blame, as the case may be. It was all Leona.'

He lifts a bushy gray eyebrow.

She barrels on, sensing the sequiturs aligning in his brain – *Leona . . . murder . . . Lily Dale is dangerous.* 'Odelia told me that Leona went on an African safari a few years back, and that's what inspired the room. She brought back those masks hanging over the bed – they're hand-carved ebony, made in Zimbabwe. And that barkcloth throw on the chair is from a tribe in Uganda. The photo album on the desk is full of pictures from her trip.'

'Fascinating. Such a shame what happened to her, isn't it?'

Bella steps back into the hall, saying only, 'I'll let you get settled in. Let me know if you need anything.'

'Will do. Thank you. And Bella? I may have overstepped a bit. What I said about crime and Lily Dale – I hope it didn't seem as though I was criticizing your choices.'

'Oh, it did,' she says with as natural a smile as she can muster.

'I'm just concerned about you and Max.'

Maybe that's true.

Maybe she's feeling defensive because Jane Anderson had also questioned her about whether Lily Dale is safe.

Maybe it's Pandora's warning, still ringing in her ears.

'I'm sure you meant well, and I appreciate the concern. Holler if you need anything.' She turns and continues on down the hall.

Hearing him close his door, she exhales in relief. She shouldn't have to defend her choices to someone she barely knows, regardless of his intentions, and she hates that he's making her second-guess herself.

Of course she and Max are safe here in Lily Dale.

She rounds a corner and cries out as a figure looms in her path.

'Sorry! I didn't mean to scare you.'

It's Jane Anderson, looking amused. And – again – vaguely familiar. She definitely reminds Bella of someone. It must be the accent – the way she says 'scare' so that it's two syllables, without an R.

'You look like you've seen a ghost. Is that what you thought I was?' Jane asks.

'No, I . . .' Pulse racing, Bella shakes her head. 'I've never seen a . . . well, they don't say *ghost* around here. It's *spirit*. Although I'm pretty sure that if you can see it, they call it an apparition.'

'*They?*'

'The locals. They're mediums. You *do* know that, right?'

'Oh, I know, but . . . it sounds like you're *not* a medium?'

'Just a boring old guesthouse manager. And a mom,' Bella adds, 'and my son is waiting for me, so—'

'I was just coming to find you because I wanted to ask you about something.'

'Is everything OK with the room?'

'It's fine. The complimentary bottle of wine is a nice touch.'

'Well, it *is* the Vineyard Room.' Bella smiles. 'There are quite a few wineries around here, if you're interested in a tour and tasting.'

'No, I'm probably just going to lie low and relax this weekend. And I thought I'd try the regional cuisine for dinner.'

'Great idea. Western New York is famous for its Fish Fry, and a lot of restaurants around here only have it on Fridays, so you're in luck. The other local specialty is beef on weck – that's roast beef on a salted roll with caraway.'

'I was thinking of Buffalo chicken wings.'

'Here they're just wings,' Bella says lightly, but she's pretty sure she sees a flicker of irritation in Jane's blue eyes.

She gives a stiff nod. '*Wings*, then. Do you know a good place that delivers?'

'I can definitely recommend some great places if you don't mind driving a few miles, but we're so far off the beaten path that delivery is hard to find.'

'Oh. That . . . that's too bad.' With a shrug, Jane retreats into her room, closing the door before Bella can elaborate.

Not that there's anything else to say. She doesn't owe Jane an apology, though she almost feels as though she did something to offend the woman. Which is ridiculous.

She's just not used to dealing with strangers in the house after two months of reservations hiatus. She'll get back into the swing of things, especially after a relaxing dinner with Drew, and a good night's sleep at last.

But right now, Max is her priority.

She descends to the second floor, knocks on his door, turns the knob, and finds it locked.

'Max?' She knocks again. 'It's Mom.'

'OK.'

The door opens, and he looks up at her, brown eyes glum behind his glasses.

'Why did you lock the door?'

'I don't know.'

'Is your hand feeling better?'

'Uh-huh. Is Dr Drew here?'

'Not yet.'

'OK, well, tell me when he gets here, and I'll come out.'

'Wait, Max? Let's talk, OK?'

She steps into the room.

On their first night at Valley View, the entire house had been deserted, and she'd let him choose where he wanted to sleep. He'd settled on this, the Train Room, with its blue and white railroad-themed décor. It reminded him of his dad, who'd ridden the commuter train to work in Manhattan every day.

Now that the room officially belongs to Max, there are mementos everywhere – framed photos of father and son, board games they used to play together, a stuffed puppy Sam had won for Max at a carnival that last summer together.

Millicent has contributed Sam's own favorite childhood belongings: favorite books, Lincoln Logs and Tinker Toys, a well-worn kid-sized baseball mitt, and countless other treasures.

Bella perches on the bed and pats the spot beside her.

Max with the enthusiasm of a patient in a doctor's waiting room. 'What do you want to talk about?'

'About that Playbox playdate tomorrow.'

'I don't want any playdates. My hand is hurting, so I can't use the Playbox controller.'

'I have a feeling it wouldn't hurt if Jiffy came home tomorrow.'

'Is he?'

'I'm not sure.'

He sighs and stares at his sneakers.

This Max – forlorn, anxious, withdrawn – reminds her of the Max who'd struggled through kindergarten back in Bedford. Sam was sick through the first half of the school year, and the second half was the aftermath of his devastating loss.

Back then, Bella feared that her son would never experience the happy-go-lucky childhood she and Sam had envisioned for him. She's pretty sure she didn't see him smile for almost a year.

Then they found their way to Lily Dale, and within the first few days, Max wasn't just smiling; he was buoyant. Jiffy had played a huge role in that transformation.

But Max really should be making other friends. Misty has never been the most stable parent around. She says she and Jiffy are coming home, but what if she changes her mind?

If not now, then in the future? Her move to Lily Dale had been spontaneous. Another spontaneous move wouldn't be out of character.

Bella can't protect Max from further loss, but she can help him foster relationships with other kids, especially if they live right here in the Dale.

'I think it's a good idea for you to play with Robby tomorrow, Max.'

'But I *hate* Robby!'

'We don't say hate.'

'I don't like Robby even a tiny bit, Mom.'

'Max, boys and girls can be good friends.'

'I know that!'

'I'm just saying, if it's because—'

'It's not because Robby's a girl; it's because she's . . .'

'Because she's not Jiffy?'

He shrugs. 'I just don't want to be friends with her.'

'Fair enough.'

'So, I don't have to have the playdate?'

'It would be awkward to cancel it now that you've said yes, Max.'

'I didn't say yes! You said yes!'

'I know, and I'm sorry. I should have checked with you first.'

'You should have! Why didn't you?'

'Because . . .' Bella closes her eyes briefly.

Because I am exhausted and overwhelmed.

She shakes her head, opens her eyes, and tells Max, 'Because sometimes, when I'm trying to do the right thing, I do the wrong thing.'

'That's called a mistake.'

'It is. You're a smart kid.'

'Thanks. And you're usually a smart mom.'

'Right. But everyone makes mistakes, Max. Even smart kids and usually smart moms. And I think it would be a mistake for you not to try a playdate with Robby.'

'I think it would be a mistake for you to make me do that.'

'I know you do.'

'So I don't have to go?'

'I have to think about it before I make a final decision.'

'For how many minutes?'

'I need longer than minutes, kiddo.' She pulls her phone out of her pocket to check the time and sees that there's a new text from Drew: *On my way.*

Buoyed, she puts a heart on his message, tucks her phone back into her pocket, and stands. 'Come on, kiddo, let's get moving. I have a few things to do, and you can set the table for dinner.'

'OK, but Mom?'

'Mmm hmm?'

'Can I set four plates, just in case Jiffy comes home and wants some pizza and wings?'

She hesitates, wanting to warn him not to get his hopes up.

But Misty *had* said they're on their way, and who is Bella to discourage hope? It's the one thing that's sustained her through the hardest days of her life, regardless of how things had played out.

Bella nods and ruffles his hair. 'Sure you can, Max.'

SEVEN

When there are no guests at Valley View, the long dining room table always has a lot of stuff on it, like puzzles Max and his mom are working on, and baskets of laundry and school projects and sometimes Chance and Spidey. When there are guests here, it only has a lacy tablecloth, candlesticks, and a vase of flowers. They eat in the kitchen unless they have company or it's a special occasion.

Dr Drew isn't really company, and this isn't a special occasion – yet. It will turn into one when Jiffy comes, even though Jiffy isn't really company either. There are two pizza boxes in the middle of the table, and there's a box of wings with celery sticks and little plastic cups of blue cheese dressing.

There's also a bottle of wine that Dr Drew brought in a shiny silver bag with a ribbon on it. He and mom are drinking it, sitting opposite each other. Max is next to Mom so he can see Dr Drew across the table, and Jiffy, too, when he comes.

Dr Drew has brown hair and eyes and wears glasses like Dad, but he's taller and he has bigger shoulders. And he usually wears plaid shirts and jeans and work boots instead of suits and ties, and he doesn't shave the fuzz on his face very often. He's super nice to Max, like Dad was, and he always tells the best funny stories, like Dad did.

'And *then* what happened, Dr Drew?' Max asks, bouncing a little on his chair, because tonight's story is extra funny.

'And *then* that silly dog coughed and coughed and coughed some more, and out came the baby's *other* shoe!'

'So he really did eat both of them!'

'He really did.'

'I'll bet the baby's mom was glad they popped back out.'

'I don't know if *glad* is the right word for it.'

'Is *excited* the right word?'

'I'll bet *relieved* is the right word,' Mom says. 'Because the dog was OK, and he didn't need an expensive operation.'

'And the baby didn't need expensive new shoes,' Max points out. 'I just hope she washed them off before she put them back on the baby.'

'Oh, I doubt anyone will be wearing *those* shoes again,' Dr Drew says.

Mom laughs and dips a wing into some blue cheese. 'Well, I'm glad everyone is OK. I like a story with a happy ending.'

'Me, too. Especially when it's about a dog,' Max adds, looking down at Hero, sitting patiently under his chair.

Mom always says not to feed him from the table, but he seems so sad that Max sneaks him the last bit of the crust from his pizza.

Hero gobbles it up and wags his tail.

Dr Drew and Mom are talking about some boring adult stuff about Odelia and Pandora and a committee, and about when Mom's car should have an oil change, and about new equipment Dr Drew needs to get for the animal hospital.

Max wishes Jiffy would get here and sit in the empty chair across from him and put some pizza on the empty plate.

Still hungry, he lifts the lid on the pepperoni pizza box and counts how many slices are left.

There are five. He already had one and Dr Drew had two. Mom only likes the veggie kind that's in the other box.

Max hates veggies. So does Jiffy, so if he comes, he'll want the pepperoni one.

'Go ahead, Max,' Dr Drew says. 'There's plenty. I might have another slice myself.'

Jiffy will probably eat at least three, but he might want four. If Dr Drew wants another slice, too . . .

Mrs Powell always says you shouldn't do math on your fingers, only in your head or on paper. But Mrs Powell isn't here, so Max puts his hand under the table and figures it out.

Five take away four equals one.

One minus one equals zero.

There won't be enough for Jiffy to have four pieces if both Max and Dr Drew have another one.

Max takes another wing instead. And a piece of celery, because he likes that even though it's green and kind of seems like a veggie. He doesn't want any blue cheese, though. He tried it once thinking he might like it because he likes his mom's blue scones. But it was disgusting, because cheese that's blue isn't delicious like berries that are blue.

As Max takes a bite of the wing, Hero sits up and looks toward the front of the house. Someone is coming in the front door.

'Jiffy's here!' Max pushes back his chair. 'I knew it, Mom! I told you—'

But then he hears someone talking, and it's not Jiffy.

It's an old lady, saying, 'No, no, Ruby, I'm certain that was Mother.'

'It *wasn't* Mother. Mother was always cheerful. This spirit was so very ornery.'

'Well, of course she's ornery, dear. She's dead, remember?'

It's *two* old ladies, the St Clair sisters. They come to Valley View a lot. Max likes them. But he wishes they were Jiffy.

'Yes, I remember! I'm not the forgetful one, Opal! You are!'

'Oh. I thought *I* was the lactose intolerant one.'

'That would be *me*. Come, let's go into the breakfast room and have a nice cup of tea before bed, shall we?'

'Breakfast? Already? I feel as though I haven't slept a wink.'

'Forgetful *and* deaf as a post,' her sister says as they step into the dining room.

Mom says they're not twins even though they look exactly alike – both with wrinkly faces and white hair piled on top of their heads. They always dress alike, too – tonight, in gray sweaters and pearls.

'Oh, hello, Bella,' one of them says. 'And my goodness, Maxwell, you've grown a foot since the summer.'

'Two feet, at least,' the other sister says, peering at Dr Drew. 'And he has a beard!'

Dr Drew stands up, smiling. 'Actually, ladies, *that's* Max.' He points at Max. 'I'm Bella's friend, Drew. And that's Hero,' he adds, pointing at the pup.

'Well, it's very nice to meet you,' the lady says, shaking Dr Drew's hand, then turning to Max. 'And you, as well.'

'Ruby, you've already met everyone! I just *knew* you were the forgetful one!'

'And my name's just Max. Not Maxwell,' Max says in a grumpy voice, remembering that Robby's mother had called him the same thing.

Mom gives him a *that's not polite* headshake, then asks, 'Did you ladies have a nice dinner?'

'I believe we did. Did we, Ruby?'

'Yes, we dined at the café across the park, and then we had a reading with Doris Henderson. Mother came through. She was in a foul mood.'

'I don't think it was Mother at all,' Opal says.

'Are you *sure* it was even Spirit?' Max asks. 'Because I know someone who's always in a bad mood and she's staying at Doris's inn. Maybe it was her.'

'Max,' Mom says in a warning voice.

'Yeah?'

Mom just shakes her head at him and tells the St Clairs to go help themselves to some tea. 'There's a teabag selection on the counter. Honey, too. And there are lemon wedges in the fridge, and milk.'

'Oh, I can't have milk, Bella. I'm lactose intolerant.'

'Opal! No, you aren't! I am!'

'You just said *you* were the forgetful one!'

Bickering, they disappear into the breakfast room.

Dr Drew turns to Max. 'So . . . *who's* always in a bad mood and staying at Doris's?'

'Robby.'

'Robby . . .'

'The new girl in Max's class,' Mom says.

'Huh. Robby's a cool name.'

'It's short for Roberta,' Mom says, mostly to Max, like that interesting fact might change his mind about her.

He makes a grumpy face and crunches a piece of celery.

Mom rolls her eyes and turns back to Dr Drew. 'Anyway, her mom invited Max over to play video games tomorrow, but he's reluctant.'

'Don't you like video games anymore, Max?' Dr Drew asks.

'I do. But I only like to play them with Jiffy, and he's probably coming home tonight.'

'Well, that's great news.'

Mom shakes her head. She looks extra, extra tired. 'I didn't say tonight.'

Dr Drew rubs his scruffy chin. 'And Robby is staying with Doris?'

'Yes, she and her mom. They seem very nice.'

'Well, they're *not* nice at all,' Max says, and his mom gives him a *look* again. 'What? You don't even know them!'

'I spoke to Robby's mom,' she says, mostly to Dr Drew. 'And *she* seems very nice. And apparently Robby is shy, so—'

'She's *not* shy,' Max says.

'Do you think I'm shy, Max?' Dr Drew asks.

'Nope.'

'Well, I was when I was your age. We moved, and I had to leave my school and all my friends. It isn't easy to be the new kid.'

'That's not what's wrong with Robby.'

'Then what's wrong with her?'

Max leans back in his chair and folds his arms across his chest, feeling like he's going to cry. But that would be even worse than tattling, even if it's just in front of Mom and Dr Drew.

For a second, everything is quiet except the wind outside.

Then Hero's tags jangle. He looks toward the parlor and barks.

Seeing the shadow of a person on the wall, Max gasps, remembering the witches.

Mom looks, too, and calls, 'Hello?'

Someone pokes her head around the doorway.

Not a witch. Just the lady who was checking in when Max got home from school.

'Sorry to bother you,' she says, looking from Mom to Max to Dr Drew to the food on the table. 'I was just about to go out in search of Buff – I mean, *wings* – and I was hoping you could steer me in the right direction.'

'Wings?' Dr Drew echoes. 'Have a seat and help yourself. There are plenty right here.' He points to the box on the table and then at the empty plate that's waiting for Jiffy.

'Oh, I couldn't . . .'

But she looks like she could, so Max points out, 'There aren't really *plenty*. Just a few.'

He expects Mom to act like he shouldn't have said that, but she nods. 'We're expecting Max's friend, Jiffy.'

Dr Drew gives her a surprised look.

'Oh . . . that's all right. I wouldn't want to take his food. I'm Jane Anderson, by the way,' she tells Dr Drew, coming over to shake his hand.

'Drew Bailey.'

'Anyway, Bella, I was just going to ask directions to a restaurant that serves them, and—' Jane stops talking, scrunching her face at Mom like she just remembered something. 'Bella!'

'Yes . . .?'

'Bella Angelo?'

Now Mom seems surprised. 'How did you know that?'

'I knew you seemed familiar! It's me! Ethel Schweinsteiger!'

EIGHT

Ethel Schweinsteiger...

'You don't remember me, do you.' Jane's – *Ethel's?* – tone is flat, and there's a challenge in the gaze she levels at Bella.

Ethel Schweinsteiger...

The name does ring a bell. It takes Bella a moment to match it to a time, place, and face.

There had been an Ethel Schweinsteiger in her high school graduating class. But she'd born no resemblance to this woman.

'You're Ethel?'

'I am.'

'But . . . you went to Dorothy Arnold High School with me?'

She nods, saying, 'Very good,' like a teacher praising a not-very-bright student.

'You changed your name.'

'Wouldn't you?'

Bella shrugs. 'My father always told me to be proud of who I am and where I came from.'

It comes out sounding a little judgmental, which isn't her intention.

Jane's frown indicates that it was received that way. 'Well, *your* father's surname starts with angel. Mine starts with pig.'

'I thought it starts with *schwein*,' Max says.

'*Schwein* means pig in German.' She gives a bitter little laugh. 'Naturally, everyone called me Pig Face. Remember that, Bella?'

'I . . . No. I don't remember that. I'm so sorry.'

'I forgive you.'

'Mom! *You* called her Pig Face?' Max is aghast.

Drew, too, is gaping at Bella.

'No! I meant that I'm so sorry I don't remember anything about it.'

'We've all done things we'd prefer to forget. And at that age,

I did look the part. Unless you forgot me altogether? I suppose I wasn't very memorable.'

'You were! I remember you!'

'Ah! Good old Pig Face, right?'

'No! I never—'

'Bella, it's OK! I'm sure you thought it was just harmless teasing. And no one has called me Pig Face in years, now that I'm not homely.'

'You were never—'

'I was, Bella. I was the ugly duckling.'

'Hey,' Max says, 'I know that story!'

She talks over him, ignoring him. 'And now I'm a swan, right?' She gestures at herself. 'So, believe me, all is forgiven.'

'Jane, I really don't think—' She cuts herself off, regroups. 'Do you want me to call you Jane, or Ethel?'

'Anything but Pig Face. Jane was my middle name, and Anderson is my married name. It's a lot easier to live with, you know?' Her forced laugh gives way to an awkward silence.

Then Drew says, 'Well, it's a small world.'

'It sure is.' Bella gestures at the chair that had been intended for Jiffy. 'Please, sit and have some wings. We can catch up.'

'Are you sure?' She hesitates, looking at Max. 'I don't want to take your friend Jiffy's dinner.'

'He's probably not coming anyway.' Max pushes back his chair. 'Mom, may I please be excused?'

'Don't you want more pizza?' Drew asks.

'I just want to be excused.'

'What about dessert? Drew brought three kinds of ice cream,' Bella reminds him.

'No, thank you. It's too shivery for ice cream right now.'

'OK, well, you can go watch TV until we're finished.'

'No, thank you.'

'No TV?' Drew asks. 'Are you feeling OK?'

'I'm just tired.'

Bella nods. 'We had a late night and a long day. Go get your pjs on and brush your teeth. I'll be up soon to tuck you in and read your bedtime story.'

He picks up his plate and heads into the kitchen with Hero at his heels.

'He seems like a nice boy,' Jane says, sitting down next to Drew. 'Very well-mannered.'

'Thank you. He is. He's a great kid.' Bella pushes back her own chair. 'I'm just going to go . . .'

She hurries after Max.

In the kitchen, she finds him scraping his food scraps into the garbage as Hero looks on wistfully.

'Make sure you put the can lid on tightly, Max, so that he doesn't get into the chicken bones.'

'I will. Dr Drew said they're dangerous for dogs.'

When he turns around, Bella presses the back of her hand against his forehead. It doesn't feel warm. He's probably just as exhausted as she is, on top of missing Jiffy.

'How come you're checking my head?'

'I want to make sure you don't have a fever.'

'I don't.'

'You said you were shivery.'

'Just a little.'

'It's drafty in here. I'll turn up the thermostat. Maybe you should take a hot bath. That will warm you up.'

'I'm not that kind of shivery.'

'What kind of shivery are you?'

'The scared kind.' He puts his plate into the sink and meets her gaze, eyes wide behind his glasses.

'Oh, sweetie . . .' She hugs him. 'What's scaring you?'

'The wind. And witches. And . . .' He looks at the floor.

'And what, Max?'

'Did you really call her Pig Face?'

'What? No!'

'She said you did.'

'Well, I didn't. I barely even remember her.'

'Then how do you know you didn't?'

'Because it's cruel, Max. You know I wouldn't do something like that.'

'I didn't think so, but she said—'

'She's wrong. Just forget about it,' Bella says, opening the dishwasher. 'Go on upstairs. I'll be up in a bit.'

He hesitates, then leaves the room.

Alone in the kitchen, she puts Max's plate into the dishwasher and washes the pizza and chicken wings off her hands, scrubbing like a surgeon.

Ethel Schweinsteiger.

Bella hasn't thought about her in years.

She was the only other girl Bella knew back then who didn't have a mother. Had hers passed away, like Bella's?

No, there was a story, wasn't there? Something dark and disturbing.

Had she run off? Disappeared? Bella can no longer recall the details.

But she's sure about one thing. Ethel hadn't been *homely*.

Everyone goes through an awkward adolescent stage. Bella remembers her with braces, bad skin, wispy brown hair, and a lumpy figure beneath the drab cardigans she'd worn like a uniform.

Bella, too, had had braces and a limited wardrobe, and had been self-conscious about her own lack of a figure, wondering if she'd ever develop. She had no mom to ask about that, or to take her clothes shopping even if they had enough money for that, which they didn't.

Her father was the kind of man who thought clothes were fine as long as they weren't frayed or torn and still fit. Bella's did, until she hit puberty, so . . .

Yeah. She had her own share of problems back then.

Being called Pig Face wasn't one of them.

As for calling someone by that cruel nickname . . .

I wouldn't do something like that!

No, the woman she is now would never. Nor would the girl she'd once been . . .

That's what she wants to believe.

It had been long ago and far away, and so many of her memories are fuzzy.

She thinks of her friend Meredith, who often recounts their school days with detailed clarity.

She pulls out her phone and texts, Are you around for a chat in about an hour?

'Bella?' Drew calls from the dining room. 'Everything OK?'

'Everything's fine. Coming!'

She sets the phone face up on the counter and carefully extracts the glass coffee carafe from the dish drying rack, buried under the pots and pans she'd washed earlier.

She keeps an eye on her phone in case response dots appear in the text window, thinking about Meredith as she fills the carafe, measures out grounds, and sets the machine to start brewing at five thirty.

They'd drifted apart during the college years, when Meredith was in Boston, but later reconnected on social media. That led to regular calls and texts, but they didn't see each other in person until Meredith invited Bella and Sam to her wedding. After that, the next – and last – time they saw each other was at Sam's funeral. But every time they talk, they pick up right where they left off.

In the dining room, Jane laughs a laugh that sets Bella's teeth on edge.

She just isn't in the mood for this tonight. She'd prefer to be alone with Drew and Max. Or one, or the other. Or even alone, alone.

Instead, she's feeling defensive, and irritated. On top of it, she's bone-tired, with a houseful of guests who will be up bright and early, and she'll have to deal with Max and his unwanted playdate.

'Bella?' Drew calls again.

'Be right there. I'm just taking care of a few things in here.'

'Need help?'

'No,' she says, and immediately regrets it.

If she'd said yes, Drew could come in here, and Jane might get the hint that three's a crowd.

Instead, she's laughing again, and Bella wonders what can possibly be so hilarious.

Jaw set, she looks around and grabs a dish towel. She might as well put away the pots and pans from earlier. But before she can reach for the precariously balanced lid on top of the heap, her phone lights up with a call.

Leaning in, she sees that it's not from Meredith.

Odelia.

Bella lets it bounce to voicemail.

A moment later, another call appears.

This time, it's Pandora.

She ignores that, too. She doesn't have to be psychic to grasp that the dance committee meeting is not going well.

A text appears. It's from Odelia.

Please call me ASAP.

With a groan, Bella tosses the dish towel aside, leaves the phone on the counter, and returns to the dining room.

Jane is still laughing at something Drew's saying, probably one of his funny animal stories. She's sitting next to him.

Right next to him, Bella notes, with another twinge of irritation and something less familiar.

Jealousy?

They look so cozy on the same side of that long table with all those other chairs Jane could have chosen.

Bella reminds herself that that place had already been set for Jiffy. Of course it's where Jane would sit.

There are wings and pizza on her plate, and there's a glass of red wine in her hand.

Bella realizes that it's one of her vintage Saint Louis crystal goblets. She keeps the pair on a high glass shelf in the built-in china cabinet. They'd been a cherished wedding gift from Millicent, so valuable and fragile that she and Sam had used them only once a year on their anniversary.

Drew wouldn't know that. He was just trying to be helpful.

Bella reclaims her seat across from him.

'You didn't!' Jane is saying.

'I did. And believe me, they never stole my lunch again,' he tells Jane, who laughs like she's at a stand-up comedy show.

He turns to Bella. 'Everything OK?'

'Everything's fine. Someone stole your lunch?'

'The third-grade bullies. I never told you that story?'

'I don't think so.'

Jane touches his arm. 'You have to tell her! She'll love it!'

'OK, well, my mom was an amazing cook,' he says, and pauses to sip some wine.

Bella can't resist her own petty need to say, for Jane's benefit, 'Right, I know that.'

'Mom felt bad that I had to eat alone when I had to start a new school, so she put half a dozen homemade cookies or brownies in with my lunch every day. She was thinking I could share and make friends and not have to eat alone. But the bullies would just steal the whole thing – sandwich, juice box, and all.'

'Did you tell your mom? Or a teacher?'

'Are you kidding? Do you know what happens to kids who tattle about being picked on?'

'I'm sure she doesn't.' Jane smiles sweetly at Bella.

'Anyway,' Drew goes on, 'one day I decided to get revenge. My mom packed a tuna fish sandwich for me. Even her tuna salad tasted like something from a fancy restaurant. That day, I doctored it up . . . with a can of cat food.'

'Isn't that the craziest thing ever?' Jane laughs as if she's hearing it for the first time.

Hoping her own laugh doesn't sound strangled, Bella agrees, 'Crazy.'

Drew tilts his head, regarding her for a moment. Then he shrugs. 'They never stole my lunch again.'

'Guess you showed them.' Bella turns to Jane. 'How do you like the wings?'

'They're great. Thank you for inviting me tonight. It's really nice not to be alone for a change.'

'It's too bad you couldn't bring your husband along,' Bella says.

'My husband?'

'You mentioned that Anderson is your married name, so I just assumed . . .'

'Oh. Right. I guess you would assume, but . . . well, we're not together anymore. That's . . . it's kind of why I'm here. I needed to get away. *Far* away.'

'I'm sorry to hear that. He's in New York?'

'Last I heard. I want you to know that I appreciate the hospitality, Bella, and I really didn't mean to crash your date.'

Bella waves her off. 'Trust me, our dates get crashed all the time, right, Drew?'

'Definitely. Sometimes, in ways that are not to be believed.'

As if on cue, the St Clair sisters toddle in from the breakfast room.

'Bella, that new herbal tea is absolutely delicious,' Ruby says.

'Oh, good. Which one did you try?'

'The fancy one in the mesh bag tied with a pink ribbon.'

'The ribbon was blue, dear.' Opal looks at Bella. 'She's blind as a bat.'

'*My* ribbon was pink. *Yours* was blue. Just like the ones Mother tied to our hair when we were girls.' She sighs. 'You've forgotten so many things.'

'Wait – teabags with ribbons?' Bella asks.

'Goodness, no. Just the ribbons. We'd have looked silly with teabags dangling from our pigtails,' Ruby says with a chuckle.

'No, I mean . . . I don't think the herbal teabags have ribbons.' Bella frowns. 'I don't even think they have strings.'

'Why, thank you,' Opal says, looking down at the rings on her left hand. 'The sapphire was a gift from a suitor, years ago. The gold one was Mother's wedding band. And this one has opals and rubies. We each have one, don't we, sister?'

'We do, dear, but Bella wasn't talking about your *rings*. She was talking about . . .' She looks at Bella. 'What *were* you talking about?'

'I was just – never mind. Goodnight, ladies.'

They say goodnight and leave the room.

Bella looks at Drew. 'I'm pretty sure they steeped my scented sachets in hot water and drank it like tea.'

'It sounds like they enjoyed it.'

'I hope you didn't poison them,' Jane says.

'No, I made the potpourri myself – dried lavender, rose petals, orange peels, and cinnamon sticks.'

'All edible. They'll be fine,' Drew assures her.

'I hope so,' she says around a deep yawn.

'You look tired.'

'I *am* tired.' She takes off her glasses, setting them on the table, and rubs her eyes.

'Max is waiting for his bedtime story,' Drew says. 'Go on up.'

'Aw, a bedtime story. That's so sweet.' In one swallow, Jane drains the wine in her glass, then eyes what's left in the bottle.

Bella pictures her and Drew finishing off the wine together and turns to him. 'We were out so late last night. You must be exhausted, too.'

'I am.' He pushes back his chair, stands, and picks up his plate. 'I'll clear the table and put away the leftovers, and then

I'll walk Hero so he won't wake you in the middle of the night to go out.'

'He hardly ever does that.'

'If I walk him, he definitely won't.'

'Drew, it's not a good night for a walk. I'll just let him out in the backyard for a minute while I do the dishes.'

'*I'll* do the dishes and let him out. You go upstairs.'

Bella opens her mouth to protest.

'No arguments. Max is waiting for you.'

'Thanks.' Grateful, Bella gets to her feet.

So does Jane. 'I'll help you, Drew. It's the least I can do.'

Bella pictures the two of them standing shoulder to shoulder at the kitchen sink. 'I can't let you clean up. You're a guest.'

'Right. I've got it,' Drew says.

'No, *I've* got it. You should get going. You've got a long drive home.' Bella holds out her hand to take the crystal goblet from Jane.

'Wait, you two aren't married?' she asks.

Bella fumbles the goblet, and it starts to slip from her grasp.

She doesn't drop it. Thank goodness, she doesn't drop it. If she'd dropped it . . .

She can't breathe. She can't speak.

'We're not married,' Drew tells Jane, who doesn't appear disappointed to hear that news.

Bella rushes from the room, heading not for the kitchen, but for the stairs.

'Bella?' Drew calls after her. 'Where are you going?'

'To read to Max, and then to bed. Thanks for dinner. Thanks for cleaning up and taking Hero out. Get home safely. Talk to you tomorrow. Goodnight!'

She barrels around the corner into the front hall and stops short, spotting a tall, dark figure looming beside the door.

But it's just the dark cloak Pandora had given her, draped over the coat tree.

Not a person.

Not something – *someone* – wicked.

Not this time, anyway.

She considers going back for the glasses she'd left behind on the table but decides against it. She doesn't need them tonight. She only wants to sleep.

In the Rose Room, she closes the door behind her, and carefully sets the goblet on the bureau beside the jewelry box that holds her wedding band and the tourmaline necklace.

'Sorry, Sam,' she whispers, looking from the glass, stained with red wine dregs but intact, to the mirror.

A gaunt stranger stares back at her.

Bella searches her face for a glimpse of the suburban wife, mother, and schoolteacher who'd assumed her future would play out precisely as she'd envisioned it.

In this moment, that woman – Sam's woman, his Bella Blue, the most capable woman in the world – belongs to a dim and distant past that might as well have been lived by someone else.

NINE

Bella is Dorothy, caught up in a tornado, and the wicked witch is chasing her, cackling and shrieking.
No, it's the wind that's shrieking, and there are three witches intoning, 'Double, double, toil and trouble . . .'

Now Bella is shrieking, and the witches are on her heels, and she can't get away, and something wet and clammy is slapping at her face, and—

She awakens with a gasp, opening her eyes to complete darkness.

No witches. No tornado.

Only Hero, bumping his wet nose against her face.

She groans and sits up. 'What's the matter, boy?'

He barks.

'Shh! We have guests.'

Another bark, trailed by a little whimper.

She sighs, hoisting him aside and sitting up in bed.

The room is *too* dark – no glow from the clock on the nightstand, no sliver of hallway light at the crack under her closed door, no glow filtering through the curtains from the lit signpost out front.

She can hear the wind, and a hard rain lashing the panes, but inside the house, all is still. Too still.

It's always quiet at night, but she's lived here long enough to recognize the absence of electronic background hum. It means the power has gone out, either due to the weather or a blown fuse in the basement.

'That's what you're trying to tell me. Good doggy.'

She reaches for her phone on the bedside table, intending to use it as a flashlight, but it isn't in its usual spot.

Why not?

She backtracks to bedtime.

She'd found Max sound asleep before she could read him a story. For that, she'd been grateful, not just because he needed to sleep, but because she did. Hero had climbed in with her, his coat damp from his walk with Drew.

As for her phone . . .

She doesn't remember plugging it into the nightstand charger.

She does remember coming upstairs with her crystal goblet after Jane had joined her and Drew at dinner and revealed that she used to be Ethel Schweinsteiger.

That strikes her anew as absolutely incredible.

It would be one thing to cross paths if they were both living in the old New York City neighborhood. Seeing her anywhere else in the city would be a pretty big coincidence.

But here?

What are the odds that an old classmate would show up four hundred and fifty miles away, right under her own roof in Lily Dale?

Lily Dale, where there are no coincidences.

Hero whines and nudges her again with his nose.

'I know, boy. I just need to figure out what I did with my—'

Ah – now she remembers. She'd left the phone in the kitchen after texting Meredith.

She quickly climbs out of bed, hoping the cats aren't underfoot. Some nights – though not last night – they follow her into the Rose Room at bedtime.

Other nights, they find their way in via Bella's closet, where a false wall hides one of Valley View's many hidden tunnels and compartments. Legend has it that they're remnants of its colorful stint as a bootleggers' haven a century ago, but they've been literal lifesavers on more than one occasion since Bella moved in.

She always leaves her closet door ajar – not because she expects to need an escape route again, but in case the cats are feeling cuddly in the night and want to crawl into bed with her.

No sign of them now, though. She makes her way through the dark with Hero right behind her.

'You're a good boy. Thanks for letting me know about the power. But you have to stay.'

She opens the bedroom door, slips out, and closes it. Hero whimpers again on the other side.

'It's OK,' she hisses. 'I'll be right back!'

The corridor is hushed. Ordinarily, it's illuminated by sconces with dimmers. Now, it's pitch black.

She painstakingly feels along the wall to the top of the stairs and descends slowly, gripping the banister. On the first floor, she goes to the front door and peers out the window.

The whole street is dark, not just Valley View's porch lamps and signpost. Beyond the windblown trees, she can see a vehicle's flashing hazard light in the distance, meaning a utility crew is already tending to the power outage.

Wondering what time it is, she heads toward the kitchen. She's relieved to have been spared a trip to the basement fuse box, but she still needs to retrieve her phone, which serves as a clock and flashlight.

Maybe there's a response from Meredith, the only person in Bella's world who will probably remember Ethel and who, depending on the hour, may be awake.

She creeps blindly through the deserted first-floor rooms, hands outstretched so that she doesn't bump into anything, aware of the eerie silence in the house, disturbed only by her breathing and the mantel clock's rhythmic ticking.

Another sound reaches her ears: a faint rustle of movement nearby.

'Chance?' she calls softly. 'Is that you? Spidey?'

Silence.

But she's not alone.

She can feel a presence. Of course it must be one of the cats, because if it were a person, they'd answer her.

Unless they were trying to avoid detection.

She moves more quickly now, needing her phone, with its glowing screen and flashlight app. As she passes her study, her bare foot slams into the cast-iron doorstop, catching it between her fourth toe and pinky.

'Ow!'

Paralyzed by pain so intense she's swept by nausea, Bella wonders if she's broken a bone. As she wills the agony to subside, something – *someone* – makes another rustling sound.

This time, she can tell it's coming from the kitchen.

She takes a couple of cautious steps in that direction, keeping her weight off her injured toes.

'Who's there? Hello?'

It might be a guest, looking for a midnight snack.

Or Max, or . . .

Oh! Of course!

'Jiffy? Is that you?'

If he's back, he'll be eager to see Max after all this time away. And this wouldn't be the first time he snuck into Valley View in the middle of the night.

'Jiffy, we're not playing hide and seek at this hour!'

Whatever this hour might be. For all she knows, it's her usual early wakeup time, which is pre-dawn at this time of year.

She hobbles one cautious step at a time from the parlor's hardwood to the kitchen tile and stops to feel for the cabinets to the left of the doorway.

Ah, right here.

As she trails the countertop with her hand, moving toward her phone, she keeps her eye on a barely perceptible shadow in the far corner of the room, between the fridge and the back door.

It's not a trick of the light, because there is no light. It's not her cloak from Pandora on the coat tree, because that's by the front door.

'Jiffy!' Her voice wobbles this time. 'Come on. This isn't funny. I hurt my foot.'

Maybe it isn't Jiffy. The shadow seems too tall.

'Pandora?'

She, too, has been known to creep around Valley View uninvited, long after – and long before – she actually owned the place.

But would she just lurk there in silence?

OK, so maybe it isn't Pandora.

Maybe it isn't anyone.

Bella's not wearing her glasses.

It's probably just her imagination, or, hey, in this moment, she'll take an apparition. Nadine, the household spirit. Any old spirit.

She pats the countertop, fumbling around for the phone. It's cluttered, as always – mail, keys, knife block, coffee maker, toaster, the drying rack still heaped with all those dishes, pots and pans she'd neglected to put away . . .

Her hand bumps the precarious stainless-steel tower. It topples to the floor with a deafening clatter.

When the final kettle lid has rattled into place at her feet, Bella becomes aware of a damp, gusty chill.

Again, she pats the counter for her phone. This time, she finds it and clicks to illuminate the screen.

It's five twenty-seven a.m.

If this were summer, she'd be up and dressed, with blueberry scones in the oven. The sun would be rising, birds would be chirping, and a blossom-scented breeze would be blowing through open screens.

At this time of year, all seems grim. At this time of year . . . *Something wicked this way comes.*

With a shudder, she tilts the phone away from her. She can't see much in the dim glow, other than that she's alone in the kitchen. No shadows lurking, human, cloak, or otherwise, and . . .

Is the back door open?

Sure is. It's wide open, which explains the wet breeze *inside* the house.

Bella limps over, slams it closed, and slides the bolt, heart racing.

TEN

Max opens his eyes, awakened by a banging sound somewhere downstairs or outside.

It's not morning yet. The room is dark.

Way too dark.

He turns toward his nightlight, plugged into a baseboard outlet by his bookshelf. It's a train engine with a smiling face and it always makes him feel safe – like he's not all alone in his room at night even if Chance and Spidey aren't here with him.

But right now, the cats aren't here. The smiling train engine guy isn't here either. Max is all alone in the night, and that's when the witches come out.

He pulls the quilt over his head and wonders how the light got turned off. He flicks it on every single night when he gets into bed, and off every single morning when he gets up.

Well, not every single morning. Sometimes, he forgets. A lot of times, he forgets.

Mom says that will make the lightbulb burn out faster.

He can hear the wind blowing all around the house.

If the nightlight was a candle, the wind would have blown it right out.

But it's not, so it couldn't have. Maybe it just burned out because of all the times he forgets to turn it off in the morning.

Or maybe someone who isn't Max turned it off.

Mom wouldn't do that. The cats couldn't do that.

Spirit could, and would.

So could, and would, a witch.

He feels shaky and shivery, thinking about the banging sound.

Mom wouldn't be outside in the rainy, windy night, and the cats never go outside at all. That might have been Spirit, or a witch, or . . .

Jiffy!

Yes! He likes to go outside alone at night, and he also likes rain, because he can jump into mud puddles and pretend he's a paratrooper like his dad . . .

His dad is dead now, so maybe he doesn't like to do that anymore.

But he likes to climb up the trellis outside the breakfast room like it's a ladder, right onto the flat roof outside Max's room. In the summer, when the window is open, he wakes up Max by saying, 'Hey, Max.'

Since the window isn't open in November, he would have to knock on it. Probably loudly, because Max is usually a good sleeper.

Jiffy is not.

'Is that because Jelly wakes you up in the night?' Max asked him once, because Jelly is a busy, bouncy puppy.

'Sometimes,' Jiffy said. 'But usually, Spirit does.'

'How come?'

'To tell me a message.'

'Why can't Spirit wait till morning?'

Jiffy told him that Spirit butts in whenever Spirit wants to, but he doesn't mind, because sleeping is boring. He said he's usually not even afraid, because most dead people are nice.

He didn't want to discuss the ones who are not.

Spirit never wakes up Max in the night.

No, but Jiffy does.

Max finds his glasses on the bedside table, gets up, and goes over to the window.

He can't see Jiffy on the flat roof, but that doesn't mean he isn't there. He likes to play tricks and hide.

Max tugs the old-fashioned metal circle thing that locks the window, which is never easy to do, and then he opens the window. There's no screen right now because Jiffy had made a hole in it over the summer and bugs were getting inside, so Mom had to throw it away and order a new one for next year.

There's a lot of bad weather blowing around, but Max sticks his head out anyway, to see if Jiffy is flattened against the house wall, hiding.

He isn't.

Max pulls his head back inside and rubs it, because his hair is wet *and* because he's thinking about the loud banging sound he heard.

Maybe it was just a dream.

Maybe it was thunder.

But maybe it was Jiffy falling off the roof again.

Last time that happened, he didn't get very hurt, dusting himself off and telling Max's mom, 'I'm fine. By the way, sometimes I jump out of helicopters with my dad, so this is no big deal.'

But now Jiffy's dad is dead and that's a big deal.

Max sticks his head out the window again.

'Hey, Jiffy?' he calls, looking all around.

What if Jiffy is lying on the ground in the storm, really really hurt?

'Jiffy! Are you OK?'

He doesn't hear anything, and it's too dark to see.

Max goes to his nightstand, opens the drawer, and feels around inside for his little flashlight.

Dr Drew gave it to him one night when Jiffy was sleeping over and they were trying to think up a fun thing to do because Max doesn't have Playbox and Mom wouldn't let them watch any more TV. Dr Drew showed them how to make shadow puppets on the wall and he let Max keep the flashlight.

He doesn't use it anymore, because you can't really make shadow puppets alone, but it would still work as a plain old light.

He turns it on, goes back to the window, and shines it all round the flat roof, then on the yard.

That's when he sees something bad.

Really bad, and really scary.

It isn't Jiffy bleeding on the ground, and it isn't Spirit, because Max can't see Spirit.

It's a witch, running across the yard in a dark, flowing robe.

ELEVEN

Fearing that the cats might have escaped into the night, Bella throws the back door open again.

'Chance!' she calls. 'Spidey!'

Her voice is lost in the wind.

'Chance? Spidey? Are you out there?'

She peers into the yard. Without landscape lighting, she wouldn't be able to see a thing, even if she were wearing her glasses.

How many times has Drew mentioned feline patients who fell victim to outdoor perils? The lake, traffic, illnesses, animal predators, human predators . . .

'It's a lot safer and healthier to keep cats inside,' he says, and Bella has always complied.

'Chance! Spidey! Get back here, right now!' she calls, as if they're kids, or dogs.

Naturally, they don't comply. Even Max and Hero don't always come running when she calls their names.

She closes the door, locks it, and yanks open a cabinet. The bag of dry food is right in front. She shakes it like a maraca.

'Chance! Spidey!'

The cats materialize at her feet, circling her ankles in anticipation of an impromptu meal.

'Thank goodness! Where were you two hiding? And how did that door open?'

She dumps a bit of kibble into each of their bowls, scenarios racing through her head.

Had Drew forgotten to turn the bolt after he'd taken Hero out?

That's not like him, but he'd been so tired . . .

No. Logic persists.

Regardless of whether it was locked, how would it have opened by itself? The wind is strong, but it couldn't have blown open unless Drew hadn't closed it all the way.

That's hard to imagine, tired or not.

But what if that steadfast, meticulous, dependable man had been somehow distracted . . .

By Jane?

Refusing to entertain that thought, Bella considers others. Like . . .

Like maybe one of the guests had left it ajar.

Nah. The guests use the front door. It does automatically lock after hours, but only from the outside.

Two different codes work with it. One stays the same, and it's only for Bella and Max. The second code is for the guests. She changes it every couple of days. So, unless someone who's here now gave it to an outsider, an intruder couldn't have gotten in that way.

The kitchen and laundry room doors have old-fashioned deadbolts. Both are off limits to guests, designated with *PRIVATE* signs.

She'd noted the silence when she came downstairs, without even the hum of appliances.

If this door had been standing wide open this entire time, wouldn't she have felt – and yes, heard – the rain and wind inside the house?

Yes, and felines are curious by nature. Surely, if the door was open for any amount of time, Chance and Spidey would have ventured out to explore.

Bella scrolls through her phone, finds the flashlight app, and turns it on. Aiming the bright beam around the room, she sees the pots and pans on the floor by the sink, and some wet leaves on the doormat. Nothing else has been disturbed.

There are no intruders. No witches, or apparitions, or Jiffy, or . . .

Jane.

Ethel.

She returns her attention to her phone.

Meredith had responded to her text last night about an hour after she'd sent it.

Hi, Bella! I'd love to chat! I'll be up till around one!

It's too late for that. Too early, too.

Bella quickly writes a reply.

Sorry I missed this until now. You must be sleeping. Call me when you wake up.

She hesitates, then adds, **It's kind of urgent.**

About to hit Send, she reconsiders, deletes the last word, and tries to come up with a suitable replacement.

Urgent implies an emergency.

Even *important* might put undue weight on the situation.

Meredith's husband Steven frequently travels overseas on business, and she's a busy, sleep-deprived mother of a newborn. She has enough to worry about right now.

Bella deletes the sentence she'd started and writes instead, **You'll never believe who showed up at Valley View!**

She hits Send, satisfied that her old friend will be curious enough to reach out when she has time, but she won't drop everything to respond the second she sees it.

Now what?

There's no electricity, which means there would be no hot water for a shower, no coffee, and not much she can get done around here in the dark.

Using her phone's beam, she hobbles wearily back up to the Rose Room and settles back into bed with Hero beside her, hoping to catch a little more sleep.

'Good doggy,' she murmurs, patting his fur. 'Thank you for waking me up to tell me about the power outage.'

Unless . . .

Her eyes snap open.

The power has gone out several times this stormy fall. Hero's never roused her because of it.

What if it was something else?

Downstairs, right before she found the open door, she'd thought she'd sensed movement in the dark. Thought she'd glimpsed a shadow in the kitchen.

What if someone really had been lurking?

What if they'd been scared off by the clattering commotion she'd made with the pots and pans, and slipped off into the night?

TWELVE

Bella had lain wide awake, fretting, until power was restored around daybreak.

Her toes are still painful, purple and swollen. She'd bandaged them and dug out the only shoes that fit her, a pair of fleece-lined brown sheepskin surfer boots. Sam had bought them the Christmas she was pregnant with Max, a size too big to accommodate her swollen feet. She'd worn them every single day until she had the baby that spring, then stored them away, along with the rest of her pregnancy wardrobe, in anticipation of the second baby they were planning to have.

Five years later, widowed and about to become homeless, she'd shoved those carefully folded maternity clothes into garbage bags destined for the donation bin. But she couldn't bring herself to get rid of the boots. Like the wind chimes, they bring comfort and memories of the kind, thoughtful husband who'd loved her and the life they'd built together.

Dressed in jeans and a blue flannel shirt, she leaves the Rose Room and looks in on Max. He's sound asleep.

She isn't sure what to do about the playdate she'd roped him into with Robby. Yesterday, she'd been feeling like it wasn't fair to make him go.

Today, it doesn't seem fair to Robby if they cancel.

Hoping time – and coffee – will bring clarity, she closes the door and heads downstairs.

In the front hall, she grabs a hoodie from the top of the coat tree and lets Hero out into the front yard. He goes about his morning business while she shivers on the porch, wishing she'd instead taken the time to dig out the down jacket that's on a lower hook, buried beneath her raincoat and Max's slicker.

At least her feet are cradled in warm, soft sheepskin.

Even in the brisk and incessant wind, she'd like to think the swaying, clanging wind chimes signify Sam's approval that she's still using his gift.

The street is littered with leaves and small branches. Down the block, orange cones surround a large limb that splintered off a massive maple. A displaced sign that reads *Terry Truman for Congress* has landed in the front yard of a neighbor who'd campaigned for the opposing candidate.

Back inside, Bella takes off her hoodie, then puts it right back on and turns up the heat a couple of degrees. The house is drafty, and the guests will be up soon.

She feeds Hero and the cats, then pads around the kitchen, sipping coffee, resetting flashing digital clocks on all the appliances, emptying the dishwasher. She keeps an eye out for her glasses, which are no longer on the dining room table, but they don't turn up. Drew must have put them somewhere for safekeeping.

The vintage radio Leona had left behind plays in the background. WDOE, a local station out of Dunkirk, is playing the Top 100 songs of 1975. It doesn't come in clearly even in good weather, but it's better than listening to the wind's lonely howl.

Or Pandora's voice, still resonating: *I'm afraid you're in grave danger, Isabella. Very grave indeed.*

Fritz Dunkle's, too: *It seems to me that this town is a magnet for criminals.*

Hero and Spidey are taking an after-breakfast nap in the back parlor, but Chance is perched on the mat by the closed back door, staring at Bella as if she's trying to tell her something.

Unnerved, Bella says, 'What is it? You know you can't go out.'

Chance just looks at her.

'And you know doors don't just open themselves. Right, so do I. So how did—'

Bella gasps, sloshing hot coffee over her hand as a face appears in the door's window.

But it's a familiar one, wearing scarlet-framed cat-eye glasses and framed by a pouf of ginger-colored hair.

Bella sets the cup on the counter, wipes her hands on a dish towel, and scoops Chance into her arms before opening the door.

'Odelia! What are you doing here?'

'Good morning to you, too, my dear. And to you, Ms Chance.' Windblown and red-cheeked, Odelia is wearing a pink cheetah-print raincoat and purple rubber rain boots with orange pajama pants tucked into them.

'Sorry, good morning.' Bella closes the door and sets the cat on the floor. 'Is everything all right? You usually sleep till at least ten on weekends.'

'Oh, believe me, I'd have loved to.'

'Did Sprout and Twixie wake you up?'

Odelia's recently adopted kittens are prone to wee-hour wrestling matches under her bed, in her bed, and right on top of her.

'No, it was that darned sailor again. He's barged in every single night since Halloween.' She wipes her boots on the mat, where Chance has once again taken up residence, then peels off her coat and drapes it on a hook. 'Let me tell you, he's one persistent spirit, Bella. I'm trying to figure out who he is and what he wants from me so that he'll move on.'

'You said the other day he's from the *Titanic*?'

'No. At first I thought so, because Luther and I watched the movie while we were away on Mackinac Island, and this spirit materialized right after that. But now I'm not so sure. He keeps showing me symbols that have nothing to do with the *Titanic* and weren't even around back then. A flashlight, a sneaker . . .'

'Do they mean anything in your Spirit shorthand?'

'No. Oh, and last night, when I asked him for more clarity, he showed me a long-stemmed rose lying on a park bench.'

'A rose! It *does* have to do with the *Titanic*, Odelia!'

'What do you mean?'

'Rose! Kate Winslet played her in the movie!'

'But she wasn't a real person. My sailor most definitely is. Well, *was*.'

'Maybe it's just his way of telling you *Titanic* was right. Everyone knows about Rose. Rose and Jack. Star-crossed lovers.'

Bella and Sam . . .

Same.

'You know, every time Sam channel-surfed and that movie was on, he watched it. And he made me watch it. We both cried at the end, every single time. Seeing old Rose remembering young Jack, and that whole long life she'd lived without him . . .' Bella swallows a lump in her throat and forces a smile. 'Spoiler alert. Sorry.'

'No worries. Luther and I have both seen it a million times. But I don't think Spirit's long-stemmed rose on a park bench means *Titanic*.' Odelia sinks into a chair. 'I'm stumped. *And* pooped.'

'How about some coffee?' Bella asks, retrieving her own cup from the counter as KC and the Sunshine Band's 'Get Down Tonight' plays on the radio.

'Brought my own, but thanks.' Odelia holds up a travel mug that bears the Buffalo Bills logo.

'Luther finally turned you into a sports fan?'

'No, but he leaves his stuff at my house, so I figure I might as well use it. You're lucky I'm not wearing his underwear.'

'We're all lucky about that.' Bella grabs the coffee pot and tops off her own cup, feeling Odelia's eyes on her.

'You're limping. Why are you limping?'

'I'm not limping.'

Lying to a medium isn't always the best idea, but she's learned the hard way that if she admits to an injury, Odelia will insist on slathering it in stinky homemade herbal and lanolin ointment.

'You are most definitely limping. Is it because you're wearing those enormous clodhoppers?'

'Hey! These *boots* were a gift from Sam.'

'Sorry. But they look much too big. I've never seen you in them before and – *what* did you do to yourself?' she asks, catching Bella's wince as her full weight lands on her bad foot.

'Nothing. I just stubbed my toe last night in the dark.'

'You might have broken it. You should go to the E.R. and get an X-ray.'

'No, I shouldn't. The E.R. is for emergencies. A stubbed toe isn't that. Plus, even if it's broken – which it's not – they can't do anything for it.'

Plus, Bella hasn't been in a hospital since Sam died. She has no desire to be reminded of those long days and longer nights at his deathbed.

Changing the subject – sort of – she says, 'Hey, Odelia, when I stubbed my toe, I was barefoot and looking for my phone to use as a flashlight! Maybe your sailor was trying to tell you about the power outage? And he was warning you to wear shoes if you went fumbling around in the dark.'

'Maybe, but . . . I don't know. That doesn't seem right. Where would the rose fit in?'

'Well . . . I was sleeping in the *Rose* Room before I hurt my foot, which happened because I wasn't wearing *sneakers* or carrying a *flashlight.*'

'That seems like a stretch.'

'Most of your visions do, at least to me.' As she sits down, Odelia pushes back her chair and stands.

'If you're not going to get an X-ray, then I'm running home to get my herbal salve.'

'No way!' Bella changes it to a more polite, but equally firm, 'No, thank you. It's *fine*, Odelia. I promise you.'

'It isn't fine. You're in pain. One ounce of that stuff will fix you right up.'

'One *whiff* of it, and Drew will break up with me.'

'You, my dear, could roll around in manure and that man would still be crazy about you.'

Bella shakes her head. 'No stinky ointment, or I'm going to slather some on *you* and see what Luther has to say about it.'

'Luther's as crazy about me as Drew is about you. By the way, I saw his truck out front when I got home from the meeting. Did he spend the night?'

'Drew doesn't spend the night!'

'He did over the summer.'

'In a spare room, and I don't have any of those right now.'

'What about the Gable Room?'

'I haven't finished the renovations yet.'

There's a moment of silence, during which the radio plays 'The Hustle' and Bella tries not to ask the question on her mind, which is . . .

'What time did you say you came home from your meeting, Odelia?'

'I didn't say. I was supposed to meet Luther for a drink, but it ran late, thanks to Pandora.'

'How late?'

'I'm not sure. Why?'

'No reason.'

Bella thrums her fingertips on the table. She'd assumed Drew had left immediately after cleaning the kitchen and taking Hero outside. But she'd been upstairs, sound asleep. For all she knows, he'd lingered.

With Jane, whom Bella can't quite bring herself to think of as Ethel.

It's not that she doesn't believe Jane is the same person, though she says she's made a remarkable physical transformation. Most people do, between adolescence and adulthood.

Anyway, why on earth would she lie about such a thing?

She wouldn't. Besides, she'd seemed vaguely familiar from the moment Bella met her.

Yet her appearance at Valley View, of all places, remains unsettling.

So does Bella's vague sense that she's flirting with Drew. And that she's silently – and not so silently – judging Bella, clinging to a misplaced grudge over some perceived childhood slight.

'Bella? What's going on?'

She looks up to see Odelia frowning at her across the table. 'What do you mean?'

'Well, you're listening to disco. That may be my thing, but I'm pretty sure it's not yours.'

Bella stops thrumming her fingers and grins. 'This is the only station that's coming in, so if a change in musical taste is grounds for concern, you don't have to worry.'

'It's not just that. I'm sensing that you're out of sorts this morning, and not just because you stubbed your toe.'

'Sensing, as a medium? Or as a friend?'

'Both. You're rundown and exhausted.'

Bella's grin fades. 'Pandora told you that, Odelia. Not Spirit. I'll bet she said I'm overwhelmed, right?'

'She did.'

'Well, I'm not. Pandora should mind her own business.'

'That, my friend, is the understatement of the year.'

'Of the *century*. Tell me about the meeting. How did it go?'

'Well, after Pandora told me that you've become a rundown wreck in her absence – and after I told her how wrong she is about that – she informed me that she'd done some research and concluded that Sadie Hawkins Day is a sexist, outdated concept. Of course I told her she's wrong about that, too, because anyone with a brain in her head knows that the precise opposite is true, right?'

'Don't look at me. I don't even know who Sadie Hawkins is.'

'You're kidding.'

'I mean . . . I've heard of her, but . . . is she a famous suffragette?'

It's an educated guess on Bella's part. The movement had deep roots right here in Lily Dale. According to her friend Calla, who's deep in her book research, Susan B. Anthony had visited the Dale even before she'd crossed over, not just after.

Odelia shakes her head. 'Sadie Hawkins isn't *real*, Bella. She's a fictional Depression-era character.'

'OK, unlike you, I wasn't alive in the Depression era.'

It isn't a dig about her age. Odelia, like Pandora, frequently references her past lives, including one as a 1930s boxcar hobo.

'Have you ever heard of the comic strip *Li'l Abner*?'

'Maybe?' Bella shrugs. 'That sounds familiar. My dad loved the newspaper cartoons. He said everyone deserved a good laugh after reading the news.'

'Isn't that the truth. Your father was a wise man. Sadie Hawkins was a man-chasing spinster in *Li'l Abner*.'

'Ouch. I hate to say it, but I can see why Pandora finds that sexist and outdated.'

'No, Bella, think about it. Back then, women weren't supposed to do the pursuing. Sadie Hawkins was *ahead* of her time. In the old days, a Sadie Hawkins dance was the one time a girl was "allowed" to ask a boy for a date. Now, it's a celebration of women – well, of everyone – choosing to be proactive about their lives. It's all about making something happen instead of sitting around waiting for something to happen.'

'You sound a little like Doris.'

'Well, she's a feminist, as am I. And she's the one who started this annual dance, years ago. It makes sense, doesn't it?'

'It does. Did you explain it to Pandora this way?'

'I tried, but she's impossible. Finally, I told her she shouldn't be at the meeting if she's opposed to the dance.'

'Good. It's probably better that she left.'

'Oh, she stayed. She insisted. And now she's in charge of the decorations *and* the refreshments, because she got into a snit with Martha Jones over having barbecue sliders on the menu, and Martha quit the committee.'

'What does Pandora have against sliders? Or Martha?'

'Miss High and Mighty thinks they're too lowbrow.'

'Sliders?'

'And Martha. All of us, really, including Sadie Hawkins.'

'I'm sorry. I never should have sent her over there.'

'No worries. She's Pandora. It's what she does. And you're Bella. It's what *you* do. I know you were only trying to help.'

'*Myself*,' Bella admits. 'I'm afraid I did it as much for me as I did for you.'

She explains how Pandora had burst in yesterday, talking about moving back to Valley View.

'You can't let her do that, Bella.'

'How can I stop her? It's her house. She has every right to live here.'

'It would be a disaster. No wonder she kept talking about how overwhelmed you are.'

'Right. She was trying to convince you – and me, for that matter – that I can't manage alone, and she'd be moving in as a favor, to help me out. Which . . . well, she'd be doing for herself as much as for me, so I guess we have something in common.'

'No, you don't. Pandora only does what would be good for Pandora. She doesn't have a charitable bone in her body.'

'I wouldn't go that far. I think she really was concerned about me,' she says, and tells Odelia about the spirit warning.

'A pastry, a waterfowl . . . and a Shakespeare quote?'

'She claimed it had nothing to do with *Macbeth*. Do you have any idea what any of it might mean?'

'Well, when Spirit shows me pastry during a reading, it's a warning about someone's health, as in . . . you'd better lay off the pastry and lose some weight.'

'Ouch. That must ruffle some feathers.'

'I try to deliver it with tact, unlike *some* people. But speaking of pastry, Bella, do you think Max might want to help me do some baking this afternoon? I know he's lonely without Jiffy, and I'm sure you can use some time to rest and put your feet up.'

'Thanks, Odelia, but Max has a playdate with that new little girl who's staying at Doris's. He's giving me a hard time about it, but—'

She breaks off as 'The Hustle' dissolves into a blast of static.

Odelia frowns, looks over at the radio, and utters a single word: 'Spirit.'

'It's just the wind.'

'Spirit manipulates electromagnetic energy, Bella.'

'So does weather, Odelia, and it's been like this all—'

'Shh. My guides are telling me something.' Odelia bows her head and rubs her palms together rapidly, back and forth, back and forth.

She often does that when she's trying to communicate with the Other Side. Bella had once asked her why. The answer had something to do with friction and energy, but – like most things around here – very little to do with any science Bella had ever learned or taught.

'Everyone who is seriously involved in the pursuit of science becomes convinced that a spirit is manifest in the laws of the Universe.'

So said the great physicist, Albert Einstein.

Luther had given Bella that handwritten quote soon after her arrival in Lily Dale. As a fellow outsider and a retired police detective, he understood her skepticism. But he'd carried that quote in his wallet ever since he met Odelia.

He'd dismissed her as a kook when she walked into the precinct saying she'd had a psychic vision about a case he was working. But the vision had merit and led to an arrest.

'I'm not saying I absolutely believe in this stuff,' he'd told Bella. 'I'm not saying there's nothing to it, either. Because, hey, if Einstein was open to Spirit, who are we to dismiss it?'

Some days, that resonates with Bella. Others . . . well, she's a former middle school science teacher, not Einstein. The concept of communicating with the dead is beyond her grasp.

She gets up, hobbles over to the radio, and silences the static. She half expects Odelia to scold her for being on her feet *and* for disrupting the conversation with Spirit, but she's in deep and doesn't appear to notice.

Now Bella can hear the wind, and the faint buzz of a chainsaw. Beyond the window above the sink, the gingko tree has gone bare overnight, the last of its golden foliage scattered like glitter over the grass. The clothesline is still attached to its poles, but the yard is littered with downed limbs.

Hearing voices in the breakfast room, and creaking footsteps on the stairs, she turns back to Odelia. 'The guests are up and about. I'd better go see if—'

Odelia shushes her again and holds up a finger, head still bent.

Bella glances at Chance, on the mat by the back door like a sentry, then out the window again at the storm-tossed mess in the yard. Most of those branches are small enough that even Max will be able to help with the cleanup, but a couple of them will require equipment and heavy lifting.

She takes her phone out of her pocket, snaps a photo of the yard, and sends it to Drew, along with a quick text: Want some free firewood?

The response is immediate. My chainsaw and I will see you this afternoon. Hope you got some sleep.

She replies to that with a thumbs up, which is true of most of the night, anyway.

Should she ask him if he made sure he locked the back door?

He'll want to know why she's asking, and it's not something she wants to explain in a text, regardless of the answer.

Instead, she asks, Where did you put my glasses?

He responds with a question mark.

Frowning, she writes, Left them on the table last night.

Three dots wobble in the message window. His reply: Didn't see them.

'Bella.'

She turns back to Odelia. 'Yes?'

'Spirit is showing me something that's . . . disturbing.'

'Disturbing, how?' She returns to the table, trying to seem casual. 'Is it the same message Pandora got, about my being in danger?'

'I don't think so.' Odelia's brows furrow above her red glasses. 'Someone is in danger. It's a woman, or a girl, maybe. She's crying, begging, and a man is shouting. He's so angry at her. He's telling her she can't leave. "*Don't you dare leave*," she says in a gruff voice, as if she's imitating his. "*If you try, I will hunt you down.*"'

Bella shudders.

'He really hurt her, Bella. Or he's about to.'

'Hurt her . . . physically?'

'I can't say.'

'Who are these people?'

'I don't know.'

'Maybe they have something to do with that sailor of yours?'

'It doesn't feel like they do.'

'Well, I don't think they have any connection to me, so . . .' When Odelia says nothing, Bella frowns.

'Do *you* think these people have something to do with me?'

'They might. With you, or with Valley View.'

'Is it Pandora and her ex-husband? She and Orville never got along.'

'No. I know Orville. He's a lot of things – yes, a wanker, among others – but not violent and dangerous. This man is.'

Bella shakes her head and rubs her tired eyes. 'Seriously, Odelia, if I start stressing about disembodied voices, I'll—'

'Don't, Bella. I didn't mean to worry you.' Odelia glances at the clock and pushes back her chair. 'I'd better get home. Luther is coming over to help me with the yard cleanup. I can send him your way.'

'Pandora might beg to differ, but I don't think I need police protection.'

Odelia smiles. 'I meant that he could do storm cleanup. But if you're concerned about the vision—'

'I'm not. Please don't bother Luther on my account. I can handle it.'

'The cleanup?'

'And everything else,' Bella says, getting up to follow her to the door. 'Don't worry about me.'

'Just be careful, please. I can let myself out. You need to stay off that foot. Put it up and ice it every hour.'

'Yes, doctor.'

'You're still standing.'

'I'm making sure Chance doesn't escape when you open the door. She's been sitting by it all morning.'

Odelia shoots a thoughtful look at the cat. 'I don't think she wants to get out. It seems to me that she's making sure no one gets in.'

Bella opens her mouth to tell Odelia about finding the door open earlier, but catches herself, saying only, 'See you later, Odelia. Enjoy your Saturday!'

'Promise you'll ice that foot!'

'I promise!'

Bella locks the door after her and sets the cat back on the mat.

This time, instead of staring back at Bella as if she's trying to tell her something, Chance is focused on the floor.

Bella follows her gaze, hoping it's not one of those big hairy spiders that sometimes come up from the basement.

Or a mouse, a possum . . .

No.

This is far more disturbing.

Leaning into the shadowy corner where the baseboards meet, she finds herself looking at a large carving knife.

THIRTEEN

After seeing the witch in the yard, Max dove back into bed and pulled the covers over his head. He was too scared to go find Mom, because the other two witches might be lying in wait right outside his door.

Now, when he opens his eyes, it's not a dark, scary night.

It's not bright and sunny, either, but it *is* morning, and the witches aren't as scary. Maybe they were a dream.

Or maybe they're just pretend witches, like the ones in the play the other night.

After it was over, he and Mom and Dr Drew waited in the lobby for Roxy to come out from backstage. It took a long time, and he almost didn't recognize her.

From the neck up, she still had on a whole lot of makeup. But from the neck down, she looked like her regular self, wearing a hoodie, jeans, and sneakers.

Mom gave her a bouquet of flowers and told her she was great. Dr Drew said she was great, too. She thanked them, then turned to Max.

'You're up so late!' she said, catching him in a yawn. 'I'm really glad you came. Did you like the play?'

'It was kind of long,' he said, and she laughed.

'It *is* long. I hope you weren't scared. It's kind of dark for someone your age.'

He was about to lie that he wasn't scared, but Mom spoke up and said the truth to Roxy.

'He was a little scared of the witches.'

'Well, *I* was a lot scared of the witches!' Dr Drew said right away, and Max was grateful and kind of surprised because Dr Drew hadn't seemed scared.

But grown-ups hardly ever do.

And even Mom nodded like she'd just remembered and said, 'You know what, Roxy? We were all scared of the witches. Do you think you could introduce us to them? Then maybe they won't seem so scary after all.'

So they met the witches, who are Roxy's friends in real life. Their names are Caitlyn, Taylor, and Maddie.

They looked like regular girls, wearing jeans, hoodies, and sneakers, like Roxy. And they didn't say things about toil and trouble. They said things like *nice to meet you*, and *thanks for coming*, and *hey, Roxy, did you do your math homework?*

Max did feel a little better after that.

And he feels a lot better now, remembering it.

Still, he stays in bed, because he remembers something else, and that's the stupid playdate with stupid Robby. He figures that if he doesn't go downstairs, Mom will have to come up to make sure he's all right. And then he'll pretend to be super sick. And then she'll have to cancel the playdate because no one wants a germy kid to come over.

That seems like a good plan at first.

But the more time that passes, the more he thinks it's not so good.

He's getting so bored lying in bed all morning with nothing to do that even Playbox with Robby doesn't sound like such a terrible idea.

Plus, he's hungry.

Plus, if he tells Mom he's sick, and then Jiffy comes home today, she won't let Max play with him.

After a while, he hears pipes creaking, water running, steps creaking, and voices talking. The guests are waking up and going downstairs to eat the pastries Mom bought for breakfast. Max wonders how many are left. He wants an apple one and a cherry one, and he should grab two for Jiffy.

He thinks of the lady who sat in Jiffy's chair and ate the pizza and chicken wings Max was saving for him, and who lied that Mom called her 'Pig Face.'

Max didn't like her when he first met her. He's not sure why. There was just something about her that made him think she was just pretending to be nice to him. And to Mom, too.

Then last night she sat in Jiffy's spot and ate his food, and then she said a bad thing about Mom saying a bad thing.

And today, she's probably downstairs eating all the cherry and apple pastries, so now he really, *really* doesn't like her.

He gets out of bed, unlocks his door, and peeks out into the hallway, checking for witches. There are none. The air smells like coffee.

On weekday mornings, he's supposed to brush his teeth, wash his face, and get dressed for school before he goes downstairs.

But this is a Saturday, so he steps out into the hall in his pajamas, with bare feet. The house is chilly, and he considers going back for a robe and slippers. But his stomach growls like it's saying 'No! Feed me!' and his brain is worrying about the pig lady eating all the pastries.

He starts down the hall then stops when his foot lands on something that's kind of crunchy and kind of slimy.

Looking down, he sees that it's just a brown leaf.

There's a smudge of dried dirt around it, and another smudge nearby, and another.

They're footprints.

In one direction, they go all the way back past his room toward the stairs to the third floor.

Sometimes Hero tracks mud through the house, but these aren't pawprints. In some spots, Max can see treads from the bottoms of someone's shoes. They're too big to be his.

Too big to be Jiffy's, too, even though Jiffy is the kind of boy who never wipes his feet on the mat.

Max follows the footsteps down the stairs to the front hall. They stop at the front door.

Wait, no – they *start* at the front door.

People don't track mud *out* of the house. They track it *in* from outside. So whoever made the footprints must have come inside and gone up to the third floor.

Wondering what kind of feet witches have, Max thinks again of the one he'd seen outside in the dark, stormy yard.

It's muddy back there. So the witch must have had mud all over her shoes.

What if she's the one who came into the house?

Max doesn't want to think about that, even in the daytime.

The pig lady is staying on the third floor. Other guests are, too, but Max decides it must have been her, because she said a lie about Mom, and she probably wouldn't care about tracking dirt on Mom's nice clean floors.

But then he walks through the house to the breakfast room, and he spots the lady in the back parlor.

She's on the couch where Max usually sits, reading Mom's library book. She has one ankle crossed over the other knee, and he can see that her white sneakers aren't muddy, even on the bottom.

She doesn't notice Max.

And she's not really reading the book. She's just holding it open on her lap, but not even looking at the words.

She seems to be thinking about something, or listening to something, like the wind outside and the St Clair sisters talking in the breakfast room.

'No, that isn't the right teabag, Ruby. That's Lipton. The one we enjoyed last night wasn't in that box. And it was tied with a ribbon.'

'What color ribbon?'

'Oh, I don't remember that now. It doesn't matter.'

'Opal, how am I supposed to find something if you don't even remember what color it was?'

'Just look for any teabag with any ribbon!'

Max stands in the dining room, wondering what to do.

If he goes into the breakfast room, the St Clair sisters will ask him to help them look for the teabag with the ribbon, and the only thing he feels like doing in there right now is eating pastry.

Mom might have put some extra ones in the kitchen, but Max can't get there without going through the back parlor, where the pig lady is sitting. She probably doesn't need help with anything, but he doesn't like her, and he doesn't want to talk to her.

Maybe he can belly crawl into the kitchen without her seeing him. Jiffy taught him how to do that one day when they were playing Army Guys.

'You're making too much noise,' he'd told Max. 'You have to be quiet. You can't keep saying ouch and sneezing.'

'I can't help it. I keep bumping my head on stuff, and it's dusty down here.'

'Well, you need to practice so you can be as good at it as I am. Then we can both be super sneaky.'

Without Jiffy around, Max forgot all about practicing.

He drops down on the dining room floor and belly crawls under the table. It's kind of like a tent under here because of the tablecloth. The rug is soft and cozy, and it's dark and quiet. He wishes he had the flashlight and his library books, because it seems like a good place for relaxing.

He hears sound, then – a very soft, quiet sound, like someone is being super sneaky.

But she's not belly crawling. Her white sneakers are tiptoeing, very slowly, through the dining room.

Maybe she doesn't want the St Clair sisters to make her help them find the teabag.

Or maybe she's hiding from someone else.

Mom?

But why?

Is it because she thinks Mom called her a pig face?

Or is it something much, much scarier?

Suddenly, the under-the-table tent doesn't seem so cozy and relaxing after all.

Max remembers how Caitlyn, Taylor, and Maddie were witches during the play and then regular people right after, wearing jeans and sneakers just like this lady.

What if her witchy clothes – and muddy shoes – are upstairs in her room? What if she's just pretending to be a regular person?

Max belly crawls to the other end of the table, just in time to see her disappear around the corner into the front parlor. He holds his breath, hoping she'll go right out the front door and never come back.

But no, he hears a very quiet footstep on the stairs, and then a creaky floorboard in the upstairs hall.

She's still here, in the house.

And she's not in a play, or a dream.

She's real.

FOURTEEN

Bella instantly recognizes the carving knife's African rosewood handle. It's part of a set that includes a matching long-pronged fork.

'Leona brought it back from her safari,' Calla commented recently.

It was on Halloween. She was next door feeding Odelia's cats while Odelia and Luther were on their Michigan trip, and wandered over to chat with Bella while Drew carved a pumpkin for Max at the picnic table. He'd used this knife.

'Make sure you hand-wash it,' Calla said. 'Leona yelled at Gammy one Thanksgiving when she caught her putting it into the dishwasher. She might come back and haunt you.'

Bella remembers hand-washing the knife, carefully removing strands of stringy pumpkin clinging to the serrated blade.

Right, and she's pretty sure she remembers drying it and putting it away.

But maybe she's mistaken. Maybe she'd left it in the drying rack, and it became buried under the tower of pots and pans. When she knocked it over, the knife might have skittered all the way over to the door.

It's a logical conclusion. Clean dishes have a way of piling up around here, just like dirty ones.

Still, she'd been as mindful of Leona's precious knife as she is of her own Saint Louis crystal goblets. And she doesn't leave sharp knives lying around where Max or one of her pets might get to them.

But the drawer hadn't opened itself, and the knife hadn't jumped out on its own.

Someone had removed it.

Someone who then lurked in the dark kitchen, armed and ready to pounce.

Someone who was startled by the clattering pans, dropped the knife, and fled through the back door.

Her phone buzzes in her pocket. She returns the knife to the drawer and quickly picks up, expecting Meredith.

Too late, she realizes she should have checked the caller ID.

'Bella? It's Robby's mom, Kay. I hope it's not too early to call.'

'Kay! Good morning. No, it's . . . I've been up awhile.'

'I figured. Robby and I are getting coffee at Sacred Grounds – well, coffee for me,' she clarifies with a chuckle, 'and we're getting some cookies for the playdate.'

'That's so nice,' Bella murmurs, wishing she'd had a chance to re-address the playdate with Max before speaking with Kay.

'Robby's so excited about it. We just wanted to make sure Max doesn't have any allergies or food restrictions?'

'No, he can eat anything, but it was nice of you to check.'

'Of course! We'll swing by to get him on our way back.'

'You don't have to do that. He's not ready yet, and I can walk him down to Doris's later.'

'Oh, I didn't mean right now. I'm going to sit and enjoy my morning coffee for a while. Robby and I both brought our books. We won't be leaving here for, say, half an hour, maybe forty-five minutes.'

'That's – I just – I hate to have you go out of your way.'

Kay laughs. 'It's just a few extra steps, and I'm happy to get them in, because these cookies look too good to pass up! Sound good? See you then!' She hangs up without waiting for a reply.

Bella returns her phone to her pocket and looks again at the knife drawer.

The sooner Max is out of here, the better. Just in case.

Time to wake him up and make sure he's ready when they get here.

With luck, he'll be more enthusiastic about the playdate when he hears about the cookies. If he still puts up a fuss, she'll remind him that a last-minute cancellation might hurt Robby's feelings.

What about Max's feelings, though?

At times like this, she longs for Sam. Most of the time, she trusts her own judgment, and if she's feeling iffy, she has more than enough friends who are willing to lend advice – solicited, and un.

But in the end, Max is her responsibility, and she alone shoulders the burden of making all the parenting decisions. If it's this challenging when he's seven, what's going to happen when he's a teenager?

You're the most capable woman in the world, Bella Blue.

Sam had faith in her. So should she.

She leaves the kitchen and starts upstairs, belatedly remembering her injured toes – yet another reason in favor of sending Max to Robby's. She'd promised Odelia she'd stay off her foot and ice it.

She looks out the parlor window to see if Luther's SUV is parked out in front of Odelia's. She may not need police protection, but it might be a good idea to run this by him.

He's not here yet, so it will have to wait.

In the front hall, she sees Fritz Dunkle on his way down the stairs. He's looking professorial as always, in a beige sweater and brown corduroys.

'Good morning, Bella.'

'Good morning, Professor.'

'Please call me Fritz.'

'Please help yourself to breakfast, Fritz,' she returns, passing him on the way up, thinking of the knife on the floor, and what he'd said yesterday about crime and Lily Dale.

'I intend to. I've been looking forward to your famous blueberry scones.'

She turns back. 'Oh – I'm sorry, but I wasn't able to make them this morning.'

'Then I suppose I'll just have to wait a little while longer, won't I? Perhaps tomorrow.'

'Perhaps,' she agrees, though she wouldn't bet on it.

'I've heard they're nothing short of phenomenal.'

'You have? I mean, *phenomenal* might be a bit of an exaggeration . . .'

'Not according to the Kyleigh Chronicles.'

'*You're* a Kyleigh follower?'

'Perhaps I'm not quite the fuddy duddy you assumed?' he says with a sly grin in his gray beard.

'I never assumed—'

'Not to worry. Most people would. And they'd be correct. But I came across the video when I was doing some research.'

'On scones?'

'On Lily Dale.'

'You googled Lily Dale and came up with the Kyleigh Chronicles?'

'Not immediately. But yes. It seems like I'm the only person in the world who hadn't heard of this young woman.'

'She's pretty popular.'

'And now, so are you. Business must be booming.'

'It's picking up.'

The online reservations system has shown a nice uptick for the off-season months ahead – not that it's any of his concern.

'I should think so. Everyone wants to be rich and famous these days, but in your case, it's probably a bit reckless, don't you think?'

'What do you mean?'

'Well, you've put your name and address out there where anyone can see it. Your whole life story – a helpless widow advertising that she lives alone in the middle of nowhere with a little boy – that's just asking for trouble.'

She clenches the banister. 'OK, first of all, I'm not helpless.'

'Of course you aren't. I didn't mean it like that. *Vulnerable* would have been a better word choice, or—'

'*Capable*, Fritz. I'm perfectly capable. I'm *not* advertising, *not* asking for trouble, *not* trying to be rich and famous. Got it?'

'I keep putting my foot in my mouth, don't I? Please accept my most sincere apologies, Bella.'

She gives a churlish nod, saying nothing, and continues on up the steps.

Rich? That's rich. She thinks of the stack of bills she can't afford to pay.

Yes, she's fortunate to have this newly non-leaky roof over her head, but it belongs to Pandora, who may very well be sharing it with her soon.

'Bella? Did you hurt your leg?' Fritz calls, still watching her from the foot of the stairs.

She stiffens. 'Nope.'

'Are you sure? You seem to be limping.'

'I'm sure. Not limping.'

And not *helpless*.

Sam's Bella Blue can do anything.

She can feel Fritz Dunkle's eyes on her until she rounds the corner in the upstairs hall, moving out of his sightline – but right into Jane's. She's just emerging from the third-floor stairway.

'Bella! Good morning!'

Her greeting is so cheerful, and her smile seems so genuine, that Bella returns both and asks how she slept.

'Like a baby. You?'

'Same,' she lies. 'I'm glad the storm didn't keep you up. That wind can sound really loud up there on the third floor.'

'I didn't hear a thing. I'm not the soundest sleeper these days, and I'm usually up at the crack of dawn, but not here.'

'Well, that's great. Everything's ready in the breakfast room, so help yourself – there's coffee, tea, juice, pastries, toast, fruit, yogurt . . . no scones, though.'

'Scones! Sounds like that would be overkill.'

And it sounds like not everyone has heard of the Kyleigh Chronicles.

'Listen, Bella . . . I was wondering if you have some time to sit and chat this morning?'

'Oh . . . sure.'

'It's just . . . I, uh . . . things have been kind of rough lately, like I said, and . . . well, I could really use an old friend to talk to.'

'Absolutely.'

This time, Bella's smile is forced, because she just noticed something.

Jane is wearing glasses. They're rectangular, with brown tortoise-patterned frames . . .

Just like Bella's.

Not *only* Bella's. They're the most popular style, according to the optometrist who helped her choose them. 'Most of my first-time lens-wearers go with something classic, like these. Later you might decide to get something more unique.'

Ah, like Odelia's red cat-eyes.

If Jane were wearing those, Bella would really raise an eyebrow. But these . . .

She's pretty sure Jane hadn't been wearing glasses yesterday.

Not that there's anything suspicious about that. After all, she herself only needs corrective lenses for distance, so sometimes she wears them, and sometimes she doesn't.

Today, she isn't wearing them because she can't find them.

Unless she just did. On Jane's face.

Which may be the least logical thought she's ever had. She resolves to put it out of her head.

'I'm going out for a bit after breakfast,' Jane says. 'But I'll be around later, whenever you have time.'

'Sounds good.'

Jane heads downstairs, and Bella walks on toward Max's bedroom door, trying to put her finger on exactly what it is about the woman that rubs her the wrong way. She was perfectly pleasant just now, and she'd called Bella a friend.

Maybe she's not the problem. Maybe it's you.

After all, Jane isn't the only one getting on her nerves today. It was all Bella could do to be polite to Fritz Dunkle.

She's probably just overtired and cranky. Plus, she's gone so long without having guests at Valley View that she's out of practice.

Then again, Fritz really was out of line, and he knew it. He apologized.

With Jane, it's different. She hasn't said or done anything overtly offensive. Her flirtation with Drew had been so subtle that Drew, being a man, might not even have been aware of it.

But women pick up on that sort of thing. *This* woman does, anyway.

Bella's never been the jealous type, and Jane is far from the first woman to flirt with Drew in her presence. She needs to let it go and move on.

She starts to unlock Max's door, then realizes that it already is. Frowning, she opens it.

'Max?'

The bed is empty.

The room is empty.

Bella turns toward the bathroom across the hall. The door is ajar. She pokes her head in anyway. 'Max?'

The bathroom is empty.

A cold sweat oozes over her as she hobbles toward the stairs as quickly as she can, calling, 'Max! Where are you?'

FIFTEEN

Max hears his mom shouting his name. She sounds super worried.

That would be a good reason for him to shout back, 'Here I am, Mom!'

But there are two better reasons not to.

If he comes out from under the table, the witch might get him, if she was real and not just a bad dream.

And if he comes out, he'll have to go with Robby and Mrs Burton when they get here, because they are definitely real.

He'd heard Mom on the phone with Robby's mother, and she was acting friendly and nice. She hadn't even tried to get him out of it.

That made him mad, so he stayed right where he was. He might even stay here all day, hiding from Mom and Robby and Mrs Burton and the witch and the sneaky sneaker lady who came back downstairs a minute ago.

Only this time, she wasn't being sneaky. He saw her shoes go past the table, right into the breakfast room. Professor Dunkle was already there, and the St Clair sisters, who'd roped him into helping them find the delicious teabags tied with ribbon.

'Can you help us, too, dear?' one of the sisters asked the lady.

'Help you with what?' she asked, and then, when the sisters explained, Max heard her say, 'Oh, no. You didn't make tea from those, did you?'

'I don't know. Did we, Ruby?'

'Of course we did. They're *teabags*. That's what you *do*.'

'Those weren't teabags,' the lady told them. 'They were some sort of poison.'

'Poison!' the sisters said in unison.

Poison! Max thought, remembering the three witches and their bubbling cauldron.

'Rat poison, maybe? Something like that. Bella told me to be sure not to mistake the sachets for tea. Didn't she tell you?'

Before they could answer, Max heard Mom coming downstairs, shouting his name.

Now everyone from the breakfast room is hurrying in to see what's going on.

'Has anyone seen Max?' Mom asks, and they all say that they haven't.

Hero is barking, running around. Dr Drew says he's part bloodhound, which means he's very good at finding foxes and bad guys, but he didn't say anything about bloodhounds finding boys. Max figures that's a very good thing.

Mom keeps calling Max, and he's starting to feel kind of bad about hiding because she's starting to sound like she does when she talks about his dad.

Everyone else is yelling his name, too, except the St Clair sisters, who are yelling, 'Maxwell!'

He watches all those feet going back and forth and all around the table – the white sneakers, two pairs of old lady shoes, and one pair of man shoes. There are some brown fuzzy boots, too, and it sounds like they're attached to Mom's voice. But it can't be her, because he's never seen her wear them before, and one of the feet is kind of dragging.

'You should call the police, Bella,' the professor says.

'The police?'

'Or the F.B.I. It appears the boy has fallen victim to a kidnapping.'

Max hears Mom make a sound that's kind of like the word *no* mixed up with choking.

'Kidnapping!' Sneaker Lady says.

'Napping! Yes, that must be it,' one of the old ladies says. 'He's taking a nap!'

'No, no, Opal, we can't nap now!' the other old lady says. 'It's much too early! We haven't even had breakfast yet.'

Hero is barking again, and Max sees his paws going around the table.

'Kidnapping is pretty extreme. Why would you even think something like that?' Sneaker Lady asks.

'Because Max's young friend was kidnapped last year,' the professor tells her. 'It stands to reason that—'

'It does not stand to reason, Fritz! My son has *not* been

kidnapped!' Mom's voice still sounds strange. Not just mad, but also scared, and almost like she's going to cry.

Max's eyes and the inside of his nose get that prickly feeling like he's going to cry, too.

He sees Chance – not just her paws, but her whole self, because she's lower to the ground than the edge of the tablecloth.

She looks right at him, and her eyes are like Mrs Powell's when she catches someone trying to break a rule. That doesn't happen very often now that Jiffy's not in school, but sometimes it still does.

Chance also looks a little like Amber Saxton, and Max thinks that if Chance wasn't a cat, she'd probably raise her paw and tell Mom right where he is.

He almost wishes she could and would. His stomach hurts from lying on it, and his head hurts because he bumped it, and his heart hurts, too, because Mom is sad, and he made her that way.

He wants more than anything to come out from under the table and throw his arms around Mom.

But he can't. Not with all these people here, and maybe witches on the loose, and Robby and her mom on their way to pick him up.

'Maybe he went outside to play,' Sneaker Lady says.

'In this weather?' The professor makes a sound with his tongue.

'Kids don't care about a little wind and rain. I think you should go look outside, Bella. I can help you if you want. You, too, Fritz.'

'No, I think we should call the police.'

'The police?' one of the sisters says. 'What about them?'

'Professor Dunkle would like to call them, dear.'

'Ah! Because Bella is trying to poison us! I had forgotten all about that!'

'You see? You *are* the forgetful one, Opal!'

Something brushes against Max's bare foot. He gasps and turns to see that it's Spidey.

He holds his breath.

'Wait, you think I'm trying to poison you?' Mom is asking, so she must not have heard Max's gasp.

Hero probably did, though, because he stops walking and sticks his nose under the table, sniffing around.

'We're lactose intolerant, and you gave us milk! Didn't she, Ruby?'

'That was last time,' the other sister says. 'This time, she gave us rat poison.'

Hero's whole head comes under the table. Seeing Max, he makes a high-pitched little whiny-barky sound, but the adults go right on talking.

'Ladies, I have no idea what you're talking about! I'm just trying to find my son.'

'I'll bet she poisoned Maxwell, too,' one of the sisters says in a loud whisper.

'Oh, for Pete's sake,' Mom says.

Max waves his hand at the dog, shooing him away. But Hero thinks he wants to play. He comes over to Max and licks his hand.

It tickles. Max pulls his hand away.

Hero barks, very loudly.

Max says, 'Shh!' very quietly.

Or maybe not that quietly, because all of a sudden, the tablecloth lifts up in front of the brown boots, and Mom peeks under.

She sees him, and her eyes get big and happy and relieved, and she says, 'Max! What are you doing under there?'

'Hiding,' he says in a small voice.

'Oh, Max.' She looks like she wants to say something more.

But then the professor asks, 'Is that the boy?'

'Yes, Fritz, it is. See? I told you he wasn't kidnapped. He's just . . . playing hide and seek. Right, Max?'

'Right.'

The tablecloth drops, leaving Max alone with Hero, who's licking his face, and Chance, who comes over and sits right next to him, purring, and Spidey, who's curled up by his feet.

'I'd appreciate it if you'd all give us a chance to talk privately,' Mom says.

Everyone leaves, and she crawls under the table. She stops right in front of Max, and she puts her chin on her hands and her face really close to his.

'Hiding, huh? Does the playdate with Robby have anything to do with it?'

And the witches, he wants to say, but instead he just nods.

'You gave me one heck of a scare, kiddo.'

'You thought I was kidnapped?'

'No! I thought you were hiding because of the playdate with Robby.'

'Is that why you didn't call the police?'

'Yes.'

'And because you didn't really try giving anyone rat poison?'

'That, too. I don't know where the St Clairs got that idea.'

'From the lady who said you called her Pig Face.'

'What do you mean?'

'I heard her telling them that you tried to poison them.'

'Oh – with the potpourri?' Mom asks, like she just remembered something. 'She was there when I told Drew that they thought the sachets were teabags, but why would she . . .'

'Why would she what?' he asks when Mom stops talking.

She waves her hand. 'Nothing. It's silly. Anyway, Max, about this playdate . . .'

'I just want to be homely today.'

'Homely?' Mom looks confused. Maybe she doesn't know what that word means.

'Yep. I learned that last night, from the lady who said no one calls her Pig Face now that she's not homely,' he explains. 'I guess she likes being away from her home because bad things happen there, but I *like* being homely.'

'Max, that's not what homely means.'

'What does it mean?'

'It's about . . . well, I don't think she liked the way she looked when she was younger.'

'You should tell her that thing about how it doesn't matter what anyone looks like on the outside. The only thing that counts is what's on the inside.'

'That's a great idea. It's important to help other people feel better when they're feeling bad, isn't it? And I wonder if Robby feels bad about being the new kid?'

'She doesn't.'

'How do you know?'

'Because she doesn't say that, and she doesn't seem like it.'

'Do you always say it when you're feeling bad inside, Max?

Or do you sometimes try to hide it? Especially at school, or with people you don't know very well?'

'I guess I hide it.'

'Do you think Robby could be hiding sad feelings about not having any friends here?'

'No. I think she's hiding mean feelings, and she doesn't even like me, so I don't know why she wants me to play at her house.'

'Why wouldn't she like you? What does she do that's mean?'

'She put a snake down my back on the bus. Not a *real* snake. But I thought it was, and she was laughing and so was everyone else and I got in trouble.'

Mom looks like she's hiding a smile. 'Why do you think she did that?'

'I just told you. Because she's mean and she doesn't like me.'

'I think the opposite. Sometimes when we like someone a lot and they don't notice us, we try to get their attention by doing something . . .'

'Mean?'

'I don't think she thought it was mean. I think she thought it was a silly trick. You said she was laughing.'

'Everyone was laughing except me. And Mr Johansen. He was yelling.'

'Poor Mr Johansen.'

'And poor me!'

'And poor you,' she agrees. 'But, Max, what if Jiffy put a fake snake down your back on the bus. Do you think that's something he might do?'

'Yep. One time he picked up a real one and he chased me around the yard with it.'

'Was it because he was mean and he doesn't like you?'

'Nope. Jiffy's not mean and he's my best friend.'

Mom nods. 'Exactly.'

'Exactly what?'

'It sounds like Robby might want to be your friend, too. I think it will be fun to have a Playbox playdate today, because you love Playbox, don't you?'

'Yes, but—'

'And you like visiting Doris's kitty cats, right? Clover and Columbus, right?'

'Right. But can I have a pastry first?'

Mom looks relieved. 'You sure can.'

'Two pastries?'

'Mrs Burton is bringing cookies.'

'But I *need* two pastries. *Please please please please—*'

'Fair enough. Two pastries it is. On one condition. Promise me you'll never hide on me again.'

'What about if we're playing hide and seek?'

'Only if we're playing hide and seek. Otherwise, no hiding.'

'What if it's about a good surprise? Like a present?'

'If you're hiding and you hear me calling you, you have to come out.'

'What if you try to trick me when we're playing hide and seek?'

'I won't.'

'But—'

'How about this? We'll have a secret code word. If you hear me say it, you have to stop hiding pronto. Got it?'

'Yep. By the way, who's Pronto?'

She laughs. 'It's not a who; it's a what. It means right away.'

'OK. Can I choose the code word?'

'Absolutely.'

Spidey brushes his twitchy tail against Max's foot again, so Max says, 'How about Spidey?'

'Perfect. The code word is Spidey. If you hear me calling you and I say Spidey, you come *immediately*.'

'OK. And if *you* hear me calling you and I say Spidey, *you* come immediately. Because sometimes I need stuff, and you say in a minute, and it turns out to be a lot of minutes.'

'Fair enough.' Mom smiles. 'You drive a hard bargain, kiddo.'

'What does that mean?'

'It means if someone wants something from you, you figure out a way to get something from them in return. Now, let's go get that pastry.'

'Two pastries.'

She laughs, and together, they crawl out from under the table and head for the breakfast room.

SIXTEEN

Leaving Max upstairs getting ready for the playdate, Bella descends the stairs and goes to the registration desk.

She checks the guest registry, hoping Jane signed it.

She did not.

Bella turns to the computer. The system shows a number of new off-season bookings – ah, the magic of starring in a viral video.

Opening Jane's reservation, she sees that the address and phone number are left blank. It's linked to an email address. Bella easily commits it to memory – her first name and last, at a popular provider Bella herself uses. There's no other info, except the credit card number Jane had used to confirm the reservation.

She logs out of the system and checks her watch.

It's too early to start her daily housekeeping rounds, so she goes to the kitchen and opens the freezer, intending to keep her promise to Odelia.

Too bad she's fresh out of ice packs – and ice. The automatic mechanism that's supposed to keep the tray full seems to be blocked by a frozen dam. This isn't the first time it's happened, and she managed to fix it in the past, but it was a time-consuming, messy project that involved an extension cord and a hair dryer.

She rummages around, looking for a makeshift ice pack. No frozen peas, but the brussels sprouts will do nicely.

Hero is dozing on the couch in the back parlor. She considers stretching out beside him, but those deep cushions are too inviting, and now isn't the time for napping.

Napping . . .

Kidnapping.

Fritz Dunkle hadn't been wrong about Jiffy being abducted last year. And it wasn't as though the prospect hadn't occurred to Bella when she found Max's bed empty.

Especially after that knife had turned up in the kitchen.

And the warnings from Odelia and Pandora.

But logic had prevailed, as it so often does. Lily Dale may be rooted in spiritualism and its lore rich with inexplicable incidents, but not everything that happens here is steeped in mystery. Most things aren't. She needs to remember that the next time her common sense is influenced by her imagination – or Fritz Dunkle.

She can hear him in the breakfast room, now filled with guests. He's pontificating on the recent election, having missed the memo about not discussing politics with strangers. Or, really, anyone.

She moves quietly past and slips into her study. Her laptop is on the desk, plugged into the wall outlet because its battery won't hold a charge for long. It's old and slow, with outdated software, and not enough memory space for an update. Still, it serves its purpose.

She unplugs it and takes it into the front parlor.

The room wafts pleasantly with woodsmoke from last night's fire and the pumpkin-scented jar candle she'd lit on the registration desk. The cats are on the window seat. Spidey is curled in a ball, sound asleep, but Chance is just sitting there, looking out.

Luther's car has yet to arrive next door.

Bella settles in a wingback chair, removes her boots, props her feet on a fringed ottoman, and drapes the bag of brussels sprouts over her sore toes. She'd taken a couple of Advil, and the pain is already subsiding. The ice should help, if she can sit here long enough and stop thinking about everything she should be doing around here . . .

And everything that may or may not have happened around here.

She opens the laptop and glances again at Chance while waiting for the hard drive to wake up.

'What are you doing, Chance? Are you looking for something?'

She doesn't flinch.

Well, of course. What's she going to do, turn around and explain why she's staring out the window? She's a cat. It's what cats do. She's probably just watching a squirrel, or a leaf flitting on the wind. There are plenty of both out there.

Bella opens a search engine, types *Ethel Schweinsteiger*, and hits Enter.

Waiting for the results to load, she looks again at the cat, then toward the kitchen.

She'd been so sure she'd heard someone prowling around in the dark with her last night.

So sure she'd seen someone lurking by the door.

Doors don't open themselves.

Nor do drawers. And knives don't jump out of them.

Common sense, Bella.

The door might not have been properly closed, and the wind might have been fierce enough to blow it open . . .

The knife might have been in the dish rack, and skittered across the floor when she knocked it over . . .

But . . .

Something wicked.

Aah. The screen has populated at last.

Bella scrolls down the list, a painstaking endeavor on this old computer. Nearly all the hits reference a popular German athlete who shares the last name, but not the first.

She goes back to the search window, adds New York, and tries again.

Again, there's a long list of hits. Glancing at the first few, she's certain none have anything to do with her Ethel.

She deletes the whole search and starts over with Jane Anderson . . . a name that is, unfortunately, shared by an award-winning actress, writer, and director.

Bella tries searching for the email address.

Still nothing.

Frustrated, she starts to close the laptop, then remembers something. Opening a new search window, she types in Kay Burton, hits Enter, waits, and groans.

'Really? Why can't anyone have an unusual name?'

Then again . . .

Ethel Schweinsteiger?

Deciding to take a closer look at the original search results, she goes back to the first page and begins slogging through. With no luck after ten minutes, she hears voices and footsteps and quickly closes the laptop.

It's the St Clair sisters, coming from the breakfast room.

As she shrinks back in the chair, hoping they won't notice her, the bag of frozen brussels sprouts slides off her foot. She grabs it before it hits the floor.

'. . . And he must have no idea what she's been doing behind his back,' Opal is saying. 'She really doesn't seem the hussy type, but I suppose it's always the quiet ones who—'

'Shh! There she is. Right there by the fireplace, see? Reading a book and snacking on little cabbages.'

'That's not Mother. It's Bella.'

'Well, yes. Why would you think it was Mother?'

'Because we were just talking about her and Clark Gable.'

'We were talking about Bella and Drew,' Ruby says in a stage whisper. 'Mother was no hussy. Besides, she and Clark Gable are dead.'

'It's *Lily Dale*. The dead aren't dead around here.' Opal raises her voice and waves. 'Why, hello, Bella! I didn't see you there!'

Bella narrows her eyes at the sisters. 'Who's the hussy?'

'Pardon?' Ruby says.

'I couldn't help but overhear, and I'm just wondering who you're talking about.'

Opal looks at Ruby. 'Oh – er, Mother?'

'Your mother was a—'

'Yes. Yes, she was,' Ruby tells Bella, and shakes her head. 'Such a shame.'

'A shame. And of course, *you're* not a hussy, Bella. Is she, Ruby?' Opal sounds uncertain.

'Of course not! Everyone knows that she and Drew Bailey are utterly devoted to each other.'

'That's right.' This time, Opal is decisive. 'Everyone knows that. Except for the woman who told us about the poisoned teabags.'

'The teabags were not poisoned! And which woman are you talking about?' Bella asks, though she knows – courtesy of Max – that it was Jane.

She must have misunderstood the sachet conversation last night.

And what? Thought you were trying to kill the St Clairs?

All right, maybe Max is the one who'd misunderstood. He's only seven.

Or maybe the St Clairs had misunderstood whatever Jane had actually said.

What about the rest, though?

Why would Jane discuss Bella and Drew's relationship with the sisters? She knows nothing about it. Nothing about Bella. And to speculate about her fidelity – or lack thereof – with a pair of elderly strangers is just . . .

It's not only inappropriate and preposterous, but it's . . .

Disturbing.

Chance jumps off the window seat, shoots Bella a long look, and strolls out of the room.

A moment later, Bella hears footsteps outside. She sets the laptop and brussels sprouts on a doily-covered table, shoves her feet into the boots, and stands, looking out the parlor window.

A woman and a little girl are climbing the porch steps.

'Excuse me,' Bella tells the St Clairs, and hurries toward the hall.

'Of course, dear,' Ruby says.

'What did she say?' Opal asks. 'Why is she leaving?'

Ruby points to the brussels sprouts. 'Flatulence. She's embarrassed.'

'Ladies, I'm not . . . I didn't—'

'It happens to the best of us,' Opal calls after her, and Bella sighs.

At least her foot seems to be feeling better, the throbbing pain having subsided to a dull ache, courtesy of Advil, ice, and elevation.

She opens the door.

Both mother and daughter are wearing jeans and down jackets. The girl is holding a white bakery bag smudged with buttery stains, and her hair is hidden beneath a Chicago Cubs baseball cap.

'Kay and Robby Burton, right?'

Kay returns her smile. 'Yes, and you must be Bella. It's so nice to meet you.' She turns to the little girl. 'Robby? What do you say?'

'Nice to meet you.'

'You, too, Robby. Welcome to Lily Dale. How do you like it so far?'

'It's fine.'

'And school?'

'It's fine.'

'You're a Cubs fan, huh?'

'What?'

Bella points to the cap.

'Oh.' Robby shrugs. 'I guess.'

'She's shy,' her mom says.

Max had denied that, and Bella is pretty sure she sees a gleam in Robby's eye that tells her otherwise, but she says, 'Believe me, I get it. I used to be a shy kid myself. Come on in. I'll get Max.'

They step over the threshold, and Kay sucks in a breath. 'Oh, wow. This place is *beautiful*.'

'Isn't it? I get to say that, because I can't take any credit.'

'How come?' Robby asks Bella.

'Well, it's not my house.'

'Then how come you live here?'

'It's like we live with Ms Henderson,' Kay tells her daughter. 'The same thing.'

'I don't think so.'

'*Kind* of the same thing.'

'It's not.' Robby scowls at her mother.

Kay ignores it and asks Bella whether the amber brocade wallpaper is original to the house.

'It is. As far as I know, all the décor and fixtures are original. There are photo albums going back over a hundred years. I can show you someday, if you're interested.'

'Absolutely! I love old houses. I've always wanted to live in one.'

'And now you do. I'm pretty sure Doris's place is even older than Valley View.'

'The Yin-Yang? But it's not nearly as grand,' Kay says.

'I've been wondering how you came across it?'

'Came across what?'

'The Yin-Yang Inn. It's usually closed from Labor Day until June.'

'Oh – I guess things changed.' She runs a fingertip over the wainscoting. 'I love the woodwork. Is it mahogany?'

'Some is. Some is walnut, or oak.'

'Where's Max?'

'Robby!' her mother says. 'It's not nice to interrupt.'

'Sorry.'

'No worries. I get it. You're not here to talk about this boring old house, right, kiddo?' Resting a hand on the newel post, Bella calls up the stairs, 'Max! The Burtons are here!'

His faint 'OK' mingles with jangling tags and claws tapping on the hardwood as Hero trots into the hall.

Robby shrinks back against Kay.

'He's friendly,' Bella says, grabbing his collar. 'But if you're afraid of dogs, I can—'

'I'm not afraid! I'm allergic!'

'Oh . . . I'm sorry. Max didn't tell me.'

'Max doesn't know!'

'Robby.' Her mother puts a hand on her shoulder and looks at Bella. 'We'll wait for Max on the porch.'

Bella steers Hero away. 'No, I'll lock him up until you go.'

'You don't have to do that,' Kay protests.

'Oh, he loves the laundry room. It's his favorite napping spot.'

'He doesn't look very tired.'

'Don't let him fool you. Come on, boy.'

Bella wrestles the hound into the laundry room and points to the baskets of dirty laundry. 'Go ahead and have a little rest. Wish I could do the same.'

At his reproachful gaze, she assures him that it's only for a few minutes and closes the door.

Back in the front hall, she finds Kay and Robby flanked by the St Clair sisters.

'. . . And then Mother had a torrid fling with Clark Gable,' Ruby is saying.

Kay, wide-eyed, echoes, 'Clark Gable!'

'Max!' Bella calls from the foot of the stairs. 'Let's go!'

'Who's Clark Gable?' Robby asks her mother. 'What's a torrid fling?'

'Oh, my,' Opal says. 'I don't remember that at all.'

'Of course not. It was before we were born. And of course, once she met Father, she was utterly devoted to him,' Ruby adds.

'Oh, yes. She didn't have an ounce of hussy in her.'

'What's a hussy?' Robby asks.

Bella mouths *sorry* at Kay, who appears amused, and calls, 'Max!'

'I hope he hasn't been kidnapped again,' Ruby comments.

'Max was kidnapped?' Robby asks, and Kay's amused expression gives way to an alarmed one.

'No! He was just hiding under the table! We were playing hide and seek,' Bella explains, and shouts, 'Max! Come on down now, please!'

'That's right.' Ruby nods. 'The Arden boy is the one who was kidnapped.'

'Do you mean Michael Arden?' Robby asks.

'No, I believe it was Jeffy Arden.'

'Jiffy Arden,' Bella corrects automatically, then bellows, 'Max!' and adds, '*Spidey!*'

This time, she's rewarded with footsteps overhead.

'Who's Spidey?' Robby asks.

'Max's cat. You're not allergic, are you?'

'Nope.'

Max trudges down the stairs with all the enthusiasm of a prisoner facing the gallows.

'Didn't you hear me calling you?' Bella asks.

He shrugs. 'I was reading.'

'Max! So nice to see you again,' Kay says, and gives Robby a little nudge.

'Hey,' Robby says.

'Hey.'

'Max, look what Robby brought!' Bella points to the white bag. 'Cookies! Isn't that nice? You love cookies!'

'We weren't sure which ones you like best, so we got two of each,' Kay says. 'You can have one now, if you'd like.'

'No, thanks. My stomach kind of hurts.'

'Oh, no. Are you sick?' Kay asks.

'Poisoned!' Opal says. 'I knew it!'

'No one has been poisoned! I'm sure it's from eating two pastries for breakfast, right, Max?' Bella fixes him with a look.

'Probably.'

Kay nods. 'That'll do it. We'll hold off on the cookies.'

'And the tea,' Opal says, heading upstairs with Ruby behind her.

'The tea?' Kay asks Bella.

She shakes her head. 'Shall we go? Playbox is waiting.'

As Bella follows them to the door, she sees that Luther's SUV is now parked at the curb in front of Odelia's.

'I'll walk out with you,' she says, digging Max's down parka and her own from beneath the rain jackets draped on the coat tree. 'I have to run next door.'

'Wait, what about Spidey? Isn't she coming?' Robby asks.

'Spidey's a boy!' Max pulls on his jacket. 'By the way, *he's* also a *cat*, and cats don't go on playdates.'

'Spidey's a crazy name for a boy.'

'You should talk!'

Robby narrows her eyes. 'Well, Spidey rhymes with Heidi, and Heidi is a girl's name.'

'Robby rhymes with Bobby, and Bobby is a boy name. By the way, so is Robby!' Max says. 'And Dobby!'

'That's not even a name.'

'Yes, it is. Didn't you ever read *Harry Potter*?'

'No! That's a big kids' book. You can't read it, either.'

'My mom reads it to me. And there's an elf named Dobby, so it's a name and it rhymes with Bobby and Robby.'

'How about lobby?' she asks with a giggle. 'Or hobby?'

'Or knobby!' Max laughs, too.

Following them out the door, Bella and Kay exchange a smile.

The yards are littered with branches and leaves, and the wind is still gusting though the rain has stopped. The wind chimes jingle in the porch eaves.

On the front walkway, Bella stoops to move an empty plastic flowerpot that must have blown in from a neighboring yard and, a few steps later, retrieves a store mailer addressed to someone who lives over on Cleveland Avenue.

'That was some storm,' Kay comments. 'I'm just glad it wasn't ice or snow. I'm not ready for that yet.'

'Oh, it's coming.'

'Today?'

Bella looks at the western sky. She's learned to recognize snow clouds – low, dark, and heavy, rolling in across the Great Lakes. These are merely gray and thick with mist.

'Not yet,' she tells Kay. 'But I'm sure we'll get a dusting or more before the month is out.'

'Robby will be excited. She's never seen snow.'

'Then I take it you're not from Chicago?' She indicates Robby's baseball cap.

'We . . . we did live in the Midwest for a while, yes, but that was . . . ah, Doris mentioned you're from New York?'

Bella nods, getting the distinct impression that Kay has deliberately changed the subject. 'I was born in the city and lived in the suburbs after I married Max's dad.'

'You're divorced?'

'Widowed. You?'

'Not widowed – unfortunately,' she adds with a bitter little laugh, then presses a hand over her mouth and shakes her head. 'I'm sorry. That was completely inappropriate. Please don't think I'm . . . well, whatever you're thinking of me.'

Bella is unsure quite *what* to think.

Her instinct is to like Kay – and Robby, too. But there's a caginess about the conversation that has her second-guessing the wisdom of sending Max on a playdate with strangers.

It would be tricky to cancel it now that it's underway. Especially when Max is forging a new friendship at last.

'You said Doris is home today?' she asks Kay. 'Maybe I'll come down and say hello. I haven't seen her in a while.'

The last time Bella ran into her, Doris tried to convince her that she seemed stressed and needed a 'Healing Touch' session – right there in the post office lobby.

'I'm sure Doris would love to have you come, Bella. You can stay for lunch.'

Bella weighs that. 'I would, but I have too much to do around here. What time should I get Max?'

'Let him spend the day. Robby and I can walk him back up the street – say, between four and five o'clock?'

'That's an awfully long playdate.'

'Look at them. They're already having fun.'

Bella turns her attention to Max and Robby, still giggling over their silly rhyming conversation, as he and Jiffy so often do.

'All right, if they get sick of each other sooner, let me know.

Otherwise, shoot me a text when you're on your way back and I'll meet him out front. Bye, guys! Have fun!'

Max waves without looking back.

Bella watches until they disappear around the corner, doing her best to ignore a pang of misgiving.

He'll be fine. Let him go.

As she turns toward Odelia's place, she spots something on the ground, poking out from under a shrub.

More storm debris, she assumes. It's hard to tell what it is without her glasses – the cover blown off a backyard grill, perhaps, or a garbage bag, or . . .

Wait a minute. Is that . . .?

She steps closer and leans in.

Yes, it is. It's a silver button. Several of them, all in a row.

Bella frowns.

What in the world is her new cloak doing out here?

SEVENTEEN

Seated across Odelia's kitchen table from Luther Ragland, Bella watches him rub his clean-shaven chin.

He is, as always, impeccably dressed – even for yard work – in jeans, work boots, and a canvas barn jacket. Handsome, Black, and broad-shouldered, he could have stepped out of an Orvis catalogue.

'You're *sure* this is yours?' he asks Bella, indicating the cloak she'd deposited on Odelia's kitchen table. The curious kittens, Sprout and Twixie, are perched side by side on a chair, balanced on their hind paws and sniffing the waterlogged heap of wool.

'It's mine. I ran back to Valley View before I came here, just to make sure. It was hanging by the door last night when I went up to bed. Now it's gone.'

'And you're sure—'

'Luther? I'm *positive*. It scared the heck out of me when I went up to bed, because it was draped over the coat tree, and it looked like someone was standing there. This morning when I went out with Hero, I grabbed whatever was right on top – which was a hoodie, and I was freezing out there. So the cloak was already gone.'

'So you think someone – a guest, maybe – borrowed it?'

'Borrowed it, *stole* it . . . but why would a guest help herself to my cloak in the middle of the night?'

'Maybe it wasn't a guest. Maybe Pandora changed her mind about giving it to you. I hear you sent her to the dance committee meeting in your place, and then she and Odelia had a falling out. She might be holding a grudge.'

'I'm sure she is, but . . . there's something else, Luther. A few things, actually.' She hesitates, looking over her shoulder.

'Odelia went back to bed. That sailor had her up most of the night again, poor woman.'

'Right – filling her head with sneakers and flashlights.'

'And roses.'

'And roses. On benches. You're a patient man, Luther.'

'Yeah, well . . . *Odelia*. And *Lily Dale*.' He shrugs. 'I'm sure she's sound asleep now, so if there's anything you *don't* want to share with her, now's the time.'

Bella quickly tells him about Pandora's warning.

'A duck floating on a pond, a Danish, and something wicked? And none of it means anything to you?'

'Only that she's plagiarizing Shakespeare,' Bella says. 'Anyway, I don't want Odelia to worry about me even more than she already does. Not that I want *you* to worry, but you're a lot more practical when it comes to these things.'

'As are you. Tell me what's going on.'

'The cloak isn't the only thing that's gone missing. My glasses disappeared, too. And this morning, I wondered if one of my guests might have been wearing them.'

He frowns and reaches for the spiral notebook Odelia uses to take notes about the recipes she's perfecting for a cookbook she's been writing. He tears out a page from the back and begins jotting down details about Jane as Bella shares them.

'Luther, I know none of this adds up to any reason to be suspicious of her.'

'Don't be so sure. A good detective is always in tune with her instincts.'

'I'm not a detective.'

'You're a finer detective than most, and that includes the pros I've known in my career. If your gut is telling you something is off, pay attention.'

'Maybe it's because of Lily Dale's mantra about no such thing as coincidences.'

'It was mine, too, long before I stumbled across Lily Dale. Uh-uh-uh, not allowed up there,' he scolds Twixie, who's ventured from the chair onto the table. He pulls her onto his lap, stroking the splotchy caramel- and chocolate-colored fur that earned her name, after the candy bar. 'Anyway, that's another thing about good detectives – they always take a closer look at anything that seems fortuitous.'

'Then you think it's no accident that Ethel showed up at Valley View? And that strange things have been happening ever since?'

'I can't say for sure. But you seem to think so, and I trust your instincts. Even if it's just a matter of her borrowing your things without permission . . .'

'My glasses? But I mean, who does that? It doesn't make sense. It might just be paranoia, because . . .'

'Because?' he prompts when she trails off.

'OK, again, I'm sure you'll agree this is nothing . . .'

'Try me.'

He deposits a squirmy Twixie onto the floor and takes notes as she tells him about her wee-hour escapade – the sense that someone was creeping around the house, and how she found the open door, then the knife.

'This just got serious, Bella. If you think this woman was armed and meant to harm you, then—'

'I don't think that! Why would she?'

He sets down his pen and steeples his hands beneath his chin. 'You tell me.'

'You think she'd, what? Stab me? Because she's fixated on this notion that I called her Pig Face when we were kids? That's insane.'

'Maybe she is.'

'Maybe she's what?'

'Maybe she's mentally ill. Delusional.'

'She doesn't seem it.'

'Bella, you know as well as I do that deranged criminals can fool you into believing they're ordinary people. What else do you know about her past?'

'Not much.' She grabs Luther's pen just before Sprout, a brownish-orange tabby with white paws, can roll it off the edge. 'We lived in the same neighborhood, and we went to the same high school. She was in my class.'

Luther holds out a palm. 'Pen, please? Which neighborhood was this?'

He writes it down, along with the name of the high school, and the graduating year. 'Where has she been since you last saw her?'

'I have no idea. I tried googling her, but I couldn't find anything under her old name or her married one.'

'Which is . . .?'

'Jane Anderson.'

'Pretty common. So you don't have her current address or phone number?'

'Only her email address. It didn't get me anywhere, but maybe it can help you.' She recites it from memory as Twixie clambers back onto the table. Bella scoops her off, saying, 'Uh-uh-uh, little lady. Not allowed.'

'Do you have any other information from her reservation?'

'Just the credit card number she used to confirm the room. I didn't run it. She paid in cash.'

He looks up. 'Cash, cash? Or by check, or Venmo, or—'

'Cash, cash. She had it ready, right down to the exact change.'

'OK, *that's* atypical behavior in this day and age.'

'Some people pay in cash.'

'People who don't want to leave a trail.'

'Some guests just like to use cash.'

'Older guests?'

'Mostly,' she admits. 'It *is* unusual for someone her age, but it might not mean she's up to something.'

'Right. But these red flags add up. Do you happen to know her husband's name?'

'Ex-husband, she said. And I don't.'

'It would help if you can find out, but I've got some contacts with access to law enforcement tools that will be a lot more efficient than googling. I'll have them see what they can find out about her.' He sets down the pen. 'In the meantime, stay away from her.'

'That's not exactly feasible, since she's a guest at Valley View.'

'Then stay away from Valley View.'

Bella tilts her head and gives him a look.

'Look, I don't think you should take any chances until you know who you're dealing with.'

'I won't. She's not even there right now. And Max is at a playdate for the day, which is the other thing I wanted to run by you.' Seeing Sprout's white paw reach out to bat the pen again, Bella snatches it from his reach. 'Did Odelia mention the new mother and daughter who are staying at Doris Henderson's?'

'Oh, yes. She told me all about how Doris dropped off the decorations committee because of it.'

'Because she has two off-season guests at the inn?'

'I guess so. Odelia thinks it was a lame excuse.'

'Well, I don't think they're here short-term.' Toying with Luther's pen, Bella explains that the little girl is enrolled in school here, and that Max is down at Doris's for a playdate.

'I'm trying to be practical about this, because he needs new friends – now more than ever, with Jiffy away. And because I tend to be over-protective.'

'Who told you that?'

'Sam, when he was alive. And ever since, when I hear him in my head,' she admits. 'Not his *spirit*. Just, whenever I have to make a parenting decision, I wonder what he'd say if he were here . . . and most of the time, I know.'

Luther reaches across the table to pat her arm. 'You're doing a great job. Take it from a guy who was raised by a single mom.'

'Thanks, Luther. I'm just . . . I have some questions about Robby and her mom, Kay. It's late for that, and it's not that I'm suspicious, and sending Max off to spend the day at Doris's seemed safer than keeping him home. But I don't know much about them, and Kay wasn't very forthcoming. Do you think you can find out about her, too?'

'I can try. But if you think there's any reason not to trust her . . .'

'I don't think that.'

'And you're not wondering if she could have been the intruder with the knife?'

'No! I don't even know for sure that there *was* an intruder with a knife,' she reminds him. 'In fact, talking it through with you is making me convinced that there wasn't.'

'Let's hope not. Tell me who I'm looking for – you said her name is Kay?' Luther flips over his page of notes and holds out his palm. Bella puts the pen into it and tells him what little she knows about the Burtons.

'I'll see what I can find out,' Luther promises as she pushes back her chair and gets to her feet.

'Thanks. What would I do without you?'

'You'd be just fine, Bella. You're the most self-sufficient person I know. But if you need me, I'll be around all day. Odelia has me on storm cleanup duty. I'm happy to give you a hand next door, too.'

'Not necessary. Drew is coming over later to help with that.'

'Good. Maybe he can stick around until we figure out what's what.'

She makes a face. 'You mean, the big strong man can protect me? Luther, I'm perfectly self-sufficient and you know it.'

'Sometimes there's safety in numbers, and *you* know it.'

'Yeah, yeah.' She heads for the door.

'Wait! What about your cloak?'

'Oh! I almost forgot. I'd better take it home and see if I can salvage it.'

It doesn't seem likely. The fabric is sopping wet and smeared with mud.

She holds it at arm's length as she heads back to Valley View, glad to see that Jane's car is gone. She'd said she was going out for a while.

Glancing again at the shrub where she found the cloak, she wonders how on earth it wound up there.

She may be wrong – and she hopes she is – but her gut is telling her Jane had something to do with it.

EIGHTEEN

Playbox is one of the most fun things in the whole world, even without Jiffy.

Max hadn't expected Robby to be as good at *Ninja Zombie Battle Armageddon* as he is, but she's way better. Maybe even better than Jiffy. The score is 21–1.

Max has 1.

'That was amazing! How'd you do that?' he asks, when her player does a flip kick into a spin attack.

The score is now 22–1.

'I play a lot,' she says with a shrug, focused on her half of the split-screen game. 'Like, all the time.'

'You're so lucky your mom lets you.'

'It's only 'cause there was nothing else to do when we—'

She stops talking for no reason.

'You do that a lot,' Max says. 'So does Jiffy.'

This time, she doesn't ask who Jiffy is like she did the first few times Max brought him up. She just asks, 'What do I do?'

'You stop talking like someone interrupted you. Even though nobody did. Jiffy does it because sometimes he hears Spirit, and Spirit has bad manners. Is that why you do it?'

'Nope.'

'Then why?'

'Because sometimes I remember something.'

'Like what?'

'Like stuff.'

'Oh.'

Max thinks about that.

'What kind of stuff?' he asks Robby, pressing buttons on the controller, wondering if he can imitate her flip kick into a spin attack.

'Just stuff.'

He can't do the move, and his player takes a punch, costing him a point. Now the score is 22–0.

If he was playing against Jiffy, Jiffy would be jumping around and shouting and making fun of Max.

But Robby doesn't do things like that, which is surprising to Max. He wants to ask her how come she's so mean to him in school and on the bus and so nice to him today, but he can't think of a way to say it.

So far, except for his score in the game, the playdate has been great. They're in a back room off Doris's kitchen. Robby and her mom call it 'the family room,' even though Doris doesn't have a family, just cats and people who stay at her inn.

When Max visited Doris before, the family room had no furniture except a sewing machine table, a cat scratch post, and a bunch of plastic storage bins.

Now it has a comfy couch and a big TV with a Playbox, and some other stuff Robby's mom showed him when they got here. Lego, puzzles, craft kits, and board games.

So far, they've only done Playbox, even though Robby keeps suggesting they take a break and do something else.

'This is getting boring,' she says again, after scoring three more points. 'Let's do something else.'

'How about *Ninja Zombie Battle Reckoning*?' Max asks, his hand still working the joystick to spring his player forward.

'No! Let's play a game.'

'That *is* a game.'

'Not another video game. I'm sick of that. Battleship is fun. Ever play it?'

A memory, long ago and far away, pops into Max's brain.

His dad: 'Hey, Max, do you want to play Battleship?'

His Mom: 'He's too young for that, Sam.'

Dad: 'He's smart. He can learn. It's all about strategy.'

Robby, bursting into his happy memory: 'Hey, what's wrong?'

Max fumbles for the controller button, and his player veers into a stone pillar, costing him another point.

'Nothing's wrong.'

'How come you look like you're going to cry?' she asks, as his score changes to negative one.

'I'm not going to cry. I just remembered something,' he adds, borrowing her phrase, hoping it will make her stop asking questions.

'What did you remember?'

'Stuff.'

'About Battleship?'

'Yeah.'

Noticing that Robby's side of the split screen is frozen, he sneaks a peek at her.

She doesn't have a mean face. She looks like she feels bad for him.

'Why did you pause the game?' he asks, doing the same with his controller.

'Because you were talking.'

'No, *you* were talking.'

'I was asking you why Battleship made you sad.'

'Because I have that game. It was my dad's when he was little.'

'Really?'

'Yeah.' Max takes a deep breath. 'But I never play it. Because he's dead, and he was supposed to teach me how. And sometimes I remember stuff about him, and it makes me sad.'

Robby is quiet for a long time.

Max stares at the stack of games on the shelf, looking for something familiar that he knows how to play that won't remind him of his dad.

Then Robby says, 'I wish my dad was dead.'

Max's mouth falls open and his eyebrows go up. He can't think of anything to say to that, but it's OK, because Robby is still talking.

'Dr Reed says it's not bad for me to say that, because he's a very bad guy.'

'Who's Dr Reed?'

'My doctor.'

'Why do you go to a doctor who's a very bad guy?'

'My *dad* is the very bad guy. Dr Reed is nice. She's not a guy. She's a lady.'

'Oh. My doctor is a lady, too. By the way, you don't seem very sick,' he adds, hoping it's not the throwing-up kind of sick, in case he catches her germs.

'She's not that kind of doctor.'

'What kind of doctor is she?'

'She's the kind who talks to people.'

'Well, my doctor talks to people, too. By the way, what's so bad about your dad?'

Robby opens her mouth like she's going to tell him, and then she closes it and shakes her head.

'Did you just remember something about your dad?' Max asks.

'No. I just want to forget something about him.'

NINETEEN

Bella searches the entire house for her glasses, including the kitchen garbage, in case she had accidentally thrown them away. She should probably be relieved they're not there amid the chicken wing bones, pizza crusts, coffee grounds, and bag of brussels sprouts she'd tossed when she got home. But really, what could have happened to them?

Jane's are so similar – nearly identical. Yet even if she'd accidentally grabbed Bella's instead of her own, they're prescription. She'd have noticed as soon as she'd put them on, wouldn't she? She wouldn't be going around wearing them.

And what possible reason would she have for taking Bella's new cloak and throwing it under a bush?

None of it makes sense.

Time to put it all out of her head and go upstairs to make up the rooms, as she does every morning. She usually begins on the second floor and works her way up, but not today.

On the third floor, she opens the linen closet. The shelves are neatly organized with extra towel sets for each room, and stacks of white bed linens. She grabs an empty laundry basket, then goes to the Vineyard Room and knocks, even though she's positive Jane is out.

Fritz Dunkle is not. His room is right down the hall, and he might be spying on her.

She enters the master code on the keypad, unlocks the door, and peeks into the room to confirm that it really is vacant.

It's one of her favorite rooms. The wallpaper is twined with vines and bunches of grapes in shades of green, dark red, and purple. The walls are decorated with framed prints of vineyards in California, France, and Italy. The bed is unmade, its plain white quilt and sheets in a tangled heap and purple throw pillows tossed on the floor.

She steps closer, intending to make the bed, then stops short, seeing a dark red splotch on the pillowcase.

Blood?

No. The complimentary cabernet from a local winery sits beside a stemmed glass on the bedside table. The bottle is nearly empty.

Bella strips the pillowcase and takes it into the bathroom. As she rinses the stain in cold water, she notes the personal items on the shelf above the sink. Toothbrush, hairbrush, makeup . . .

Contact lens solution and a plastic case.

So Jane really is vision-impaired.

Relieved, Bella wrings out the pillowcase and tosses it, along with a damp purple bath towel and washcloth, into the laundry basket. As she heads back toward the hall to grab a fresh pillowcase and towels, she notices Jane's rolling suitcase on the luggage rack.

It's closed and zipped, and there's no way she's going to snoop through it, but . . . is that an identification tag, dangling from the handle?

She steps closer.

It is not. It's a checked baggage tag from an airline.

It's from a recent cross-country flight – LAX to JFK. The date is early September. There's a bar code, but no identifying information.

Bella takes her phone out of her pocket, snaps a photo of it, and sends it to Luther accompanied by a text: **From Jane/Ethel's suitcase, in case it tells you more than it does me.**

Then she moves on, aware that she's violated Jane's privacy. Unacceptable if she turns out to be innocent.

If she isn't, then Bella has other problems to worry about.

Back downstairs an hour later with the rooms all made up, she sorts laundry and sprays stain treatment on the wine-splotched pillowcase, unable to put Jane out of her mind. She suspects it's much too early for Luther to hear back from any of his contacts, and resists nudging Meredith again. This is hardly a matter of life and death. Bella is sure she'll reach out when she has time.

She does, however, allow herself to call Kay Burton to check on Max.

'Oh, hi, Bella! Is everything OK?'

'Yes, I was just making sure that's the case on your end. I

know how challenging it can be to entertain a pair of seven-year-olds.'

'It's a lot less challenging than entertaining *one* seven-year-old. They've moved on from video games to building . . . uh, *something* . . . out of Lego. It might be a robot. It's hard to tell. But they're laughing a lot.'

'That's so nice to hear.'

'Doris is making lunch for them right now.'

'Oh, thank her for me.'

'She's right here, if you want to talk to her.'

'No need. Thanks again. And if they're sick of each other after lunch, or you're sick of Max, give me a call.'

'I will, but I'm sure that I won't,' Kay says with a laugh.

Bella hangs up, grateful for the reassurance that Max, at least, is in good hands. She leaves Hero snoozing on a pile of towels waiting to be washed and goes to the kitchen.

The ice had worked wonders earlier, but her toes are starting to ache again. She roots around in the freezer for a suitably expendable substitute for the brussels sprouts and settles on a bag of meatballs Odelia had made.

Pina colada meatballs – another test recipe for the so-called 'creative' cookbook she's hoping to publish.

Definitely expendable.

Back in the parlor, Bella eyes her laptop, tempted to open it and resume her online search for Jane.

But if the battery hasn't already died, it's probably about to. Anyway, that's Luther's department now. He and his former law enforcement colleagues can do it far more efficiently.

She carries the laptop back to her study and plugs it into its charger. Then she retrieves her book from the back parlor, eager to lose herself in something that has nothing to do with anything that's gone on around here in the last twenty-four hours.

But when she settles back with the meatballs on her foot and opens the novel to the bookmarked spot, she finds that the story in progress has nothing to do with . . . well, anything.

'Who the heck is *Babette*?' she mutters.

Turning to the previous page, she scans the text in an effort to jar her memory. 'And who's *Colin*?'

She checks the front cover.

Right book. Wrong characters.

And why are they using French phrases and eating baguettes and talking about the war? *Which* war?

What happened to Hank and Sandy, who were eating barbecue at a picnic table in Houston when Bella left off?

She backtracks six pages before she finds the spot where the author introduces Babette, Colin, and a new setting and time period. According to the scene heading, the action has shifted from modern-day Texas to *Côte d'Azur, 1942* – which explains the war, the baguettes, and the sprinkling of *Mon Dieus*.

Thumbing her way backward to Hank and Sandy, she resumes the story at last, making it through three whole paragraphs before she hears a car crunching through the leaves out front.

She puts her bookmark between the pages, closes the book, and gets up to look out the window.

Jane is back.

Bella watches her climb out of the car and reach into the back seat to remove several large, bulky shopping bags. When she straightens, Bella sees that she has a pair of glasses on her head.

Not sunglasses.

As she pulls them down over her eyes, Bella is pretty sure they're the same pair she'd had on this morning.

Remembers Luther's warning, she starts toward her study. The door locks. She can barricade herself in there, and—

She stops short.

And what? You're not being chased. You're not under attack.

It's one thing to avoid Jane in the dead of night, but now? In broad daylight, with other guests up and about?

No way. Sam's capable Bella Blue doesn't run scared. Cowering and hiding won't get her anywhere.

She puts on her sheepskin boots and pats her back pocket, making sure her phone is there. If she feels the slightest threat, she can call for help. Or even scream for help. Luther is right next door.

She reaches the front hall just as Jane steps inside.

Mustering a light, breezy tone, Bella says, 'Welcome back! Looks like you went on a shopping spree!'

'Oh – yes. I just needed to pick up a few things.' Jane glances down and quickly twists one of the bags so that it's not gaping open, but not before Bella glimpses the corner of a cardboard box – a shoe box?

The woman starts for the stairs.

'Wait, Jane. You said you wanted to talk?'

'Oh! That would be nice, whenever you have time,' she says, as if it's Bella's idea.

'Now's good.'

Jane stops and turns back, eyes startled behind her glasses. 'What?'

'I have time right now.' Bella gestures at the front parlor. 'We can sit and chat.'

'Ah . . . Sure. I'll come back down in a bit and find you.'

'I only have a few minutes.'

'Why?'

It's such a strange, forthright question that Bella stumbles over a reply. 'You know . . . it's just a crazy day, and I, uh, I have a million things to do.'

'With your boyfriend?'

'My . . .'

'Your boyfriend. Drew. Didn't you say he was coming over?'

'Did I?'

'Maybe he said it. Someone did. I don't want to keep you from him.'

'He's at work.'

'But he's coming over afterward?'

'I'm not sure,' Bella lies, wishing Drew would walk through the door right this second. But he'd texted her half an hour ago to say he was still seeing patients and would be awhile longer.

'If this is the only time you can spare for me, I'll just run this stuff upstairs. Be right back.'

Bella forces a smile. 'I'll be here.'

She watches Jane hurry on up the flight, wondering what can possibly be in those bags.

Buying new shoes isn't exactly incriminating. Unless she's using the box to smuggle something else into the house.

Like what? Heavy artillery?

Uneasy, Bella gets the bag of meatballs from the front parlor, takes it to the kitchen, and deposits it into the trash can.

She pulls her phone out of her pocket to text Luther and sees that there's a missed call from Misty.

Bella returns it immediately without bothering to see if she'd left a message.

She answers on the first ring. 'Hi, Bells!'

She smiles. Misty is the only one who's ever called her that. And it's nice to hear her sounding like her old self.

'I saw that you called. Where are you?'

'We're driving. Well, *I'm* driving.'

Bella hears Jiffy laugh in the background. 'Yeah, I can't drive yet!'

He, too, sounds like his cheerful old self, despite all he's been through.

'I have you on speaker phone,' Misty says. 'Jiffy wanted me to let Max know we're on our way.'

'Home?'

'Yes. We just left Toronto. We should be in the Dale before dark.'

'Aren't you stopping in Niagara Falls?'

'No, Jiffy just wants to get back and see Max. He's – uh-oh, is that a cop behind me again?'

'Nope, it's just a car with a ski rack,' Jiffy says.

'Oh, phew. The last thing I need is another speeding ticket.'

Bella frowns. 'Misty? How many speeding tickets have you gotten?'

'Today? Or ever?'

'She only got one today,' Jiffy reports. 'So far.'

'No, he didn't give me a ticket,' Misty says. 'Because I started crying and I told him about Mike.'

'Misty!' Bella shakes her head, exasperated.

'It wasn't fake, Bells. I really was upset. The grief hits you in the strangest moments, you know?'

Bella can't argue with that.

'Anyway, we're just trying to get home, because we've been gone for way too long. We miss everyone. And Jiffy especially misses Max, so he wants to have a sleepover tonight.'

'Here?'

'Did you get Playbox while I was gone, Bella?' Jiffy asks.

'No.'

'Then no. At my house. Can I talk to Max?'
'He's not home right now.'
'Where is he?'
'He's . . . he's down at Doris Henderson's for . . .'
Bella hesitates. It might hurt Jiffy to know that Max has made a new friend in his absence.
'For what? Is he playing with her cats?'
'Probably.'
'As long as he's back by the time we get there,' Misty says. 'Bye, Bells!'
She hangs up and texts Luther.
Any info yet?
When there's no immediate response, she goes into the laundry room. A window above the cluttered countertop faces Odelia's house next door. Luther is out there, perched atop a ladder, pulling sticks and leaves out of the gutters.
Reassured by his presence, Bella turns away to see that Hero has awakened and is sitting by the door, tail wagging in anticipation.
'You need to go out, boy? OK, but it's too chilly out there for me right now.'
She lets him out into the fenced garden area. In the summer, it's alive with blooms and pollinators. Now, the beds are full of bare brown stalks and dead leaves. The mulched pathway is mostly mud, with puddles in the spots where Hero likes to dig.
Bella keeps an eye on him as she looks for an empty basket to hold the finished load in the dryer. There are none – some are filled with clean, folded laundry, some with sorted dirty laundry. One contains the sodden cloak she'd found under the shrub.
She picks it up, wondering what she should do with it until she has a chance to get it cleaned.
'Oh, there you are!'
Bella gasps and whirls to see Jane in the doorway.
'Sorry, Bella. I keep spooking you, don't I? I promise, it's not on purpose.' Her gaze shifts to the swath of wet wool in Bella's hand. Something flickers in her expression, then is gone. 'What's that?'
'I'm not sure. I found it outside.' Bella holds it up. 'Any ideas?'
'It looks like an old cape or something.'

'No, I mean, I know what it *is*. Just not why it was outside. It's mine. A gift from a friend.'

'From Drew?'

'Not Drew.' Bella tosses the cloak back into the basket, swallowing a comment about Jane having brought up Drew – *again*. She glances at Hero, happily digging in what's left of the petunias, then opens the dryer. 'What did you want to talk about?'

'Should we go into the other room?'

'I'd *love* to, but I have to fold this stuff.'

It's the truth. She does need to catch up on the laundry. But Luther's presence right outside the window makes her feel a little more comfortable about being alone in a room with this woman.

Just in case something really is off about her.

Dangerously off.

'I'd tell you to have a seat,' Bella says, 'only there's nowhere to sit. Unless you want to hop up on the counter? I can clear a spot.'

'I don't think I'm allowed.' Jane points to the *PRIVATE* placard on the door.

'That's just to keep the guests out of parts of the house that are as messy as this.' Bella nods toward the laundry heaped all over the room. 'You should see the kitchen. It's a real mess most of the time. And now you know my dirty little secret.'

She intends the last comment to be light and flippant, but Jane doesn't crack a smile.

Uncomfortable, Bella turns to the dryer, pulling out a warm bath towel. 'You mentioned you've been having a rough time?'

'Yes. Right. I am.'

'What's going on?'

'It's my ex. He's . . . I don't even know how to say it.'

She falls silent as Bella swiftly folds the towel into thirds, and then again, sets it on top of the dryer, and reaches in for another one.

'What's his name?' Bella prods. 'Your ex.'

'Tom?' There's an expectant tone in Jane's reply. It's more of a question.

That's how Pandora introduces her own ex in conversations.

'Orville Holmes?' she'll say, and then pause, waiting for the other person to be suitably impressed. If they don't recognize the name – Bella had not when they first met – Pandora grows a bit haughty, explaining that he's *the* Orville Holmes – the Hollywood medium whose *other* ex-wife is movie starlet Jillian Jessup.

Pandora hasn't forgiven the trollop for stealing her husband, nor Orville for running off with another woman. That doesn't stop her from name-dropping.

In this case, with Jane, Bella isn't quite sure why – or whether – *Tom* is supposed to strike a chord with her.

'Tom,' she echoes.

'Yes.'

Still, she seems to be waiting for a reaction. Either that, or she's fascinated by Bella's towel-folding skills, because she's watching her intently.

'How long were you married?' Bella asks, for lack of a better question.

'Until someone better came along.'

'Oh. Then he—'

'Left me for another woman. Yes.'

'I'm so sorry. I know how painful that must be for you.'

'*Do* you?'

About to grab another towel from the dryer, Bella notes the palpable chill in her tone.

'Your husband was unfaithful, too, then?' Jane asks.

'What? No!'

'I didn't think so.'

Bella takes out a towel, tempted to swaddle herself in its warmth and to avoid Jane's gaze. She does neither.

'Sam and I didn't get divorced, Jane. He died. I thought I'd mentioned that, but maybe I'm wrong.'

'No, you did. But there must have been someone in your life before Sam?'

Flabbergasted, Bella just shakes her head and focuses on lining up the towel edges with unnecessary precision.

'I mean, I remember you back in school, Bella. You were the girl every guy wanted to date.'

'Um, you must have me mixed up with someone else.'

Jane waves off the comment. 'You don't have to be modest. It's *me*,' she adds, as if they're best friends.

Or friends at all.

Bella frowns.

Yes, she'd outgrown the braces and acne and developed a figure before high school was over. She'd made friends, gone to parties, dated, even fleetingly had a boyfriend, but . . .

'I wasn't exactly Miss Popularity,' she tells Jane.

'Oh, please, Bella. You literally had the *kissing* disease!'

'What?'

'Senior year! You weren't in school for a month.'

It's true – she'd been out sick for weeks, highly contagious and with the worst sore throat of her life. 'You mean, when I had mononucleosis?'

'Mono. Yes. Also known as the *kissing disease*.'

Bella's jaw drops. She doesn't even know what to say to that. It's almost as if Jane is . . .

Jealous?

Yes. That's the word. From the moment she arrived, she's seemed jealous of Bella, irrationally so.

'And look at you now,' she goes on. 'You lost Sam, but you have Drew. You have this house, and Max, and so many friends. You're a lucky woman.'

Lucky? To have watched her beloved husband die? And in the wake of that tragedy, to have lost her home, her livelihood, her entire life as she knew it?

She opens her mouth, then swallows a sharp retort.

Maybe she's the one who's being tone deaf. This isn't about her.

She takes a deep breath. 'I haven't always been lucky. We all go through our share of struggles. I'm sorry for whatever you're dealing with right now.'

'It's really bad. I'm worried about what he's going to do.'

'What do you mean?'

'He's dangerous, Bella.'

'Dangerous how?'

'He's been making threats.'

'But . . . I thought you said he left you for another woman?'

'I did say that. I guess he's changed his mind. He wants me back. He's stalking me.'

'*Stalking* you? How? What is he doing?'

'What do stalkers do?' Jane snaps. 'They *stalk*!'

Bella closes her mouth and puts another folded towel on the pile.

She looks out at the garden. Hero is rolling around in a puddle.

'Sorry,' Jane says. 'It's just . . . I'm a nervous wreck over this. I don't know what to do.'

'Did you call the police? You can get a restraining order.'

'They're useless.' Jane shakes her head. 'A piece of paper isn't going to stop anyone who wants to get to you. If you get caught, you spend a few days in jail and pay a fine. Big deal. That's why I had to get away, to a place where he'd never find me.'

Unless he followed you.

Bella is reluctant to voice the thought.

Jane is not. 'I just hope he didn't follow me.'

'From New York? You're still living there, right? And he's there?'

'Let's hope so.'

'Last night . . .'

No. She shouldn't get into it. She isn't even sure it wasn't her imagination.

But Jane isn't going to let it go. 'Last night, what?'

'Last night – actually early this morning – I thought someone might be prowling around the house. I found the door open, and . . .' She shakes her head, reluctant to share the knife incident and perhaps needlessly frighten Jane.

Jane, however, doesn't seem frightened. 'It was him. Tom. I know it was.'

'How do you know?'

'Who else could it have been? He must have found me.'

'But you drove, right? Wouldn't you have noticed if someone was behind you on the road? You must have been looking, making sure.'

'Yes. I was. Definitely. I would have noticed.'

Bella exhales.

'But he might be following me some other way.'

'You mean electronically? On your phone, or something?'

'Or with some sort of tracking device, I suppose. I'm probably just paranoid. I hope so. He's dangerous. The way he shouts at me . . . I'm terrified he's going to hurt me.'

Odelia's warning about an angry man and a terrified woman come back to Bella.

'Look, Jane, if you think he knows where to find you, then you need to do something.'

'Like what?'

She thinks again about calling the police. But that likely means summoning Lieutenant John Grange to Valley View . . . *again*. And while he's dutifully competent, he's hardly the type of man who's going to handle this sensitive situation in a sensitive manner.

'I think you should get out of here,' she tells Jane. 'Otherwise, you're a sitting duck.'

Pandora's vision comes to mind.

Duck on a pond . . .

Sitting duck?

Yeah, it's a stretch.

'I already paid for three nights here,' Jane says. 'Am I just supposed to leave after one, and then spring for some other hotel? I'm not made of money, you know!'

Taken aback, Bella says, 'I'll refund you for the whole stay. The cash is still in the drawer. You can have it. I just want to make sure you're safe.'

'And I'm not trying to be difficult. But where am I supposed to go?'

'Is there a family member you can stay with? Your dad?'

'He's dead.'

'Someone else, then?'

'There's no one else. No other family.'

'A friend?'

'I *am* staying with a friend.' Jane's smile is weak.

'What I mean is . . .' Bella glances out the window at Luther, still on the ladder. 'I think you should report this.'

'The police can't do anything unless he violates the restraining order. Right now, it would be my word against his. He'll deny everything.'

'Not if there's evidence. Has he been calling you? Texting you?'

'No. He's just . . . look, he's out to get me. He's watching me. Call it intuition, or who knows? Maybe I'm psychic. But I can feel it. *You* must understand that, don't you? Living here?'

'I do. And I hope you're wrong,' Bella says.

'Yeah. So do I. But this morning, when your little boy went missing, I was worried that Tom might have something to do with it.'

Bella's blood runs cold. She fights to keep her voice level. 'Why would you think that?'

'Because I have no clue where he is, or what he's capable of. So it's probably a good thing Max is over at the Yin-Yang.'

Bella wonders how she knows that.

She could have overheard. But even if she had, it isn't the kind of detail a guest would retain. She could have just said he's on a playdate.

'Hey – I think your dog needs you.'

Bella follows her gaze and sees Hero on the doorstep, shaking himself off. Muddy water droplets spatter the glass.

As she grabs a couple of towels from the pile and goes to let him in, Jane heads out of the room.

'You don't have to go,' Bella says over her shoulder, reaching for the doorknob. 'I have time to talk. The laundry can wait. We can go sit down. Maybe I can help you figure out—'

'No, it's OK. I need to lie down for a little while.' As she disappears around the corner, she calls back, 'Just be careful, Bella. I wouldn't want anything to happen to you.'

TWENTY

Battleship turns out to be a fun game, even though Robby beats Max three times in a row.

'Let's play again,' he says, as they pull the pegs out of their little plastic boats after the third game, which was a lot closer than the first two. 'I bet I can win the next one.'

Robby shakes her head. 'I'm sick of this. Let's play something else. You can choose.'

Max gets up and walks over to the shelves of games. 'I like checkers.'

'That's boring. Can you play chess?'

'Is it like checkers?'

'Not really. I can teach you.'

'Is it easy?'

'Nope.'

'Then no, thanks.'

He doesn't feel like losing more games in a row. Robby's good at a lot of things, and she knows a lot of things, and she can read big words. She's kind of like Jiffy, if Jiffy was a girl and not a psychic.

Robby isn't. They talked about that. Her mom isn't, either.

'Hey, Robby? How come you live in Lily Dale if you and your mom aren't spiritualists?' Max asks her now.

'You and your mom live here, and you're not spiritualists, either.'

'I know, but my mom's job is to run Valley View.'

'Oh, yeah.'

'So why are you and your mom here?'

'Because we . . .'

'Because you what?'

'We just are.'

'Max?' Doris comes into the doorway.

She's a nice lady. She has short gray hair and a wrinkly face like Max's grandma, except she wears jeans, and she has a tattoo, which is not at all like Max's grandma. Max once heard his mom tell Dr Drew that Doris is a 'hippy.' When he asked her about that, she said for him not to ever tell Doris she said that, so it must mean something bad.

She holds up her phone. 'You've got a call.'

'Is it his mom again?' Robby asks.

Max sighs. 'Can you just tell her I'm fine?'

'It's not your mom.' Doris is smiling. 'I'm pretty sure you'll want to talk to this person.'

Max gets up and takes the phone. 'Hello?'

'Did Doris get a new cat?'

'Jiffy! Hi! Where are you?'

'I'm in the car. My mom said we can call Doris's house because your mom said you're there playing with her cats. Does she have a new one named Robby?'

'No! Robby's a kid in our class.'

For a second, Jiffy doesn't say anything. Then he asks, 'By the way, does he sit next to you, in my seat?'

'Nope. And he's a she. By the way, some lady I hate sat in your seat at my house last night. Dr Drew got pizza and wings, and I wanted to save some for you because my mom said you're coming home.'

'I am and I want pizza and wings. Can you bring them over to my house when you sleep over?'

'I think the lady ate them all.'

'Is that why you hate her?'

'And because she sneaks around, and she says bad things about my mom. By the way, when are you coming home so I can sleep over at your house?'

'Today!'

'Today? Yippee!' Max shouts, and then he sees that Doris is looking at Robby. He looks at Robby, too, and she seems kind of sad.

'Max,' Doris says, 'why don't you take your call in the other room? I'd like to have a word with Robby in private.'

'OK.' Max goes into the hallway with the phone and asks Jiffy, 'What time are you coming today?'

'Mom says we'll be there before it gets dark out if she goes fast enough. But she can't go too fast, because the police might chase us again.'

'Why were they chasing you?'

'I think they thought we were bank robbers.'

'Jiffy!' Misty shouts in the background. 'Nobody thought that.'

'I guess they thought my mom was speeding,' Jiffy tells Max. 'It was just like a car chase on TV, with sirens and everything.'

'You mean your mom didn't stop?'

'Well, she stopped. But not right away.'

'Because there was nowhere to pull over!' Misty says. 'I stopped as soon as I could.'

'Were you scared?' Max asks Jiffy. 'Being in a car chase?'

'I'm never scared, remember?'

'Oh, yeah.' Jiffy wasn't even scared when he got kidnapped.

'By the way, we should play wild west cops and robbers when I get back. I went to a place called Deadwood. Some gunslingers and outlaws and bank robbers used to live there.'

'Did you see them?'

'Only one. Her name was Calamity Jane, and she talked to me while we were there. Only I don't think she was a bad guy. Just a lady. By the way, she was dead.'

'Hey! Jane is the name of the sneaky lady who ate your food. Only she's not dead. But she might be a bad guy. Or a witch.'

'Does she have a black dress and a green face and a pointy nose?'

'No, but sometimes witches look like regular people.'

'I know.'

Max wonders if he'll ever get to know anything interesting that Jiffy doesn't already know. Probably not.

Oh, yeah, there is one thing.

'If you get back before I get home, make sure you call my mom and tell her Spidey. That's our secret code word.'

'You have a secret code word? What does it mean?'

'Well, sometimes it means come downstairs right away . . .'

'How come you can't just say come downstairs right away?'

'Because it's a secret code.'

'Secret code words are for when something really, really scary is going on,' Jiffy says. 'Like if you saw a bank robber. An alive one. They're not for coming downstairs.'

'I know. We use it for that, too,' Max says quickly. 'Like if we see a bank robber, or a kidnapper.'

Doris sticks her head out of the family room. 'Max? Are you finished with your call?'

'Almost.' He says into the phone, 'Make sure you call as soon as you get home, OK?'

'OK. And I'll use the secret code word. Bye, Max.'

'Bye, Jiff.' He hangs up, steps back into the family room, and gives Doris her phone. 'That was Jiffy.'

'He's on his way home, huh?'

'Yep.'

'I'm sure you're looking forward to seeing him. And I'll bet Robby would like to meet him.'

'She will, because he's in our class.'

'Maybe you can introduce her before that. I'll bet the three of you would have fun playing together,' Doris says.

He looks at Robby. She seems grumpy, sitting cross-legged on the floor, putting the pieces back into the Battleship box.

'Maybe sometime,' he says.

'Lunch is almost ready. I'll call you to the table in a few minutes. You two can play until then.'

'I don't feel like playing anymore.'

'Well, I feel like it,' Doris tells Robby. 'I'd love nothing more than to play a game with both of you after lunch.'

'Battleship is only for two people. So is chess.'

'But we have lots of games for three. Why don't you pick something fun and bring it into the kitchen?'

She shrugs. 'Max can pick. I don't care.'

'Someone pick.' Doris leaves the room.

'You can,' Max tells Robby, because she seems sad. Or mad. Or both.

'No, *you* can.'

As Max looks over the stacks of games, Robby is quiet.

He thinks back to what they were talking about before Doris came in.

'Hey, Robby?'

'Yeah?'

'Where did you live before you came to Lily Dale?'

'Far away.'

'Buffalo?'

'No.'

'New York City? That's where I was born. And then we lived in Bedford. That's in Westchester.'
'Not New York City and not Bedford and not Westchester.'
'Then where?'
'It's a secret.'
'From me?'
'From everyone.'
'How come?'
'It just is.'
'Well, I'm great at keeping secrets.'
'So am I,' Robby says, as she plunks the box top back on Battleship and gets to her feet. 'Come on. It's time for lunch.'

TWENTY-ONE

Crouched beside Hero on the back step, Bella gives his wet, filthy fur a vigorous rubdown with fluffy white towels that are still warm from the dryer.

Maybe she should go next door to Odelia's to tell Luther in person about Jane's stalker ex-husband.

But what if he really is lurking around here, watching the house, watching Jane – watching Bella?

She glances around the yard, and then at the lake beyond. She supposes someone could be hiding behind a tree or shrub. Or even watching her from the opposite shore, with a telescope trained on her right this moment.

Or a gun.

'OK, that's crazy,' Bella mutters. 'Stop. He's not after *you*. Or Max.'

Hero lets out an anxious bark, and she stands.

'Come on, boy. You're clean enough. Let's go back inside.'

She follows Hero back into the laundry room and throws the muddy towels into the heap of dirty ones on the floor. She should have taken them from there in the first place, or at least have chosen some that aren't white, but Jane's unexpected revelation has robbed her of her common sense.

She steps back outside with the wet woolen cloak and a couple of clothespins and hangs it on the line. The wind will whip it dry in no time, and she'll bring it to the dry cleaner next week.

Back inside, she locks the door. Then she texts Luther the new information about Jane's ex-husband, watching him on the ladder to see if he pulls out his phone as soon as the text goes through.

He does not. He must not have it in his pocket. That means he won't see the message until he finishes with the gutters. It also means that if his contacts who are looking into Jane have tried to follow up, they haven't gotten through to him, either. For all Bella knows, he hasn't even gotten in touch with them yet.

That strikes her as uncharacteristically cavalier behavior. Yet when she'd spoken to him earlier, she'd downplayed her concerns. There was no reason for him to believe Jane's presence here was anything other than annoying. She'd reiterated that she wasn't even sure there was an intruder, and that she was sure there was a perfectly benign explanation for the open door, the knife, and even paying cash for the room.

Knowing what she knows now, well . . .

It all makes sense.

There's no way a woman on the run from a dangerous ex would use a credit card or a check. But that doesn't mean he couldn't have found her some other way.

If he knows where she is, then he might very well have been prowling around Valley View in the dead of night, looking for Jane.

Just be careful, Bella. I wouldn't want anything to happen to you . . .

But *she's* the one in danger. The only one he'd want to harm. Jane. Not Bella. Certainly not Max.

When your little boy went missing, I was worried that Tom might have something to do with it . . .

Bella grabs her phone, pulls up Kay Burton's number, and places a call. As it rings, she paces with an anxious Hero at her heels, and she tries to think of a good reason she'd need to check on Max yet again.

She can tell him Jiffy's coming home, that he wants a sleepover.

But he'll probably lose interest in Robby. He might want to come home right now.

After four rings, she hasn't come up with another excuse to be calling, and when the call bounces into voicemail, she decides she doesn't need one. She has every right to call simply to make sure her son is OK – and what if he's not?

Why, oh why, is she getting voicemail?

The person you're trying to reach is unavailable. Please—

She hangs up. Since the outgoing message is the robotic default one, she probably just dialed the wrong number.

That makes sense.

Except, checking her phone, she sees that the number she'd just called matches the one she'd dialed earlier, when Kay answered.

Kay had assured her that the kids were just fine.

But that doesn't mean they are.

She'd even offered to let Bella talk to Max.

But that doesn't mean she was really going to put him on the line.

What if Kay isn't who she claims to be?

Who does she even claim to be? Bella knows nothing about her. She'd volunteered no information about her life. In fact, she'd been so cagey that Bella had resorted to asking Luther to see what he can find out about her.

This is crazy. How could she have been so irresponsible? If anything were to happen to Max . . .

No. No way. Nothing can happen to Max.

'It can't,' she tells Hero, now sitting at her feet, watching her intently. 'It *won't*.'

Bella returns to the first call and presses redial with a trembling hand. Again, it rings once . . . twice . . . three times . . . four.

The person you're trying to reach is—

Bella hangs up, scrolls through her contacts to the Hs, finds Doris Henderson's number, and places a call. She leaves the laundry room, dogged by the dog, heading for the front door as the line rings once . . .

'Come on, pick up!' Hero, behind her, lets out a little whine.

Her heart sinks as the line rings again.

In the front hall, she grabs her car keys from a drawer and fumbles for a jacket on the coat tree.

The line rings a third time.

And then, 'Hello?'

'Doris! Is Max there?'

'Bella?'

'Yes! It's Bella! Is Max there?'

'Of course he is. We were just—'

'Can I talk to him, please? I was trying to get ahold of Kay, but—'

'She's right here. Is everything all right?'

'Can you just put him on? Please?'

'Sure. Hang on a second.'

She hears Max's voice in the background. 'Sorry! Sorry!'

And Kay, shouting, 'You'd better look out! I'm going to get you for that!'

Bella throws the front door open. She and Hero burst out of the house. She has to get to Max before something horrible happens.

'Mom?' He's on the line, sounding like he's crying.

'Max! What—'

'I'm having the best time!'

He isn't crying. He's laughing.

Bella stops in her tracks and grabs Hero's collar.

'We're playing Sorry! It's the most fun game ever, and I have to ask Santa to bring it to me for Christmas!'

Bella's legs wobble. She sinks onto the porch swing. Hero, concerned, climbs up beside her.

'And guess what? I'm winning! I keep making great moves and sending everyone back to the start!'

'You won't get away with this! I will have my sweet revenge!' Kay calls in the background, laughing.

Bella finds her voice. 'Max, that's . . . that's fantastic. I'm so glad you're having fun.'

'Yep. What do you want? Because they're waiting for me.'

'I just wanted to make sure you still want to stay for the afternoon.'

'I do! Thanks, Mom!'

'OK, sweetie, I'm here if you change your mind. Have fun. I love—'

He's already hung up.

'—you.' Bella exhales and leans her head back, eyes closed, clutching the keys so hard they dig into her palm.

Hero whimpers, and she reaches out to give him a reassuring pat. 'It's OK. Max is fine.'

Of course he is. He's having fun. Playing a game. Everything is as it should be.

She listens to chainsaws buzzing, someone raking leaves, and the tinkling glass angels in the porch eaves. Not Sam, trying to warn her from the Other Side, but the wind. It's brisk, and she's not wearing a jacket, but she can't seem to make herself move just yet.

She doesn't have to worry about Max in this moment.

But Jane's ex-husband really has tracked her to Valley View . . .

Then Pandora's vision makes sense.

Odelia's, too.

Someone is in danger . . . A man is shouting. He's so angry at her . . . He really hurt her. Or he's about to . . .

He's so angry at her. He's telling her she can't leave . . .

The man's voice, speaking through Odelia: *Don't you dare leave. If you try, I will hunt you down . . .*

Every detail she'd shared had been reflected in Bella's conversation with Jane. If Bella was convinced that spirit guides are feeding information to the mediums, Odelia's would be dead on.

Hero shifts position on the cushion beside her, and she hears, 'Bella!'

She opens her eyes to see Calla Delaney waving from the park across the street. She appears to be coming back from her daily run, lean and fit in blue Lycra, with a sweatband beneath her brunette bangs and tied around her ponytail.

She removes her earbuds and jogs toward Valley View, calling, 'What are you doing outside in the cold without a coat?'

'That's a good question.' Bella stands, hugging herself.

Wagging his tail, Hero goes over to the edge of the porch to greet Calla. She climbs the steps and bends over to pet him.

'Hey, buddy. Who's a good doggie?' She looks up at Bella. 'Is everything OK? How's your foot?'

Bella rolls her eyes. 'News travels fast around here. Who told you?'

'Gammy.'

Odelia. Of course.

'My foot feels better. But everything is definitely not OK.'

'What's wrong? And where's Max?'

'He's fine. He's on a playdate at Doris Henderson's.'

'Isn't she a little old for that?'

Bella manages a smile. 'A mother and daughter are staying with her, and the girl is in his class.'

'Oh, right. I heard.'

'Gammy again?' At Calla's nod, Bella says, 'Then I'm sure she told you all about the dance committee situation.'

'*All* about it. What's going on here?'

Bella lowers her voice. 'Something strange. If you can come in for a few minutes, I really need to get your take on it. Just . . . shhh. I don't want to be overheard.'

'Do you want to go talk at Gammy's instead?' Calla offers, gesturing next door. 'I'm pretty sure she's home, and I see Luther working in her yard.'

'Luther already knows. He's looking into something for me. And I don't want to give your grandmother more to worry about than my foot. It's already feeling much better thanks to her suggestions.'

'Ice, rest, elevation?'

'She told you?'

'No, but it's the usual remedy, along with this god-awful salve she makes. You don't stink, so I'll assume you've been spared.'

'By the skin of my teeth.' She opens the door and gestures for Calla to step inside, then follows her over the threshold. 'We can go into my study. It's private and—'

Too late, she realizes they're not alone in the front hall.

Fritz Dunkle is just descending the stairs.

'Calla Delaney!' he says, wide-eyed.

'Yes?'

'Fellow wordsmith here. Fritz Dunkle.' He extends his hand. 'I'm a fan of your work.'

'Thank you.'

'I was thrilled when Bella said you'd be willing to lend some advice about a book I'm working on.'

'Oh, ah . . . she did?' Calla flicks a glance at Bella.

'I . . . did,' she admits, recalling her offhanded remark yesterday, when Fritz asked. 'Sort of. But it wasn't—'

'I'll confess, I wasn't expecting you to show up so soon,' Fritz plows on, 'but I'm happy to tell you about it if you don't mind an informal presentation.'

'Presentation?'

He nods. 'My research isn't complete. It's nonfiction, about Lily Dale.'

Calla, whose work in progress is also a nonfiction book about Lily Dale, raises an eyebrow at Bella.

She jumps in. 'Oh, Fritz, I'm afraid Calla isn't—'

'You were saying we can use your study?'

'Calla's not here to talk about your book! She's here for . . . I need her to . . .'

Calla rescues her. 'I'm doing a reading for Bella.'

'Is it from your work in progress? I'd love to sit in!'

'Not that kind of reading. I'm a medium.' Calla hooks her arm through Bella's and steers her away. 'Nice meeting you, Fritz. Talk soon!'

In the study, Bella tosses her keys and phone on the desk. She winces as she bends to move the doorstop, handling it with care. Yesterday, she'd narrowly escaped being impaled on it. This morning, it had been a painful obstacle in the dark.

She closes the door and slides the old-fashioned lock. Not that she thinks Fritz is going to burst into the room uninvited. It just feels . . . safer.

'Sorry about him, Calla. I can't believe how presumptuous he is.'

'It's OK. Happens all the time. Is he the problem you're dealing with?'

'I wish. And I hope he doesn't become the problem you're dealing with, since he's writing the same kind of book.'

'Is his under contract with a publisher?'

'I don't think so.'

'Then I'm not worried.'

'Good. Anyway . . . have a seat.'

'Looks like someone beat me to it.' Calla gestures at Chance, asleep on the window seat. 'You don't mind being a lap kitty for a bit, do you?'

She picks up the cat and holds her, stroking her fur. Chance doesn't open her eyes, and Bella can hear her contented purring as she sits down at the desk.

Decorated in summery shades of sun and sky, with crisp white woodwork, the room is an uplifting oasis during the Dale's monochromatic off-season weather.

Bella's laptop is on the desk, plugged into the charging cord after her earlier futile search.

Jane's ex-husband's name will give her more to go on, though she'll probably have hundreds, thousands of Tom Andersons to wade through.

She opens the computer, intending to allow it to boot up as

she brings Calla up to speed, talking in a low tone. 'So there's this woman staying here for the weekend, and it turns out she's someone I knew back in—'

She goes still, staring at the screen in horror.

'Bella?'

She turns the laptop toward Calla, its screen completely smashed.

TWENTY-TWO

A full five minutes after she discovered her shattered laptop screen, Bella's heart is still racing.

She'd told Calla everything, at first in a panicky rush, and again in a more coherent manner after reality had set in, prompted by Calla's questions about Jane, the past, and everything that's gone on here in the past twenty-four hours.

Calla remains on the window seat, but Chance is now perched on the wooden surface beside the damaged laptop, her tail twitching as it does whenever she's on high alert.

'I feel like she knows something,' Bella says, gazing into the cat's unblinking green eyes. 'I wonder if she saw who did it?'

'Maybe.'

'I wish she could talk. I don't suppose you can read her mind? Channel her thoughts? Whatever you call it?'

'Sometimes,' Calla says. 'But not right now. I'm hoping Spirit will help me understand what's going on here.'

'Do you feel like this man – the ex-husband, Tom – do you think he did this?'

It seems to Bella like the obvious question, and one that should have an obvious answer, but Calla shakes her head.

'I don't feel his energy here.'

'He's not dead, though,' Bella clarifies. 'He's—'

'No, I know he's not. What I mean is, I feel negative *female* energy.'

'You think *she* did this? Jane?'

'I don't know. Maybe.'

'But why would she?'

'You said you had done an online search for her name?'

'Yes. *Both* her names.'

'Could she have seen that?'

'Seen that I was searching? No, I was alone in the parlor until . . .' She backtracks through the sequence of events. 'The

St Clairs came in, and then Kay and Robby showed up to get Max for the playdate.'

'Where was the laptop?'

'On the table in the parlor. I closed it before Ruby and Opal even came into the room, and I didn't open it again until just now.'

'How did it get from the parlor to in here?'

'I moved it after I got back from your grandmother's. The battery dies quickly when it's not plugged in.'

'So you left it untended for a while? And Jane was in the house?'

'Not for very long. She left and went shopping while I was next door.'

'It doesn't take long to smash a computer screen, Bella.'

'But why would she do that?'

'Maybe she snooped and saw that you were looking into her background. Do you think she could have figured out your password?'

'There is no password.'

'What? That's—'

'I know.'

'You have so many strangers coming through here.'

'I *know*. But I never do anything that requires that much privacy.'

'*Everything* requires privacy these days. The least you can do is use password protection, and even then, you're vulnerable unless—'

'Calla, do you know how long it takes me just to turn this thing on? It's ancient. Having to log in with a password would make it take even longer. I've been trying to save up for a new one, but . . .'

'Maybe Santa will bring you one for Christmas.'

'You must be channeling Max,' Bella says with a wry smile. 'That's what he just said about Sorry.'

'Sorry?'

'Remember that old game? He's playing it with Robby and her mom.'

'Sorry,' Calla says again, this time almost to herself.

'It was around when we were kids,' Bella elaborates. 'Remember it?'

'Mmm.'

'Anyway, about the laptop—'

'Wait!' Calla closes her eyes.

'Are you—'

'Shush!'

Bella shushes, aware that Calla is listening to Spirit, although she doesn't rub her hands back and forth as her grandmother does.

Sitting back in her chair, Bella channels her own common sense. There must be a plausible, non-nefarious scenario that would explain the damage to her laptop.

Could it have been an accident? Had someone – Jane? Her ex-husband? Another guest? – picked it up and dropped it?

Bella looks again at the screen and rules that out. It isn't just a network of cracked glass. There are gouged areas, as though it was hit with something sharp and heavy . . .

Like the cast-iron fleur-de-lis doorstop.

The study isn't off limits to guests. She imagines someone coming across the laptop, opening it, and realizing that Bella was searching for Jane.

But they must have known that simply destroying the computer wouldn't eliminate Bella's ability to search? She can still use her phone, or ask someone else to look it up, or even use the desktop computer behind the reservations desk.

Whoever did this wasn't ruled by logic. It must have occurred in a moment of sheer rage.

Maybe she's mentally ill. Delusional.

Luther might be right about that.

'Bella?'

She looks at Calla. 'Hmm? Are you getting something?'

'I am, but I don't think it's connected to the laptop.'

'Then what's it about?'

'I'm not sure. When you mentioned that board game Max is playing, I felt like there was something . . .'

She trails off.

'Something what? Something about the game? Sorry? Is someone saying they're sorry?'

'Oh, he's not sorry.'

'Who's not sorry?'

'This man.'

'I thought you were getting a woman?'

'That was before. This is a man, and he's furious.'

'It's Jane's ex-husband. The stalker.'

Calla shakes her head. 'I don't feel like it is. I don't think he's connected to her.'

'Is he a spirit?'

'I don't know.'

'Could he be the sailor who's been hanging around next door, haunting your grandmother?'

'The sailor from the *Titanic*?'

'No, she thinks she had the wrong shipwreck. She's trying to figure out what he wants, and who he is. He's showing her a sneaker, a flashlight, and a rose lying on a park bench.'

'A rose? That's the *Titanic*. Rose was—'

'In the movie,' Bella says. 'I know. But your grandmother doesn't think that's right, since she was a fictional character.'

'Well, I really hope Gammy's sailor isn't tied to this man, because he's . . .' Calla shudders.

'Do you think he's here?' Bella asks. 'Whoever he is – is he in Lily Dale? At Valley View?'

'I don't think so.'

'But you don't know.'

'It's not a perfect science.'

'Right.' Bella sighs. Even science isn't a perfect science. 'I'm not sure what to do about any of this. I can't have Max under this roof until I'm positive we're safe. Because if someone really was here last night . . .'

'You're sure there were no signs of a break-in? Did you make sure all the windows were locked? The basement, too?'

'I checked everything. If he was here, he walked through the front door.'

'Which anyone with the code can do.'

'The only other people who have it are the guests who are here now, because I change it. Oh, and I have my own code that never changes.'

'Who else has it?'

'Just Max. And Drew. And Pandora, because she owns the place now. And your grandmother, because she fed the cats for me a few times over the summer – and she probably gave it to Luther . . .'

'She gave it to me, too,' Calla says. 'One day when you weren't home and she couldn't get here herself. That's a lot of people who can get into this house, Bella.'

'But they're all people I know and trust.'

'Except the guests.'

'They're already *in*. Why would they share the code? Especially Jane. She's trying to keep this stalker *out*.'

'What about the other doors?'

'The deadbolt in the laundry room was locked. So was the one in the basement.'

'And the back door? You said it was wide open, and you're not sure whether Drew locked it when he left?'

'I'm sure he did. But, Calla, we're talking about Valley View. This place is full of false walls and secret passageways and compartments. You're sitting on one right now.'

'What?'

'Under the bench. For all we know, there's a trapdoor somewhere that leads to a tunnel with a hidden entrance to the house.'

'Well, if you don't know about it after living here for this long, what makes you think an intruder does?'

'I don't, but—' Bella breaks off as her phone buzzes. 'This is probably Luther.'

'Go ahead and take it. I'll run home and shower and change. Let me know what he says. I'll be back in a little while, or sooner if you need me.'

'That's fine. Thanks.'

'Be careful, Bella. And there's no way you and Max can spend the night here until you figure out what's going on.'

'*If* anything's going on. And don't worry. Max is spending the night at Misty's.'

'They're home?'

'On their way.' Bella pulls out her phone as Calla leaves the room, closing the doors behind her.

The call isn't from Luther.

'Meredith!'

'Spill it! I'm dying to know!'

Bella can't help but smile. Same old Meredith.

'First, how are you?' Bella asks. 'And how's little Cassandra?'

'*I'm* tired. Cassandra is *not* tired. Ever. Never. This baby does not sleep, Bella. What's up with that? But other than the not sleeping, she's absolutely perfect, and of course I'm not biased.'

'Of course you aren't.' Bella smiles, remembering how head-over-heels she'd been for newborn Max.

'I finally just got her down for a nap so I can get something done around here.'

'I won't keep you! This isn't—'

'*Please* keep me. I'll talk to you while I clean. I'm dying to know who showed up at Valley View. Is it Jillian Jessup?'

'What? No!'

'I thought she was married to the guy who owned it before you did.'

'I don't own this place, Mer. I just manage it,' she says, trying to keep her voice down. 'And Jillian Jessup *was* married to him, but I'm not talking about her.'

'Then who? The Long Island Medium? Oh, wait – John Edward? He's a famous medium, right? Or . . . is it one of the Kardashians?'

'The Kardashians aren't mediums.'

'But they're famous. Are they there?'

'No, they're not here!'

'Who is it? Ooh, what's the name of that guy who won the Oscar for that movie we both hated? Remember? We thought he was hot, but that movie—'

'Meredith! This is not a celebrity!' Bella hisses. 'It's Ethel Schweinsteiger.'

Meredith's upbeat tone dissolves with a single word. '*What?*'

'Remember her? From school? She was—'

'What is she *doing* there, Bella? She's dangerous!'

TWENTY-THREE

'She's dangerous? What do you mean, Meredith?'
'Just . . . you know what happened with her, right?'
'With Ethel?' Bella whispers the name, keeping an eye on the French doors. They're covered in curtains that are sheer enough for her to keep an eye out for wandering guests – or Jane/Ethel herself.

'Yes, with Ethel. I'm sure you don't know. I didn't, either, until I moved back to the neighborhood last spring, and . . . wait. What was that?'

'What was what?'

Meredith groans. 'I heard something. I hope she's not awake. I haven't even emptied the dishwasher yet. Anyway, I ran into Mrs Dubinski at the deli . . . remember her?'

'Young Mrs Dubinski or old Mrs Dubinski?'

'Well, they're both pretty old now, but this is Mr Dubinski's wife. Not his mother.'

'What did she say about Ethel?' Bella whispers the question.

Meredith whispers back something unintelligible.

'I can't hear you, Mer. *You* don't have to whisper.'

'I do. I'm peeking in on the baby. I think she's still asleep.'

Bella hears a door creak. Then another creak. Then Meredith whispers again, something about Ethel.

'Wait, *what*? Did you say she jumped in the deep end to save her mother?'

'No! Hang on.' Bella hears movement on the other end, and then Meredith is back on the line, speaking in her normal voice. 'Sorry. I said, she went off the deep end, like her mother.'

'Ethel did?'

'Yes, Ethel! Who did you think? Cassandra? Although that might be accurate, depending on the day. Or night.'

'I didn't think Ethel *had* a mother. Not in the picture, anyway. Wasn't she sick or something?'

'She was mentally ill, in a psychiatric hospital for years. By the time she got out, Ethel's father had divorced her and was dating another woman. Her mother made this huge scene about it — you really don't remember any of this?'

'She made a scene at school? Was I there?'

'No, it happened on the street. But everyone was talking about it, in the neighborhood and at school.'

'Why do I not remember?'

'It was senior year. You were probably too busy being in love with Tommy Zavala.'

'Tommy Zavala!'

'Don't tell me you forgot all about him, too!'

'No. Him, I remember.'

She'd dated Tommy briefly at the tail end of high school, and they'd gone to the senior prom together. Their breakup, not long after graduation, was by mutual agreement — they were headed to different colleges in August.

'Well, I can't believe you don't remember the whole thing about Ethel's mother,' Meredith says.

'Maybe it happened when I was out for a month with Mono?'

The kissing disease, as Jane called it, with that bizarre, almost accusatory attitude.

'Probably,' Meredith says, running water on her end. 'Anyway, her mother got arrested for threatening to kill Ethel's father and his new girlfriend.'

'She threatened to *kill* them?'

'That's not the worst thing. When I ran into Mrs Dubinski at the deli, she filled me in on everything that went on around here while I was living in Boston.'

Of course she did. Now that Bella lives in a small town, she recognizes that in some ways, the old urban neighborhood had operated like one. People knew each other and looked out for each other, and there were a couple of busybodies who made everyone else's business their own.

'Mrs Dubinski told me that Ethel's father eventually married this other woman. It was when we were away in college, so I didn't know about it. And unless your father told you, you probably didn't know either.'

'My *father*? Come on, Mer, I'd be lucky if he told me *he'd* gotten married again.'

'Good old Frank. Yeah, he was never the most communicative guy on the block. But he was a good dad.'

'The best,' Bella agrees, feeling her throat tighten with unexpected emotion.

Meredith is one of the few people – possibly the only one – in her life now who knew Frank Angelo. Or, for that matter, who knew Sam.

She'd only met him once, and it was at her own wedding, but when she hugged Bella goodbye, she said, 'He's special. I'm so glad you found each other.'

'So Ethel's father remarried this woman,' she prompts. 'Then what?'

'Then Ethel kind of went crazy. She hated her, just like her mother did. Even though everyone says she was a wonderful woman.'

'The stepmother? Who says that?'

'Mrs Dubinski. She used to hear Ethel screaming at her stepmother, making threats. And get this. The stepmother somehow fell off the fire escape and died.'

'That's horrible!'

'I know.'

'But why was she on the fire escape? Was there a fire?'

'No. Nobody knows why she was out there. People think she was trying to get away from Ethel.'

'Which people?'

'Well, Mrs Dubinski said Ethel was trying to kill the poor woman in a jealous rage. Apparently, she succeeded.'

'What do you mean?' Bella asks, heart pounding.

'She doesn't think the stepmother fell. She thinks she was pushed.'

'*Ethel* pushed her?'

'Who else? There weren't any eyewitnesses, other than people who heard them arguing that night.'

'People? Like Mrs Dubinski?'

'Yes. The fire escape was above an alley. By the time someone found the body, and the police went to the apartment, there was no one there. Ethel's father worked nights, and of course Ethel had an alibi,' Meredith says, clattering dishes.

'The police questioned her?'

'I guess so. She said she was out late with friends. Which is odd, because she was always such a loner back in school.'

'She was bullied. Kids called her Pig Face because of her name.'

'Wow. That's mean. I didn't realize that.'

'Neither did I.'

'I guess everyone is just wrapped up in their own stuff at that age. I feel bad that we didn't know what she was going through, but at least we weren't bullies, right?'

'I don't know. She seems to think I was part of the name-calling.'

'*You?* Definitely not. You were quiet. And sweet to everyone. Why would she say that?'

'I have no idea. It's the craziest thing – she seems like she's holding a grudge against me.'

'Because of Tommy? She had such a crush on him. She even asked him to go to the prom with her, remember?'

'*What?* Were they dating?'

'No. But he was like you. He was nice to everyone. Including Ethel. They were both in my calculus class, and I remember that he made it a point to talk *to* her, not about her, after what happened with her mother. Maybe she read into it and thought he liked her.'

'And this was when I was dating him?'

Is that why she'd made that misguided comment about all the guys wanting Bella back in high school? Because she'd had an unrequited crush on Tom?

'Probably around that time. But I do remember when she asked him to the prom, because it was so out of left field. She kind of blurted it out one day in the hall right after calculus. Everyone overheard, and his friends were teasing him about it afterward.'

'What did he tell her?'

'I'm sure he made up some excuse. He was such a nice guy. That's what everyone called him, wasn't it? Mr Nice Guy.'

'Yeah, I guess some nicknames are better than others.'

'What ever happened to him?'

'I have no idea. He didn't live in the neighborhood, remember?' Like all New York City public high schools, theirs had drawn students from every borough. 'I haven't kept up with anyone from school except you.'

'So you and Ethel haven't been in touch? You didn't invite her to Valley View?'

'No! I didn't even know it was her at first.'

'What does she look like?'

'Long hair, nice figure, pretty face, blue eyes, glasses.'

'Sure you're not looking in a mirror?' Meredith asks with a laugh. 'Because you're the one with the blue eyes, not her. And other than the glasses, that sounds like you.'

'I wear glasses now, and what do you mean about blue eyes?'

'*Yours* are blue. Hers are brown.'

'Hers are blue.'

'No, they're not. She has brown eyes. Look at the yearbook. You'll see for yourself.'

'I had to get rid of almost everything I owned when we lost our home,' Bella tells her. 'The yearbook didn't make the cut.'

'I'm sorry. That stinks. I have mine right here. Want me to take a picture of her senior portrait page?'

'Would you?'

'Sure, hang on a second.'

Bella stands and paces the tiny study, all of three steps in any direction. Chance is sitting beside the closed doors as if she wants to leave the room.

'Just one minute,' Bella tells her. 'I just need to see . . .'

If it's really her? Yes. That's what she's wondering.

Maybe the blue-eyed woman claiming to be Ethel is an imposter.

OK, but why? What does she possibly have to gain from that? It doesn't make sense.

'Just sent it,' Meredith informs her as her phone vibrates.

'Thanks. Let me look.'

Bella lowers her phone.

She enlarges the headshot.

It jars her memory. That's Ethel, all right.

She isn't homely. She's not even unattractive. She's just young, and awkward. Her hair is frizzy and flyaway. Her outfit is drab and mismatched – a patterned beige blouse with a gray sweater. She's wearing no jewelry, and no makeup. She's not smiling, just gazing dutifully into the camera like she's posing for a passport photo, or a mugshot.

She bears enough resemblance to Jane Anderson for Bella to rule out that she's an imposter. That's the same square jaw, visible even in her fleshier young face. That's the same nose and those are the same eyes.

Except that Meredith was correct. Ethel's eyes are, indeed, brown.

'It's her,' Bella says, back on the line. 'She must be wearing colored contact lenses.'

'Why?'

'I have no idea. It's not like she's trying to hide her identity. She's the one who told me who she is.'

'So she admitted she came to Valley View to find you?'

'No, she only recognized me once she got here.'

There's a moment of silence. Then Meredith asks, 'And you bought that?'

'Shouldn't I?'

'I wouldn't believe a word she says.'

Before Bella can reply, she hears a shriek on the other end of the line.

Meredith groans. 'Naptime is over. She's awake.'

'I'll let you go. Thanks for sending this. I need to figure out what's going on with her.'

'It's nothing good. She's not stable. You need to get her out of your house before something terrible happens.'

'It's not that easy. It's a guesthouse. She's a guest.'

'A guest who killed her stepmother and got away with it.'

'You don't know that for sure. Mrs Dubinski's suspicion doesn't make it the truth.'

'I know. But I don't like this. Just . . . whatever you do, don't trust this woman, Bella.'

TWENTY-FOUR

As rattled by the conversation with Meredith as she is by the shattered laptop, Bella stares at the photo of Ethel on her phone.

'What do you want from me?' she whispers. 'Why are you here?'

Only one thing is certain. It's no accident.

The way she'd mentioned *Tom*, as if she expected Bella to recognize the name . . .

But of course it hadn't clicked. She'd called him *Tommy* after they started dating. That's what his closest friends called him, he said. It's how she thinks of him whenever she remembers him . . .

Which isn't often.

Theirs had been a fleeting high school romance. They'd broken up not long after graduation, bound for separate colleges. She hasn't seen him since.

And now . . .

Now it turns out that Ethel had a crush on him, back before, as she put it, the ugly duckling became a swan.

Had she gone on to marry him? Is he the stalker ex-husband? No – she'd said Anderson is her married name, not Zavala.

Unless he goes by a different name now? An alias?

Or *she* does?

Bella's gut instinct is that there's no way Tommy was hiding a cruel, violent side.

Nor does she want to believe that Ethel is.

Bella may not remember her being bullied, but that doesn't mean it isn't true. As Meredith had said, most teenagers are self-absorbed. Self-conscious, too. Even if she'd exaggerated the cruelties of her classmates, she had to be going through a difficult time, given what had happened with her mother.

Bella looks into those brown eyes, searching for vulnerability, seeing only that they're guarded.

It must have been so hard for her to work up her courage to ask Tommy to the prom. She must have been devastated when he turned her down. Anyone would be.

And wouldn't anyone be jealous of the girl who went with him in her place?

Of course. It's only natural . . .

When you're seventeen or eighteen.

But then life moves on and so do you. You don't cling to something like that years later, unless . . .

She's not stable, Meredith had said.

And, *She was trying to kill the poor woman in a jealous rage.*

Unsettled, Bella puts the phone face down on the desk. She can't bear to look at the girl she'd once known, can't bear to imagine that she could have done such terrible things.

She glances again at the laptop screen. Not just cracked. Pulverized.

She needs to show Luther. *Now.*

She goes through her desk drawers, looking for something she can use to smuggle the laptop past anyone who might be hanging around between here and the front door. She settles for a zippered fireproof pouch that holds original documents she and Sam had kept in a bank safe deposit box – birth certificates, social security cards, their marriage certificate, their will. An envelope labeled *Sam Jordan – death certificate* has since joined the contents.

She manages to keep her emotions in check as she quickly and methodically empties the pouch. The laptop fits perfectly. She zips it inside, tucks it under her arm, opens the study door, and peeks out to see if there's anyone nearby.

The coast seems to be clear. But as she steps over the threshold, she hears voices in the front of the house.

'Why, yes, yes, I have,' Fritz Dunkle is saying. 'It's beautiful at that time of year.'

Oh, no. Poor Calla. He must have cornered her before she could leave.

'Lovely, isn't it? Though you must see it in winter, beneath a mantle of freshly fallen snow.' Not Calla – Pandora.

What is she doing here?

'Such a poetic turn of phrase,' Fritz tells her. 'Are you certain you're not a fellow wordsmith?'

'Quite.' Pandora adds, with characteristic immodesty, 'Though I've been told that my writing is brilliant, and that my life would make a fascinating book.'

'You don't say? Tell me more.'

Terrific. It's going to be awhile. Bella can't get past them to the front hall without being seen, so she hurries in the opposite direction, through the back parlor, kitchen, and mudroom.

Wishing she'd left a jacket on the hooks beside the back door, she slips outside coatless. The wind has died down, but the air feels even chillier than it had earlier.

Feeling as though she's being watched as she cuts across the yard toward Odelia's, she glances back at Valley View just in time to see a curtain flutter in a third-floor window.

It's the Vineyard Room.

Looking out the window isn't necessarily suspicious behavior, Bella reminds herself. But Ethel seems to have ducked out of sight just as Bella looked back.

Next door, the ladder is still leaning against the house, but Luther is no longer on it.

Odelia answers her knock. 'Bella! What's going on? Where's your coat? You're going to catch your death.'

'Is Luther here?' Bella asks breathlessly.

'Yes, he's on the phone. Come on in.'

Bella steps into the kitchen. It's chaos, as usual – every surface covered with bowls, pans, liquor, baking ingredients, and baskets of fruits, vegetables, and nuts.

Sprout is perched on top of the refrigerator among boxes of cereal. Twixie is on the floor, batting a shelled walnut around like a ball.

Bella eyes a pear, remembering that she'd forgotten to eat lunch – breakfast, too.

'Odelia, do you mind if I—'

'Help yourself.'

Bella starts to reach for a pear, then pauses, sniffing the air. 'Is something burning?'

'It was me. I set my hair on fire,' Odelia says offhandedly, patting her pumpkin-colored coif. 'Not on purpose.'

'I hope not! How did it happen?'

'I was working on a squash flambé' for the cookbook, and I aimed the torch in the wrong direction.'

'Are you OK?'

'Oh, I'm perfectly fine. It's out now.'

'Yes, I can see that.'

'Is that Bella?' Luther calls from the next room.

'It is. Hi, Luther.'

He appears in the doorway, phone in hand. 'Come on in here. I've got some information for you.'

Bella looks at Odelia, who shakes her head. 'Don't worry, I'm not even going to ask what's going on. I'm heading out as soon as I finish this recipe. I made an emergency appointment at Shear Magique to cut off the singed hair.'

Luther frowns. 'Just remember what we said. No more torching unless I'm in the room.'

'That's what *you* said, Luther. I said that if worse comes to worst, I'll stop, drop, and roll.'

'The woman is incorrigible,' he tells Bella, leading the way into the living room.

'That's why you love me!' Odelia calls from the kitchen.

'She's right,' Bella tells him.

'Of course she is.'

Still chilled through from the short walk, Bella sits on a wingback chair, close to the glowing space heater. The cottage may be winterized, but like Valley View, it's well over a century old, and just as drafty.

Luther sits on the adjacent couch. 'What's in the pouch?'

'It's—'

'Hang on,' he says, as his phone buzzes. He looks at it, and then at Bella. 'I've got to take this. Be right back.'

He steps out of the room.

Wishing she'd grabbed that pear in the kitchen, Bella stares at the candy dish on Odelia's coffee table. It's filled with jellybeans, and it's been there since Easter. Summer's humidity coagulated it into one enormous jellybean – green, because that's the leftover flavor Odelia doesn't like. Bella asked her a few months ago why she doesn't just throw it away, but she says she's trying to think of a way to use it in a recipe.

'It would make a nice gastrique. Or maybe I can add it to my no-apple apple pie.'

Bella knew better than to ask about that. And as a frequent unwilling taste-tester for Odelia's cookbook concoctions, she's relieved that the jellybeans have yet to become an ingredient.

She reaches into her pocket for her phone, thinking Luther will probably want to see the photo of Ethel, but it isn't there.

Uh-oh.

She must have left it back at Valley View – a reckless move, considering what happened to her laptop. She'd better run back over and get it. She starts to get up, but Luther is back, looking somber.

'Was that about Jane?' Bella asks. 'Or should I say Ethel?'

'Probably Ethel. Her middle name was Mildred, not Jane.'

'So she lied.'

'Oh, she lied. Where's Max? Is he still down at Doris's?'

'Yes. Why?'

'I see Jane's car out front. She's at Valley View?'

Bella follows his gaze out the window and nods. 'Yes. She's up in her room. But I did talk to her, and I've got more information for you. Did you see my text? About her ex-husband stalking her? I sent you his name. It's Tom. So if you look for Tom Anderson—'

'Bella, I saw your text. But when I said she lied, it wasn't just about her middle name being Jane.'

'What do you mean? Her married name isn't Anderson?'

'It is not.' Luther levels a look at her. 'She's never *been* married. This stalker ex-husband of hers doesn't exist.'

TWENTY-FIVE

Max and Robby are standing on chairs, building the tallest Lego tower in the world, when Mrs Burton comes into the family room. Clover, Doris's fat black-and-white cat, comes in with her.

'I hate to break this up, but it's getting late. I just texted your mom, Max. I told her that we'll head up the street in a few minutes.'

'What about our tower?' Robby asks.

'Maybe you can work on it again tomorrow.'

'And the next day, too, because we don't have school,' Max says. 'I bet Jiffy will want to help.'

'Now there's a great idea. Robby is looking forward to meeting him. Aren't you, Robby?'

'I guess so. No! Clover!' She grabs the fat black-and-white cat before she crashes into the tower. 'Mom, can you keep her in the other room?'

'Yes. But wrap it up, guys, OK?' She looks at her phone. 'You've got five more minutes.'

'Is that what my mom says?' Max asks.

'No, she hasn't texted me back yet. She said she'd be home, but . . .'

'She's probably busy. She's busy a lot.'

'Probably.' Mrs Burton smiles and leaves the room with Clover.

'My mom used to be busy, too,' Robby tells Max. 'Really, really busy.'

'Did she run a guesthouse?'

'No, she—' Robby closes her mouth tight.

'She what?'

'I can't say.'

'Well, my mom used to be a teacher. That was when we lived in Bedford. Why can't you say what your mom used to do? Don't you remember?'

'I remember. But it's a secret.'

They're both quiet for a few minutes, carefully snapping Lego blocks onto the top of the wobbly tower.

Max wonders what Robby's mom did that's so secret. Maybe she was a real-life superhero. Or maybe she was a real-life bad guy. It must be something like that. And he really, really wants to know, so he decides to drive a hard bargain.

'Me and my mom have a secret, too,' he says. 'But it's not about my dad. It's about a code word.'

'What is it?' Robby asks.

'If I tell you, will you tell me?'

'I'm not supposed to tell anyone.'

'I won't. I'm great at keeping secrets.'

'You already said that, by the way.'

'By the way, you sound a lot like Jiffy.' For some reason, that doesn't make him sad.

He tells her about the secret code word, 'Spidey.' About how if he or his mom says it, it means they have to come right away.

'Spidey! I thought that was your cat's name.'

'It is. That's why it's such a great secret code word. Now it's your turn. What was your mom's secret job?'

'She worked in an office.'

'Doing top secret stuff?'

'No! Doing regular office stuff.'

'But that's not a real secret.'

'It is a secret. Because I'm not supposed to tell anyone.'

Max shakes his head. 'You need to tell me a better secret, because I'm driving a hard bargain.'

Robby looks around, like she's making sure no one is listening. Then she leans close to Max and whispers, 'My dad is a really bad guy. He's always mad at my mom and me. He yells at us all the time. And he said he was going to hurt us. So, we had to sneak away in the night, and we can never go home, ever again.'

'That's a really, really bad secret,' Max says, kind of wishing he hadn't decided to drive the hard bargain after all. 'And no one else in the whole wide world knows about it?'

'Well, some people do. Some ladies who help other ladies who are in trouble. Doris is one of them. That's why she's letting us hide here, at her house.'

'You don't seem like you're hiding,' Max says, remembering

how he belly crawled under the table this morning, and how the lady in the white sneakers seemed like she was hiding, too, when he saw her with Mom's book.

'We are. And if my dad finds us, he might do something bad. So that's why I can never ever tell anyone. And you can never ever ever tell anyone, either. Do you promise?'

'I promise. And you can never ever tell anyone about mine, either,' Max says, even though he already told Jiffy. And even though having a secret code word isn't a dark, scary secret at all, unless you're using it because of a bank robber or a kidnapper.

TWENTY-SIX

Luther lets out a low whistle, staring at the laptop Bella set on Odelia's coffee table between the jellybean bowl, the stacks of outdated magazines, and Sprout, who'd made his way down from the fridge and onto the table at some point during their conversation.

Still reeling from the revelation about Tom, Bella asks, 'Do you think Ethel did this? Maybe because she saw that I was looking into her background?'

'I do.'

'She was giving me way too much credit. I never would have found out on my own that she was lying about her ex-husband, although . . . I can't believe I didn't pick up on it.'

'Sounds like she's a skilled liar.'

'I don't know about that. I think I bought it because Odelia had a vision this morning that seemed to be describing exactly what she told me. It was about an angry man, and a woman in danger, and – oh!' Bella breaks off, clasping a hand to her mouth.

'What is it?'

'She was eavesdropping! She must have been. She heard Odelia telling me this, and she borrowed the story to manipulate me. She realized it would make me want to help her.'

Luther nods. 'That makes sense. But it doesn't explain why she's here in the first place.'

'No, it doesn't. Maybe it really was a coincidence.'

'Bella—'

'No, Luther, hear me out. You and I both know that people come to Lily Dale from all over the world because they're going through some kind of personal struggle and they need spiritual guidance or healing. Why should Ethel be any different?'

'She's had a troubled past, Bella. She—'

'Exactly! She's troubled. Maybe once she recognized me, she thought I might be able to help her. Maybe she remembers that

I was always kind to her. I really want to think she's looking for friendship.'

'Then why did she lie?'

'Maybe because she feels like people have always been against her?'

She shares what Meredith said about Ethel's mother's very public display of rage over her ex-husband's new girlfriend, resulting in her arrest.

And about how the neighborhood gossip mill later perpetuated the myth that Ethel, too, had treated her stepmother with jealous rage and even tried to kill her.

'And she died in an accidental fall from the fire escape on a night when Ethel was there?' Luther shakes his head.

'No one saw her push the woman to her death, Luther. She had an alibi.'

'Why are you trying so hard to defend her?'

'Because somewhere inside her, there's a hurt little girl who didn't have a mother at a time when all the other girls did,' Bella says. 'And because I don't want to assume the worst about her, like everyone else.'

'But, Bella, I've uncovered a history of violent behavior.'

'Her mother's?'

'*Hers.* Ethel served time for assault. A number of people have restraining orders against her, and she's been arrested for violating all of them.'

They're useless, she'd told Bella. *A piece of paper isn't going to stop anyone who wants to get to you. If you get caught, you spend a few days in jail and pay a fine. Big deal.*

Bella had assumed she was speaking from experience, but as the victim. Not the stalker.

'She's wanted for questioning in a vandalism case involving a former roommate on the west coast,' Luther goes on. 'It happened in the beginning of September. The luggage tag you photographed coincides with that date.'

'I shouldn't have done that. I was violating her privacy.'

'Sounds like Ethel suffers no guilt for anything, Bella. If these things are true, then she's dangerous.'

That's what Meredith said.

But what if they *aren't* true?

'Luther, if everyone picked on her because she didn't fit in when we were kids, then can all this just be more of the same? People judging her, assuming the worst about her because of the way her mother was. The neighbors, the roommate . . .'

'She's a grown woman with a police record. And she lied to you about why she's here. It sounds to me like she's carrying out some kind of vendetta against you.'

'Because of someone I went out with for about five minutes in high school?'

As she tells him about Tommy, Sprout explores the table. He turns away after nosing around the candy bowl, clearly not a fan of green jellybeans. Nor of smashed computers. He gives Bella's laptop a cursory sniff, then he jumps down and up onto the windowsill.

'Where is Tommy now?'

'I don't know. I haven't seen him since we broke up that summer.'

'Let's see if we can find out.' Luther pulls out his phone. 'What was his full name?'

'Tomas – without the h – Zavala.'

'Any other details you remember?'

'He's my age – his birthday is in May, I remember, because we were dating when he turned eighteen. He went to the same high school, but he lived in Brooklyn. And he was going to Texas for college. A&M, maybe? Or Austin? Something with an A, I think.'

As Luther types and scrolls on his phone, Bella idly stares at Sprout on his windowsill perch. It takes her a moment to realize that Drew's pickup truck is out there, parked in front of Valley View. He must be wondering where she is.

'Hey, Luther? I need to go back over to Valley View and . . .' Seeing the look on his face as he looks up from his phone, she asks, 'What? What did you find?'

'Tommy never made it to Texas, Bella.' He clears his throat. 'He was killed in an accident that summer.'

She gasps. '*What?*'

'I'm so sorry.'

'But . . . are you sure? Maybe there's someone else with the same name, and . . .'

'The details fit. Is this him?'

He shows her his phone. She finds herself looking at a photo of Tommy, smiling in his cap and gown, beneath a newspaper headline that reads *Recent Grad Killed in Hit and Run*.

'Yes. It's him.'

'I'm so sorry,' he says again.

'No, it's . . . I mean, he wasn't . . . we weren't . . . he was just a really nice guy, you know?'

He was nice to everyone, Meredith had said.

Including Ethel.

'Did they arrest the driver who hit Tommy?' she asks Luther.

He checks his phone. Types. Scrolls. 'Doesn't look like it.'

'Then do you think . . . do you think it wasn't . . . an accident? Do you think . . . is there any way . . . Could Ethel have . . .' She swallows hard, unable to even suggest it.

'There's no evidence that it was anything more than an accident, but—' He breaks off at a clatter and crash in the kitchen. 'Odelia?'

'I'm fine,' she calls back. 'I'm just – ouch, ouch, ouch, ouch!'

'Are you on fire again?'

'It's OK, I'm putting it out!'

He's on his feet and rushing toward the kitchen.

Bella, too, jumps up. But she makes a beeline out the front door.

Luther will make sure Odelia's OK.

It's up to Bella to do the same with Drew.

Her chest is tight as she hurries back to Valley View. Part of her can't bear to suspect Jane of anything more than immature jealousy. Another part of her is on the verge of panic over what she might be capable of. What she might have done.

The sky is overcast now, and there's a hint of dusk. It gets dark so early at this time of year. Max will be heading home soon. She needs to find her phone and ask if he can stay a little longer. Just until she makes sure that there's nothing to worry about here at Valley View.

She can hear sirens in the distance, out on Dale Drive. She reminds herself that they have nothing to do with Valley View, or Jane. As she climbs the front steps, the rotting jack-o'-lantern seems to leer at her, and the wind chimes tinkle ominously in the porch eaves.

Throwing open the door, she hears jaunty samba music coming from the upright piano in the parlor. Voices are singing 'The Girl from Ipanema.'

'What in the world?' she mutters.

'Drew!' she calls. 'Drew?'

Sticking her head into the parlor, she sees Pandora at the keyboard, with Fritz standing behind her, shaking maracas.

Chance, perched on the window seat, gives Bella a beleaguered look.

'Pandora!' Bella calls above the music. 'Have you seen Drew?'

She pauses singing but not playing to say, 'He didn't want to join in. Says he can't carry a tune.'

'Where is he?'

'He was looking for you and Max.'

'I saw him go upstairs,' Fritz says over his maracas and then to Pandora, 'Next verse, en español!'

'How long ago did he get here?' Bella asks.

But they're back to their duet. *'La niña de Ipanema camina . . .'*

Bella gives up, hurrying back into the hall and up the stairs.

'Drew?' she calls. 'Drew, are you up here?'

She opens the door to the Rose Room. It's just as she left it. No Drew.

Seeing that Max's bedroom door is ajar, she heads there, calling, 'Drew?'

He isn't in Max's room, either. Spidey is on the bed, curled up beside a book that's lying open and face down. He must have been reading it before Robby and Kay arrived to pick him up.

It's Hans Christian Andersen's *The Ugly Duckling*.

She starts to turn away, then whirls back, staring at the cover. The name Andersen . . .

It's the Danish spelling of *Anderson*.

The cover depicts a duck, floating on the water.

Pandora's vision comes back to her.

Duck . . .

Danish.

Even the story fits.

'I was the ugly duckling,' Jane had said last night. 'And now I'm a swan.'

'No,' Bella whispers. 'You're Something Wicked.'

She hears Hero barking then. Outside.

She goes to the window and sees him in the yard. He's looking directly at Bella, as if he's trying to tell her something.

She sees Drew's chainsaw on the ground near a bunch of large branches he must have collected from around the yard.

He's dragging another one over to the heap.

He's not alone.

Jane – Ethel – is out there with him.

Her hair is in a ponytail, like Bella's. She's wearing glasses and a blue plaid flannel shirt and jeans tucked into a pair of brown sheepskin surfer boots.

What in the world?

She's dressed like me. She's trying to look like me. She's even made her eyes blue.

She's talking to Drew, walking alongside him.

He's not looking at her, but he's listening. Bella can't see his face, but she's familiar with his body language after all this time together.

He's uncomfortable. Whatever Jane is saying is making him squirm.

He tosses the branch on the pile and turns to her. He's speaking, shaking his head.

She stares at him as he talks. Now she, too, is shaking her head. Slowly, as if in disbelief.

Drew pivots and starts walking away from her, as if he's had enough.

As Bella watches, Jane reaches for the heavy limb he'd just dropped. She lifts it and swings it, high and hard, into Drew's head.

'Noooo!' Bella screams as he crumples to the ground. 'Noooo! Drew!'

Bella races from the room, down the stairs.

'Pandora, call for help!' she screams as she races past the parlor.

The piano music stops abruptly. 'Isabella?'

'Call 911! Tell them we need an ambulance!'

She explodes through the back door. Drew is sprawled on the ground. Hero is standing over him, barking wildly.

Jane is nowhere to be seen.

As Bella reaches Drew's side, she hears a car engine start out front.

Jane. She's getting away.

It doesn't matter. Nothing matters but Drew, lying so still, eyes closed, blood trickling from the back of his head.

TWENTY-SEVEN

'Ah, there she is!' Robby's mom waves her phone at Max. 'Your mom just texted me back.'

'Is it time to walk me home?'

'No, she said she's coming to pick you up.'

'Why?'

'I'm not sure. Maybe she got her wires crossed. But – oh! Here she comes now.'

Max sees his mom's car swing around the corner. She's driving really, really fast. He wonders why she's in such a hurry.

'I hope you had fun, Max,' Mrs Burton says.

'This was the most funnest playdate I ever had,' he says as the car pulls up at the curb. He opens the back door and climbs in, remembering to call, 'Thank you!' before Mom even has to remind him.

'See you tomorrow!' Robby shouts.

Max closes the car door and buckles his seatbelt. Then he notices something.

'Hey, Mom, you forgot to buckle *your* seatbelt.'

She doesn't say anything, just presses the button that locks the car doors, and starts driving toward the gate.

'Where are we going?' Max asks.

Still, she doesn't say anything.

He frowns at the back of her head. Her ponytail looks a little different than it usually does.

He looks at her face in the rearview mirror. He can't see all of her. Just her eyes.

And they're blue, and they're wearing Mom's glasses, but . . .

'Hey!' Max shouts. 'You're not my mom!'

TWENTY-EIGHT

Crouched on the grass beside Drew, Bella fights back tears. 'No, Drew. Please, please, wake up. Please. I love you. I need you. Don't you dare die on me.'

His eyes open, and then his mouth does. 'OK.'

It's more of a groan than a word. But he's alive.

Hero whines, still by his side.

'What happened?' Drew tries to say something more and winces.

'No, don't move. You have a head injury. She hit you.'

He murmurs something.

'Shh, help is coming. Try to just stay still.'

He says it again. This time, Bella makes out, 'Sadie Hawkins.'

Hero gives a sharp bark, and she hears someone shouting.

It's Luther. He's running across the yard toward them.

'Oh, Luther, thank goodness! He's hallucinating. He thinks I'm Sadie Hawkins.'

'What happened?'

'It was Jane! She hit him with a branch.'

Pandora and Fritz have emerged from the house. He's shouting into his phone, 'Yes, and an ambulance. There's a man here, and he's been badly injured.'

'I saw her, Bella,' Luther says. 'She was dressed exactly like you.'

'She went shopping, remember? She must have bought the same clothes I have on right now. It's like she wants everything I have. Including Drew. She did this and then she got away.'

'In your car,' Luther tells her. 'I was just coming to find you. I saw her jump in and drive away.'

'In *my* car? But how? The keys are . . . Oh, no! I left the keys on my desk.'

'She must have grabbed them.' He turns to Fritz. 'Tell them we have a stolen vehicle, too!'

'The cloak!'

Bella sees Pandora gesturing at the clothesline.

'Isabella, what is it doing out here? It's ruined!'

'Pandora, it was her! I didn't—'

'Fritz! Tell them this beastly woman has damaged a delicate woolen garment, as well!' Pandora kneels on the ground beside Drew. 'Now then, Dr Bailey, what's befallen you?'

'Sadie Hawkins,' he moans.

'Goodness, no. It's Pandora Feeney. You're delirious!'

'What's the make, model, and plate of the car?' Fritz calls.

Bella tells him, then turns to Luther, thoughts racing. 'My phone was with my keys. What if she took it, too? What if Max needs me and tries to call me? Wait, where are you going?'

'After her,' he says, striding away.

'I'm coming with you!'

'No. She's dangerous. Stay with Drew.'

'I'm coming! Pandora, can you please stay with—'

'Of course. And don't worry about a thing, Isabella. He's in splendid hands. I was a battlefield nurse during the Great War.'

'Past life?' Luther asks as Bella catches up with him.

'I'm assuming.'

As they scurry past Fritz, Bella hears him saying into the phone, 'Yes, it's Valley View Guesthouse on Cottage Row. You must know the place. It's a hotbed of crime and debauchery.'

'Debauchery?' Luther asks Bella.

'I'll explain later.'

'Looking forward to it.'

He gets behind the wheel of his SUV and Bella jumps into the passenger's seat. He throws the car into gear, and they barrel down Cottage Row and around the corner.

'Wait! Luther! Stop!'

The Yin-Yang Inn is just ahead. Bella can see Doris out on the porch, talking to Kay. She sees Robby, too.

Fear sweeps over Bella.

'Where's Max? *Where's Max?*'

She rolls down her window and screams the question.

They look over. All three register startled recognition – and then dismay.

'It wasn't you!' Doris says. 'I knew it! It was your car, but it wasn't you!'

'Where is Max?' Luther asks, and the words mingle with the sound of distant sirens. 'Where is he?'

Bella knows the answer before Kay utters the dreaded reply. 'She took him!'

TWENTY-NINE

Max is kind of surprised that he's being kidnapped, because Jiffy is the only one who ever gets kidnapped around here.

But it's definitely happening to him, because the lady who isn't Mom drives right out of the gate, way too fast.

She's Jane Anderson.

He's remembering the mean things she said about Mom, and how she sneaks around, so it makes sense that she's a bad guy in real life. Maybe a bank robber like Calamity Jane, because her name is Jane, too.

Or she might be a witch.

Maybe even a zombie.

He wonders if she has a secret lair, and if that's where she's taking him.

He wishes he had a flaming scythe so he could fight her.

Sometimes the ninjas fight back with moves instead of weapons, like the combo punch attack, or the flip kick into a spin.

Except Max can't even do those things with the joystick controller, and anyway, this isn't a game.

There must be some other way to save himself.

He can't jump out of the car, because the back seat doors have had a safety lock setting ever since the time Mom was driving Max and Jiffy and Jiffy thought he saw his puppy Jelly running in the park and he opened the door to chase him. Only it wasn't even Jelly. And even though the car wasn't going fast, Mom got really, really mad.

So now the doors are locked until she unlocks them. The windows aren't, because it's an old car and the lock is broken.

But Max can't roll down his window and dive out because they're going way too fast and he would get hurt.

As they speed around the corner onto Dale Drive, the tires make squealing noises like they're in a car chase.

Max remembers that Jiffy wasn't scared when he was in a car chase, or even when he got kidnapped, so he tries not to be scared, either.

Except he is, kind of.

Dale Drive runs along the shore. It has sharp turns, and Jane is going so fast now that it almost seems like she's going to crash the car.

It skids as they go around a curve, and she slows down a tiny bit and turns the wheel really hard. Then she speeds up again and they go flying around the next curve even faster.

Max squeezes his eyes closed, sure they're going to crash. Maybe even into the lake. That would be bad, because the water would be very cold at this time of year, and even though Max had swimming lessons this summer, he can't go in over his head yet, like Jiffy.

Plus, he's locked in the car, so he can't get out and swim away even if the water isn't over his head.

He hears the lady shout a bad word.

But when he opens his eyes, he sees that it isn't because they're crashing.

It's because there's a flashing red light in front of them.

There are two cars. One is a police car. The other is Misty's.

Max sees Lieutenant John Grange, standing by the driver's door. Misty is behind the wheel, and her window is down. Jiffy is in the back seat. His window is also down.

Lieutenant Grange waves his arms at Jane like he's gesturing for her to stop.

She speeds up instead.

Max rolls down the window. As they pass Misty's car, he yells, 'Spidey! Spidey!'

'Shut up!' Jane shouts, and she rolls the window up from the front seat and tries to lock it.

She doesn't know the lock is broken.

Max rolls down the window again. 'Spidey! Spidey!'

He hears screeching tires. Then sirens.

Looking back, he sees Lieutenant Grange in his police car, right behind them.

'You have to stop!' he tells Jane. 'It's the police!'

'Shut up!' She rolls up his window again.

'No! You shut up, you . . . you pig face!' He rolls down his window, shouting, 'Pig Face! Spidey! Pig Face! Spid—'

Then the car is skidding again, and Jane is spinning the steering wheel, and this time it isn't helping. This time, they really are going to crash . . .

Into the lake.

The car bumps over the narrow strip of grass at the edge of the road and lands in the water with a splash.

Jane isn't wearing her seatbelt. She flies forward and bumps against the windshield, and she goes very still, leaning against the steering wheel so that the horn is making one long, hard honking sound.

Max unbuckles his seatbelt, climbs on the seat, and puts his right leg through the open window.

The water is dark. There are little waves in it, because of the wind. He hears the sirens coming closer, and the police car screeches to a stop and so does another car – Luther's!

The horn is still honking because the lady is still leaning on the steering wheel, not moving. The car seems like it's still floating in the lake, but it's probably going to sink any second now. There might not be enough time for Lieutenant Grange and Luther to rescue him, so he'd better rescue himself.

He quickly swings his left leg over so that he's sitting on the edge of the car window with his feet dangling above the water.

He counts out loud, just like he and Jiffy always do when they're being brave army guys.

'*One* . . .'

Except that's just pretend. This is real.

And Max isn't aways brave inside, like an army guy. Or like Jiffy.

He's afraid of a lot of things. Like deep water. And snakes, even when they're not real. And witches, even when they're not real.

And Jane, although . . .

'*Two* . . .'

Maybe he's more mad at her than afraid of her. She told lies about Mom, and she's trying to look like Mom, and she crashed Mom's car, and she tried to take him away from Lily Dale. Away from Mom, who would be so sad if she didn't have Max.

He can't let that happen. He's not going to let Jane take him away and he's not going to sink to the bottom of the lake with the car. He's going to escape, because he learned how to swim, and he's going to get to go home to his house and his bedroom and Hero and Chance and Spidey and all his friends, best of all, to Mom.

'*Three!*' he shouts, and he closes his eyes and jumps, just like a brave army guy.

His feet hit the water, and it's super cold, and—

And then they hit the bottom, and—

Hey! It isn't deep at all. This is the shallowest part of the lake. It's only up to his knees.

'Max!' someone shouts, and he turns to see Mom running toward him. Luther is right behind her, and Lieutenant Grange is out of his car, too, shouting on his phone as he rushes toward the lake.

Max raises his arm and shakes it around in the air, pretending he's holding a flaming scythe like a ninja warrior who won the battle.

'Bella, stay back!' Lieutenant Grange tries to catch her, but she ducks and slips right past him.

She runs right into the water even though she's wearing those clumpy brown boots. She's crying, and laughing. She throws her arms around Max, so he has to stop pretending he's a ninja warrior because they don't have moms who hug them.

Lieutenant Grange and Luther are both holding guns, walking through the water toward the front seat. Max wants to turn around and watch, but Mom won't let him, which is another thing that doesn't happen to ninja warriors.

'Are you OK, Max?' she asks, keeping both of her arms around him as they wade to the shore.

'Yep. I can't wait to tell Jiffy that I got kidnapped *and* I was in a real live car chase *and* I crashed into the lake *and* I rescued myself by jumping into the water like a brave paratrooper! This turned out to be the best day ever.'

'Oh, Max . . .' She's crying again, squeezing him so tight he can hardly breathe, and this time he doesn't even mind at all.

THIRTY

Sitting beside Drew's bed, Bella watches him sleep, pale and so still, his broad shoulders draped in a hospital gown, his head wrapped in a bandage. She's as jarred by his unfamiliar appearance as she is by the all-too-familiar hospital night sounds.

Medical equipment hums and beeps. Carts rattle past the room. The intercom pages doctors. There's a chatty conversation at the nurses' station down the hall.

'. . . So I gave him an ultimatum,' someone is saying. 'If we're not engaged by Christmas, I move out.'

'Do you have someplace else to live?'

'Of course not! He'd better be ring shopping.'

There's laughter, and good-natured teasing.

Bella is reminded of another group of nurses, another hospital, another night . . .

The night Sam died.

It was someone's birthday – a nurse, an orderly, someone. There was chocolate cake. She heard them speculating about the calorie count and whether there was almond in the filling. The chitchat would be innocuous among playground moms or lunching friends, but it was all wrong in that setting, on that night in particular. How could anyone be celebrating anything when the world was ending?

Toward dawn, it was over – Sam was gone. Bella was numb, all cried out, leaving.

In the corridor, she passed a garbage can filled with paper plates and plastic forks. Smears of frosting, crumbs. The white cake box, stamped with the name of an Italian bakery.

She knew the place. She'd been there with Sam, many times – for struffoli and pizzelle at Christmas, for gelato on hot summer days. It would never happen again.

In that moment, her staggering loss hit her full-on.

In this one, she's doing her best not to relive it.

Drew is not Sam. This isn't a deathbed vigil.

He has a concussion. He's just here for observation and will be released tomorrow.

It's going to be OK. Everything is going to be just fine. The ordeal is over.

Max is none the worse for wear, thrilled to have Jiffy back home and at Valley View for a sleepover. Even Jiffy seems to be his happy-go-lucky self. He was far more interested in hearing about Max's short-lived kidnapping than in discussing his two-month road trip or his recent loss. Max was all too happy to regale him with the tale, which grew more harrowing with each retelling.

He didn't embellish, though, when he spoke to the lead detective handling the case. Flanked by Luther and Bella, he answered all their questions and provided additional details.

Afterward, the detective said, 'I've interviewed a lot of witnesses in my career. I wish they were all as keenly observant as you and your son are, Mrs Jordan.'

It was past midnight when Bella tucked the boys into bed in Max's room, with Hero, Chance, Spidey, and Jiffy's dog Jelly curled up at the foot of the bed. She was certain no one was going to get any sleep, but when she peeked in on them five minutes later, only Hero was awake.

He met her gaze as if to say, *I'll keep them safe.*

Luther had provided updates all evening, speaking to Bella on Odelia's phone. Her own had been confiscated during Jane's arrest and was part of the case evidence.

Luther said he'd told Drew that Jane is in custody, but not that she'd abducted Max.

'Now isn't the time to worry him, even though Max is safe. His vitals are good and he's sleeping,' he told Bella about an hour ago. 'You should get some rest, too.'

'I will, but not now. I'm on my way over.'

'Bella, you're exhausted. I'm here. He's stable.'

'I know, but . . . I want to be there. I . . . I *need* to be there.'

And her friends needed to be at Valley View. Odelia, Calla, Pandora, and Misty. Despite her protests, they'd insisted on staying, making dinner, cleaning up, and dealing with guests.

'Don't worry about a thing. We'll hold down the fort while you're gone,' Calla said when Bella left for the hospital, borrowing Odelia's car.

'Do give Dr Bailey our warmest regards for a speedy recovery, Isabella,' Pandora said.

'Yeah, tell him to get his butt back here soon,' Misty put in.

Odelia hugged Bella fiercely and whispered, 'Go be with him, honey. We've got you.'

Walking out the door, Bella nearly cried, thinking of all the times she'd felt alone in the world.

Now she's watching Drew's chest rise and fall beneath the blanket, waiting for Luther to come back with two cups of coffee.

It's taking longer than it should. Either the cafeteria is crowded at this hour, or he's trying to give her time alone with Drew, even if just to watch him sleep.

It could have been worse. So much worse.

To think that she'd felt sorry for Jane, had tried so hard to give her the benefit of the doubt, when the woman is responsible for hurting Max, and Drew . . .

And Tommy.

After all these years, it might be impossible to prove that she'd played a role in his death, but Bella's instinct is that she had.

Seeing Drew's eyelids flutter and then open, she leans in, touching his shoulder with a hushed, 'Hey. Hi.'

'Bella?'

'Yep, it's me.'

'You're blurry.'

Uh-oh. Had the blow to his head damaged his vision?

'Are my glasses . . .'

'Oh! Your glasses!' No wonder he doesn't look like himself. Well, that, and the gown and bandage. 'I don't know where they are, but I can go ask.'

He grabs her wrist. 'Don't go. Blurry Bella is better than no Bella at all.'

She smiles. 'How do you feel?'

'Like someone dropped an anvil on my head. What time is it?'

'Around two thirty.'

'Afternoon?'

'Night. Well, morning.'

'What are you doing here? Where's Max?'

'Home, in capable hands.'

'Bella, you shouldn't be—'

'No, shh, it's fine. Jiffy's back, and he's thrilled.'

'I wouldn't call that "capable hands."' Drew wince-smiles.

She laughs. 'The whole gang is at Valley View keeping an eye on them, so they'll be fine. And they all send their love to you.'

'That's nice.' He's still clasping her wrist, but now slides his fingers down to squeeze her hand.

His grasp is reassuring – warm and strong. He doesn't let go. She doesn't want him to.

'Well, then, I'm glad you came, as long as Max is safe and Jane's in custody.'

'What happened, Drew? Between you two? I saw you with her, out by the lake, before she hit you.'

'It was bizarre. She was acting like we were . . . I don't even know how to explain it.'

'Like you were a couple?'

'Yeah. At first, I was trying to be nice, because I knew she was your old friend.'

'She was *not* my friend.'

'I didn't realize that then. But the more she talked, the more I could tell that something was off. And when she asked me to go to the dance with her, I decided I'd had enough.'

'Like . . . a high school dance?' Bella asks, thinking of the prom, and Tommy.

'No, the Sadie Hawkins dance.'

'So she wasn't hallucinating, stuck in the past, thinking you were . . . someone else?'

'Oh, no. She knew exactly who I was. I think she snapped when I told her I already have a date for that.'

'You do?' She raises an eyebrow.

'Yes. You. Unless you had someone else in mind?'

'Trust me, Drew Bailey. I have *no one* else in mind!'

'Good to know.'

Someone clears his throat loudly behind them. She looks over her shoulder and sees Luther in the doorway holding two cups of coffee.

'Sorry to interrupt, but the nurse is on her way in. She said Bella and I need to clear out of here for a few minutes.'

'You should both go home to bed. I'm fine here.'

Bella looks at Luther. 'I'm staying. You go.'

'I'm staying.'

'We're staying, Drew.' She gives his hand a final squeeze, then lets go and stands. 'See you in a little while.'

She follows Luther out into the hall. He hands her one of the coffees, takes a sip of his own, and makes a face.

'Bad?' she asks.

'It's vending machine coffee.'

'Really? I figured you went to the cafeteria. Or Starbucks – you were gone for so long.'

'No, Ethel's down there.' He nods toward the end of the corridor. Bella turns to see a pair of uniformed troopers flanking a doorway.

She gasps. 'She's *here*? This close to Drew? What if she—'

'She won't. She can't. She fractured her head and broke a couple of ribs when she crashed into the lake. Anyway, she wouldn't get past those two even if she weren't in restraints. Which she is.'

'You saw her?'

He nods. 'From a distance. She was sleeping. I spoke to the detectives handling the case. She waived her right to an attorney. She's been interrogated. She confessed to assaulting Drew, and to stealing your glasses, your phone, your car.'

'And my *son*? Why would she do this, Luther?'

'She said you've always had everything that should have been hers.'

'But . . . I haven't even seen her in years.'

'Apparently, she stumbled across that viral video of you, and it triggered her. She came to Valley View to find you, Bella.'

'To kill me?'

'I don't know if that was her intention at first. But then she met Drew, and she wanted to get you out of the way. She said she should have done that years ago.'

Bella's hands are icy, clasped around the hot coffee cup. 'She really was there, then? Last night? In the kitchen? With the knife?'

'Yes. Wearing your cloak as a disguise. She was planning to stage a robbery so that it would seem as if an intruder had broken in and . . . you know.'

'And killed me,' Bella says with a grim nod. 'But then I came downstairs and interrupted her plan.'

'Thank God you did. You scared her off when you made that commotion in the kitchen, just like you thought.'

'So she dropped the knife and ran out the back door.'

'Exactly. She ditched the cloak outside and let herself back in later, through the front door.'

'And came up with a new plan? Because Max told the detectives he saw her eavesdropping this morning in the back parlor while I was in the kitchen with Odelia. I'm guessing she decided to borrow the vision and came up with the story of a violent ex-husband.'

'That's about right.'

'I keep thinking about how she took my glasses, and then went out and bought the exact clothes I'm wearing.'

'She wanted to become you. I think on some level, she believed she could take on your identity and step into your life, be with Drew. As if he'd ever have eyes for anyone but you, Bella.'

Despite everything, the words warm her.

She glances again at the sentries posted at Jane's door, then turns away, pushing the what-ifs from her mind. It's over. The people she loves most in this world are safe.

Back in Drew's room, they find him asleep. Bella and Luther sit quietly beside his bed. After a while, Luther dozes off.

Bella leans back in the chair, weary, unable to keep her eyes open. It's been an exhausting, emotional night, on the heels of an exhausting, emotional day. An exhausting, emotional two years, building a new life with Max. She's come a long way since the last time she sat at a hospital bedside in the middle of the night.

But there's so much further to go. Uncertainties in her path, crushing responsibility on her shoulders; so many things could go badly.

Daunted by the harrowing road ahead, she feels alone again, and terrified.

How am I ever going to get through?

She hears someone whisper her name.

No . . .

Not *just* her name.

Someone whispers, 'Bella Blue.'
She opens her eyes.
He's there. Right in front of her. Sam.
'You've got this, Bella Blue. And I've got you.'
She gasps.
Then he's gone.
'Bella?'
It's Drew. Awake. Watching her.
'Are you OK?' he asks.
'I'm . . . I just . . .'
'Bad dream?'
'What?'
'You seemed like you were startled in your sleep.'
'I wasn't sleeping.' She frowns. 'Was I?'
'I think so.'
Sam was here, though. In the room, or in her dream . . . Either way, he was here.

Bella leaves the hospital after seven. Stepping out into the cold air, she sees that the eastern sky is glowing. It looks like the sun is actually going to make an appearance today, although . . .

Red sky at night, sailor's delight. Red sky in morning, sailors take warning.

She'd heard that somewhere, once.

But she's had her fill of warnings. Today, she'll take a sky that isn't gray.

She gets back into Odelia's car to head back to Valley View. When she turns it on, an old disco song, 'Play that Funky Music,' blasts over the radio.

She thinks of Odelia's comment in the kitchen at Valley View, about Bella listening to disco.

Was that really just twenty-four hours ago?

Odelia's vision had been eerily accurate – not pertaining to Jane, or to her ghostly sailor, but to Kay.

After the ordeal was over and they, too, had been interviewed by the detectives, she and Doris came by Valley View to apologize for what had happened.

'I should have made sure that was you in the car, Bella,' Kay said. 'I never should have let him drive off with a stranger. If anything had happened to Max, I'd never forgive myself.'

'It isn't your fault. She was driving my car, impersonating me.'

'But I'm always so careful. I know what it's like to have a child in danger.'

She told Bella, then, that she and Robby had come to Valley View to escape her violent ex-husband. Doris, a volunteer with a domestic violence organization, is sheltering them until permanent arrangements can be made.

Bella still doesn't know their real names, or where they're from, and probably never will. It's safer that way, for everyone. She'd promised not to tell anyone what's really going on.

Including Odelia.

Even though she seems to know things she can't possibly know and sees things she can't possibly see.

If you believe in that stuff.

You've got this, Bella Blue. And I've got you . . .

Sam's words had been just what she needed to hear in that moment, just like Odelia's comment to her earlier, when she was heading to the hospital.

The logical presumption is that Bella's subconsciousness had recreated that, conjuring Sam.

But he'd seemed so real.

And she's almost certain she hadn't been asleep.

On the radio, the song ends, and the disc jockey speaks. 'This is Dan Palmer on WDOE radio bringing you this morning's countdown of the top songs of 1976.'

Ah, 1976. Yesterday, it had been 1975.

'Let's throw back to that fall, when Jimmy Carter was elected president, Johnny Bench and Pete Rose led the Cincinnati Reds to a World Series Championship, and Gordon Lightfoot had a hit song about a Great Lakes shipwreck that had taken place just a year earlier.'

The D.J. gives way to the familiar opening strains of 'The Wreck of the Edmund Fitzgerald.'

Bella listens idly to the lyrics about the gloomy skies of November.

She thinks about red skies . . .

Sailors . . .

Shipwrecks.

Johnny Bench. Pete Rose.

Gordon *Light* . . . *Foot.*

'Wow, Odelia,' she whispers, realizing she might just have solved the puzzling vision.

Of course, it could be another coincidence . . .

If you believe in those.

Coincidences . . . visions . . . spirit warnings . . . dead husbands manifesting in hospital rooms, or in dreams . . .

Driving on beneath a red November dawn, Bella yawns deeply.

Right now, she doesn't know what to believe about any of that, or the afterlife. But in this one, the nightmare is over, and she's going home to Valley View.

EPILOGUE

Thanksgiving Day

Peering into the oven, Bella frowns.

The turkey certainly *looks* good – golden brown, basted in butter, roasting on a bed of fresh herbs and stuffing.

'Think it's done yet?' Calla asks, peering in beside her.

'Do you?'

'It looks done on the outside.'

'It could be raw inside. The last thing I want to do is poison everyone on a holiday.' Bella pauses to clear her throat. 'Or, you know . . . ever.'

Someday, she probably won't be reminded of Jane – Ethel – with a sick, twisting feeling in her stomach.

Not today, though. Not yet.

She closes the oven with a sigh. 'I wish your grandmother would get here with the meat thermometer.'

After a fruitless last-minute search through her own kitchen drawers, she'd asked to borrow Odelia's.

'You know Gammy. She's probably turning the house upside down looking for it.'

'I just wish I'd thought of it sooner. I never had any need for one.'

On past Thanksgivings, she'd relied on the plastic buttons that pop up to let you know when a small pre-packaged, storebought turkey breast is done.

This is the first time she's cooked a fresh bird, a twenty-nine pounder she'd purchased from a nearby farm. It's large enough to feed her crowd of a dozen guests for the holiday feast, with plenty of leftovers for everyone, and then some.

'Sandwiches, pot pies, soup . . . this'll get you through the storm,' the farmer had assured her yesterday when he'd delivered the massive turkey.

'Storm?'

'You didn't hear? Big one coming Friday morning. It's going

to last into early next week. They're predicting about seventy-two inches.'

'Of snow?'

He grinned. 'That, and my waistband after four or five days snowbound with pie. My wife makes the best around. Apple, pumpkin, pecan . . . Sure you don't want to add a couple to your order? I've got a bunch in the truck.'

'Thanks, but I'm set. Happy Thanksgiving!'

Pandora is baking four pies. Everyone insisted on bringing something – a potluck Thanksgiving, so that Bella doesn't have to do all the cooking single-handedly.

It had been Max's idea to include pets. After grudgingly accepting that the cats and dogs can't join the humans at the dining room table, he, Jiffy, and Robby spent yesterday afternoon making elaborately illustrated placemats for the floor feast.

First thing this morning, Jiffy was back, with his barking puppy in tow. 'My mom sent me over to help you, Bella, because she's busy doing her hair and figuring out the cranberry sauce. By the way, do you have any breakfast? 'Cause Jelly and me are hungry.'

Drew came shortly after, accompanied by Peewee, the ironically named greyhound he'd rescued last year. He brought two quarts of heavy cream, several pounds of butter, a huge sack of potatoes, and the biggest stainless-steel pot Bella has ever seen. He'd put Max and Jiffy to work with peelers, and later taking turns with the masher.

Now, he's outside letting Peewee, Jelly, and Hero romp around the yard, and the boys are setting the table.

Calla, who'd shown up on time with Li'l Chap, her Russian Blue kitten, and a case of champagne, winces at a loud clatter from the dining room. 'I hope that's not your good china.'

'No, it's the everyday stuff. I needed service for twelve, so I have just enough. I even have matching bowls for the menagerie.'

'Happy Thanksgiving, Bells!' Misty breezes in. Her long hair is streaked with bright orange and yellow, and she's clutching a drugstore shopping bag. She opens it and removes six cans of cranberry sauce, plunking them on the counter one by one.

'Don't worry,' she tells Bella. 'I'm going to open them all

myself. All I need is a can opener. And a bowl. And spoon. Sorry.'

'No, it's fine. I just . . . I thought you were making fresh cranberry sauce.'

'Fresh! Was I supposed to?'

'When Jiffy said you were figuring it out, I just assumed . . .'

'No, I was figuring out where to buy it. Do you know how many stores are closed on holidays? Sheesh. Lucky for me, CVS was open, and they had tons of it. And hair dye, too. Do you like my fall colors? I think it's chic. Of course, Mike hates it.'

Gotta love Misty, who'd recently told Bella that her late husband is in touch with her and Jiffy far more frequently now than he ever was in life. 'The way he's always hanging around, I don't know how I'll ever be able to date. You're lucky Sam doesn't do that to you, Bells. At least you and Drew have some privacy. Am I right?'

She winked, and Bella blushed.

Misty, she'd learned early in their friendship, often says the wrong thing, but her heart is always in the right place. In that sense, she's a lot like . . .

'Yoo hoo, Isabella!' Pandora calls from the front hall. 'We've arrived!'

'We?' Calla asks, looking at Bella. 'The royal we?'

'I'm sure she means the cats. And her spirit guides.'

Turns out she's wrong about that. After handing Misty a can opener, bowl, and spoon, she follows Calla to the front hall.

Pandora is there with a cat carrier, accompanied by Fritz Dunkle, who's bearing what appears to be a large, blanket-draped box.

'Happy Thanksgiving,' he greets Bella. 'Thank you for inviting me.'

'Oh . . . uh, Happy Thanksgiving, Fritz. I'm so glad you could make it.'

'You invited him?' Calla asks in a low voice, close to Bella's ear.

She gives a subtle shake of her head, her bright smile a little strained.

'The more, the merrier,' Pandora says gaily, hanging her red cloak on the coat tree. 'That's what you always say, isn't it, Isabella?'

'Do I? I just . . . I'm not sure the guest rooms are—'

'More the merrier,' a disembodied voice says. 'More the merrier.'

Startled, Bella looks around and sees only Chance and Spidey, who have appeared in the hall. They're staring at Fritz, tails and whiskers twitching.

'No worries, I won't be staying here at Valley View,' Fritz informs her. 'It's a bit too large and drafty for my taste. Cotswold Corner is much more my cup of tea. It's so wonderfully cozy. And safe . . .'

Uh-oh. Here we go. Bella braces herself for a tirade about crime in the Dale.

'. . . for Mrs Nickleby. Your cats seem a bit . . . fierce.' He points at Chance and Spidey. 'Pandora's Lord Clancington and Lady Pippa are a little more docile.'

'They are,' Pandora says, opening the carrier. 'Though today, they're quite chuffed about their first American Thanksgiving.'

As the chubby Scottish Folds yawn and go back to sleep, Calla comments under her breath to Bella, 'I'm guessing chuffed means fat and lazy.'

'Fat and lazy,' the disembodied voice says. 'Fat and lazy.'

It seems to have come from the large, blanketed rectangle Fritz is holding.

Bella points at it. 'Is that . . . Pandora's pies?'

'No, no, I'll run back to fetch those. Where shall I put Mrs Nickleby?'

'Excuse me?'

He pulls the blanket away to reveal a birdcage that contains a large, red-tailed parrot. It squawks and says, 'Mrs Nickleby,' as if by way of introduction.

'She's an African Grey,' Fritz says. 'Beautiful, isn't she?'

'And so very clever,' Pandora says. 'Her vocabulary is brilliant! And she's named after the Dickens character.'

'Wasn't that Nicholas Nickleby?' Bella asks.

'*Mrs* Nickleby was Nicholas's mother,' Fritz explains. 'Based on Dickens' own mother.'

'And quite the chatterbox. Have I mentioned that my ancestors knew the Dickens family quite well?' Pandora asks.

'Yes!' Bella and Calla say quickly, in unison.

'You can put the birdcage on a table in the back parlor, Fritz,' Bella says. 'Just make sure it's locked – with a house full of cats, we don't want our feathered friend to *become* the Thanksgiving feast.'

'How dreadful, Isabella!' Pandora shoots her a glare, then turns back to Fritz. 'The pies are on the kitchen table, love. And don't forget my sheet music portfolio.'

'Wait – sheet music?' Calla asks.

'Of course. For the singalong.'

'Singalong?' Bella asks.

'Of course. I've been working on the set list all week. Do hurry along, Fritz.'

'And when you come back, just leave the pies on the dining room sideboard next to the dessert plates,' Bella tells him.

Mrs Nickleby echoes, 'Dessert!'

Bella smiles. 'Oh, and I've got vanilla ice cream to go with the pie.'

'How dreadful!' Pandora says.

'Pie a la mode is an American tradition!'

'These are not *dessert* pies, Isabella.'

'*Not* dessert,' Mrs Nickleby scolds, sounding almost as haughty. '*Not* dessert!'

Pandora goes on, 'I made one fish, one shepherd's, and two steak and kidney.'

'How dreadful!' Mrs Nickleby says, and Bella couldn't agree more.

Doris, Kay, and Robby are next to arrive. Doris is carrying the cats, Clover and Columbus. Robby has a stack of board games. Kay bears a large foil-covered tray.

'Lobster macaroni and cheese,' she tells Bella. 'A family tradition where we come from.'

'How nice of you to share it with us.'

'You don't know how happy Robby and I are to be included today. Holidays can be hard.'

Bella nods. It's not easy to leave behind everything you've ever known to make a fresh start among strangers. With luck, Kay and Robby will be as lucky as Bella and Max have been.

'Guess what, Bella? It's finally going to snow tomorrow!' Robby tells her.

'I heard!'

'So much for that dusting you predicted,' Kay says. 'They're saying we're going to get about six feet!'

'I guess I was a little off,' Bella admits with a grin. 'But then, I'm not Al Roker *or* a psychic medium. I'm just Bella.'

Bella Blue . . .

In the front parlor, Pandora and Fritz are singing a Motown medley. In the back parlor, the others are devouring appetizers.

In the dining room, Bella is squeezing in a mismatched place setting for Fritz, when Luther and Odelia show up.

She's carrying a covered baking dish, and he greets Bella with a kiss on the cheek and a large bouquet of flowers. 'Happy Thanksgiving, Bella!'

'Sorry we're late! I've got the meat thermometer for you, Bella, and the side dish you asked for.'

Ah, yes.

Last night on the phone, Bella had unsuccessfully tried to convince Odelia not to bring a thing. 'It's fine. Really. You've been away all week. You must be exhausted.'

'I'm not. Now that my sailor's finally at peace, so am I. I'm sleeping like a baby.'

After Bella figured out that Odelia's phantom sailor might be from the *Edmund Fitzgerald*, Luther had done some homework. It turned out that when he and Odelia came back from Michigan on Halloween, they traveled right past the spot on Lake Superior where the ship had gone down. The sailor's spirit seemed to have 'hitched a ride,' as Odelia put it.

Further research on Luther's part – along with meditation on Odelia's – had allowed them to identify the sailor, who'd been from Cincinnati. Odelia tracked down his surviving middle-aged sons with an offer to visit them and attempt to reconnect them to their father.

She'd told Bella about that last night on the phone. 'He and his wife were going through a rocky divorce. The last time the boys saw him was a few weeks before he died. He wanted to do something special, you know, to make up for not being around as much. He got tickets to Riverfront Stadium to watch the first game of the World Series. He bought the boys their favorite players' Jerseys.'

'Let me guess – Johnny Bench and Pete Rose?' Bella asked.

'Yes. They still have them.'

Of course they do. Just like Max still has a few precious gifts from Sam.

'Now, getting back to Thanksgiving, what can I bring?' Odelia asked.

'Just yourself, Luther, and the kittens.'

Odelia wouldn't hear of it. 'It's a potluck, Bella. Everyone brings a dish to share. That's how it works. I can bring my sauerkraut cake, or—'

'Veggies!' Bella said quickly. 'Just bring veggies.'

Now, she takes the casserole dish from Odelia. 'Thank you so much for this. What is it?'

'Rutabaga-farro soufflé.'

How dreadful, Bella thinks, but she smiles and says, 'Sounds yummy.'

'Oh, it is. I'll bring it to the kitchen and take the turkey's temperature.'

As she leaves the room, Luther winks at Bella and holds up a big box. 'Don't worry. I've got something to make up for the rutabagas. Apple Danish crumble from the Brown Bear Bakery in Cincinnati.'

Danish . . .

Bella is reminded of the stormy November day when all she wanted was peace and quiet, but then Pandora came along with her vision, and Ethel showed up at Valley View, and—

'Hey, Bella? You OK?' Luther asks.

'I'm fine. Just . . . I wish I could put certain things out of my mind forever.'

'You can. Just forget she even exists.'

'I'm trying. It's just . . . I'll have to face her again in court someday.'

'The trial's a long, long way off, Bella. Just try to focus on healing and moving on.'

Drew pokes his head into the room, holding two glasses of champagne. 'Should we get this party started?'

'Looks like you already have. Double-fisted, huh?' Luther asks with a grin.

'One is for Bella.'

'And the other is for me?'

'Sorry, pal, you're on your own.'

'I can take a hint. You want to be alone with your girl. I guess I'll go find mine.' Laughing and shaking his head, Luther heads for the kitchen.

Drew hands Bella a champagne flute and clinks his own against it.

'What are we drinking to?'

'You decide.'

She pauses, eyes closed, smiling, breathing . . . listening.

She hears no tinkling wind chimes. No whispered, 'Bella Blue.' Maybe she's missing it. Him. Sam.

Maybe she just can't hear him because there is no peace and quiet.

There are a million conversations all at once, pot lids clattering, the stove timer beeping, voices singing, children laughing, dogs barking, cats meowing, and a parrot saying, 'How dreadful! How dreadful!'

No peace and quiet. Just noise. The old house is filled with it, alive with it. Loud, chaotic, beautiful, wonderful noise.

Bella wouldn't have it any other way. She opens her eyes, looks up into Drew's, and nods.

'Got it?'

'Got it.' Smiling, she clinks her glass against his and offers a simple, heartfelt toast. 'To home, to family, to gratitude.'